# McGARR and
# the Sienese Conspiracy

# McGARR and the Sienese Conspiracy

by Bartholomew Gill

CHARLES SCRIBNER'S SONS / NEW YORK

Copyright © 1977 Mark McGarrity

Library of Congress Cataloging in Publication Data
McGarrity, Mark, 1943-
   McGarr and the Sienese conspiracy.

   I. Title.
PZ4.M14348Mae    [PS3563.A296]    813'.5'4    77-24570
ISBN 0-684-15185-5

1 3 5 7 9 11 13 15 17 19 H/C 20 18 16 14 12 10 8 6 4 2

Printed in the United States of America

# Characters

| | |
|---|---|
| AGNOLLO, REMIGIO | Turin car maker |
| ALFORI, ALDO | Carabinieri commandant, Chiusdino |
| BATTAGLIATTI, FRANCESCO | Chairman, Italian Communist party |
| BROWNE, C. B. H. | Former C. of SIS |
| CERVI, PAOLO | Servant to Enrico Rattei |
| COLE, DR. PATRICIA | Professor, chemistry department, Trinity College, Dublin |
| CROFT, SIR SELLWYN | London solicitor |
| CUMMINGS, SIR COLIN | C. of SIS; appointed British ambassador to Italy |
| CUMMINGS, ENNA RICASOLI | Wife of Sir Colin |
| DELANEY, RICHARD S. | Detective inspector, Garda Soichana |
| DRAKE, ROD | American oilman |
| FALCHI, CARLO | Carabinieri commandant, Siena |
| FOSTER, MOSES | Former SIS operative |
| FRANCES, JOHN | Irish Ambassador to Britain |
| GALLUP, EDWARD | Assistant commissioner, CID |
| GARZANTI, MARIA | Opera diva |
| GREAVES, HARRY | Detective inspector, Garda Soichana |
| HITCHCOCK, E. L. J. | Former C. of SIS |
| HITCHCOCK, GRAHAM | Wife of E. L. J. Hitchcock |
| MCKEON, BERNARD | Sergeant of detectives, Garda Soichana |
| MCGARR, PETER | Chief inspector of detectives, also superintendent, Garda Soichana |

| | |
|---|---|
| McGarr, Noreen | McGarr's wife |
| Madigan, Hugh | Private detective, London |
| Mallon, Dermot | Lieutenant, Garda Soichana |
| O'Connor, Kathleen | Householder, Slea Head |
| O'Shaughnessy, Liam | Superintendent, Garda Soichana |
| Pavini, Umberto | Historian |
| Rattei, Enrico | Chairman of ENI, Italian oil cartel |
| Scanlon, Terrence | Superintendent, Garda Soichana, Dingle |
| Sclavi, Vicenzo | Official, Monti dei Paschi di Siena |
| Simpson, Robert | Lieutenant, RAF |
| Sinclair, William | Detective inspector, Garda Soichana |
| Ward, Hugh | Detective inspector, Garda Soichana |
| Zingiale, Oscar | Italian industrialist |

# 1

McGarr glanced out the window of the lurching express train, then looked down at his hand. If my thumb sprouts a rose, he thought, I'll let my fingers become serpents. He placed the hand on his wife's thigh. She didn't stir from her sleep. They were in Italy.

Since Florence, a mauve line had been forming on the eastern horizon, silhouetting the cypress trees on the hilltops. All the farmhouses now had lights in upper windows. In the courtyard of one, a shawl-draped woman, surrounded by chickens, was strewing grain from a basket. Near the barn of another, a young boy was leading cows through a vineyard toward open fields. Even though McGarr could not as yet see the olive trees through the ground fog, he knew they were there, could feel their presence on the hillsides—fecund, gray green, ancient witnesses to the evanescence of man.

Such as the vendors, who with vans loaded tall were driving toward Siena on this, the day of the Palio. The festival had begun as a horse race among the seventeen *contrade,* or sections, of the medieval city. Since then, however, it had become much more: a parade of bright costumes, a flag-throwing exhibition, a religious ceremony, a bacchanal, a highly profitable business week, and finally a mad, bareback scramble through a vortex of people in an exquisite Renaissance square—brief, impassioned, tempestuous. Half the riders never finished. In the heat and excitement, women swooned, men cried, the church bells of the victorious *contrada* rang for a day. In short, McGarr believed the Palio to be a little bit of everything that was characteristically Italian. Pomp, beauty, family, passion, sport, and greed—it was here in Siena twice yearly that Italians were most unabashedly themselves.

Separate but identical murders in a vacation house near Slea Head in southwestern Ireland had brought McGarr to Italy. McGarr believed an experienced killer—a former agent of SIS—had been a party to these executions and now planned to kill the man whose head was nodding in sleep across the compartment from the chief inspector. He was Sir Colin Cummings, who had recently been appointed British ambassador to Italy. His wife, the former Enna Ricasoli, was awaiting them in her family's palazzo on the Piazza del Campo in Siena. Nearly forty years before, one of her disappointed suitors had promised to kill the Englishman if he dared return to the city. All facts that McGarr had learned in his investigations of the Slea Head murders pointed to this same man, who was rich and powerful enough to fulfill his vow. Yet McGarr felt serene—deeply content to be hurtling through the dark Tuscan countryside where, remembering his Petronius, he believed everything, even protecting a man's life among 125,000 revelers, was possible.

In the compartment behind him, McGarr had stationed Garda Superintendent Liam O'Shaughnessy. Because of his neutral Galway accent, he was pretending to be an American tourist. In the compartment in front of him, Inspector Hughie Ward was dressed in the cassock of a Jesuit priest studying at the Vatican. At the Excelsior Hotel in Siena, Sergeant of Detectives Bernie McKeon had already secured two suites of rooms. The balconies offered views of the Stadio and Siena's Duomo, and the Excelsior was only a ten-minute walk to the Piazza del Campo where the Palio would be held. There Ward would be staying in the Palazzo Ricasoli with the Cummingses. McGarr could do no more for the ambassador.

McGarr looked out the window again. With the rising sun an azure tint had begun to suffuse a cloudless sky. The weather would be perfect for the Palio.

The events that brought them to Siena had begun nearly a week and a half before. McGarr remembered the day well, since after fourteen straight days and nights of rain the sun had suddenly broken through a lowering sky. Traffic rushing to Dublin that morning slowed; nobody tooted. When McGarr got to his office at Dublin Castle, his staff, their faces pasty and winter-worn, had collected around Sergeant Bernie McKeon's desk. They were drinking tea and staring out an open window.

The sun catching in its chrome and black enamel, a limousine passed in a fiery blur. The tires hissed on the wet macadam. The wind off the Liffey was soft now, mild and welcome. McGarr walked into his dark cubicle to answer the ringing phone which everybody had ignored. Indoors, things seemed dusty and old.

It was Superintendent Terrence Scanlon, commandant of the Dingle Garda barracks. They had found a dead man in an outbuilding of a vacation home on Dingle Bay. His arms and legs had been trussed behind him, wrists to ankles, and he had been shot once in the back of the head.

"An execution," said McGarr. He was a short, thickset man with red hair gone bald on top. Off the cap of a wooden match he flicked his thumb. He held the flame to the tip of a Woodbine, then sat on the edge of his desk. He glanced over at his staff and the open window. Dingle would be glorious on a day such as this, he thought. "IRA?"

"Don't think so," said Scanlon. "That's why I called. The murderer either dropped or ignored the shell casing. The gun seems to have been a twenty-two, nothing an IRA gunman would choose."

"If the choice were his." An IRA gunman would use anything with a trigger, McGarr well knew.

"But this is different, sir. The man's name is Hitchcock with three initials. He has a London legal address. Rumor has it he's a retired civil servant—Coal Board, I think—but nobody, not even my brother, knows who he is." Scanlon's brother was the Kerry C.O. of the regular IRA. "A quiet sort, it seems. Didn't frequent any pubs whenever he was here; even stayed in the car when his wife completed the sale of the place at the barrister's office. And it's some place, it is—stretches half a mile, I should think. He must have *owned* the Coal Board and several other utilities as well."

"Where is she?"

"London, I believe."

"Does she know yet?"

"Only found him this morning when their laborer let out the donkey. The smell it was, you know."

"How long dead?"

"A week. I was wondering if you wouldn't mind coming out here, sir. I might have missed something important, not being used to this sort of thing and all. If this isn't an IRA affair, mightn't we have a chance of learning the facts?"

"Dingle, you said," McGarr said in a loud voice. A fringe of the Gulf Stream struck Ireland near Dingle, and on a day when Dublin was balmy, the southwest coast of the country might well be tropical.

As one, his staff turned to him.

"Well," said Scanlon, "it's actually far Dingle. You can see the Great Blasket from the shore."

"You can? The weather must be fair out there too, Terry."

"Smashin', at last. Puts me in mind of Portugal where the missus and me—— but that's another story and not one for the phone."

"Portugal-like, eh?"

"We went there over Easter. Can we expect you?"

"Early afternoon." McGarr rang off.

When he raised his head, a dozen expectant faces were looking at him. The silence was complete. "I won't be in today, men. I've got a little field work to do." McGarr fitted on his derby, then tossed his dark raincoat over a shoulder and made for the door.

"But that damn car fits five at least," roared Bernie McKeon. "What—do you think the rest of us enjoy this great, gloomy dungeon?" Histrionically, he swept his arms about the room. His face was now scarlet, eyes bulging. "Or messing about with this slick tissue?" He grabbed some papers off his desk and tossed them over his head. He then approached McGarr truculently. "Get a hold of yourself, Chief Inspector. You're not a dictator around here, you know. This isn't a penal colony. We'll just have to choose up to see who gets the dirty duty of carting your carcass out to Dingle and back. Have a seat." McKeon pulled out a chair for McGarr and eased him into it. "Now then—you make up the tickets, Ward, and I'll get the hat." He reached behind him and plucked the derby off McGarr's head.

All the men laughed. Only McKeon could treat McGarr like that and get away with it. McKeon was a chubby, blond man who spoke in a rush. His eyes were small, very blue, and mischievous.

Ward put twelve slips of paper into the derby. On four of these he had marked an *X.*

McKeon did not win.

As Ward, Delaney, Sinclair, and Greaves started for their coats, McKeon said, "Wait just one minute, you blaggards. This was a put-up job. Today, I'm going to have to pull rank on one or the other of you two. And, if you give me any lip, neither of you will go." He meant Ward or Greaves, who asked, "But why? It was all above-board. Didn't you hold the hat yourself?"

"That's why I lost. By the time I got to choose, there was only one ticket left and blank at that."

"Chance," said Sinclair.

"Luck," said Delaney.

"Rank," said McKeon again, heading for the coat rack.

Greaves glanced at Ward, who shrugged and reached into his pocket for a half-crown to flip.

McGarr stood, picked his derby off the table, and fitted it on his head. "C'mon, we'll take the Rover. That way all five of you can go."

"But the energy crisis!" said Boyle from his desk. He hadn't chosen an *X.*

"—the energy crisis," McKeon advised.

"Why don't we take two Rovers?" another asked.

"Or a staff car and two tanks." McKeon shut the door. Taking McGarr by the elbow as they walked down the long, gloomy hall, he observed, "Gripers. I've never seen the like. They complain all the day long. And such a pleasant day, what?"

They were in the courtyard now. The sun made McGarr pull the short brim of his derby over his eyes. The men removed their rain gear and suit coats and folded them into the trunk.

Lowering himself into the front seat beside Ward, who was his driver, McGarr said, "Scanlon will think half the Dublin office has nothing better to do than take a junket to Dingle for the day."

"Sure," said McKeon, sinking back into the plush rear seat of the new Rover, "and we haven't, have we?"

And between the elements a most pleasant tension obtained that day—rivers, streams, even the roadside drainage ditches were rush-ing with clear winter water that was made to seem all the more frigid in the bright sun. Every so often a cool breeze off a cow pond would cut through the heat. All Ireland, it seemed to McGarr, had revived in this first burst of warmth. Whole families, mile after mile, were working their fields, repairing walls, cleaning barns, stables, and outbuildings. Cottage doors were open, bedding hung on wash lines, babies playing among the chickens by the back doors. Deeper into the country, near Limerick, the crack of an ash sapling turned McGarr's head to a field in which young boys, clubs whipping, were playing hurly. In the Shannon, salmon were running. From boats men were tossing nets into the black, swift water.

Near Foynes they stopped at an inn that was perched on a hill. From their window seat McGarr could see Ennis and Lough Dergh to the north and east, and Kilrush down the sparkling Shannon estuary to the west. The color of the spring grass in Ireland, he thought, has no equal, especially, like now, after a long rain.

They ate salmon that had been roasted over a special spit made in the form of an oblong cage and situated, as part of the fireplace, in the middle of the dining room. The fresh whole fish, so the chef told McGarr, who conversed with him in a French made colloquial during his seven-year stint with Criminal Justice and after with Interpol in Paris, was stuffed with a julienne (thin strips of carrots and celery hearts cooked in butter to which truffles, an equal amount of mushrooms, and some sherry had been added, all bound with a thick béchamel sauce). The fish was then covered with bards of bacon fat held in place with twine. It was placed in the cage and braised before a hot fire for fifteen to eighteen minutes, basting often. Before taking the salmon off the spit, the chef removed the bacon bards and allowed the fish to color. He served the dish with fresh lemons and dispatched the bar boy to the cool depths of the second cellar to retrieve a few bottles of a select white Graves from Illats that he favored with the dish.

As McGarr talked with him, the chief inspector noted that the only other diners in the inn were two men who were seated on the other side of the room, directly across the open, circular fireplace from McGarr and his men. One was a black man whose girth was only somewhat less remarkable than his broad forehead and close-set eyes. At first McGarr thought he must be slightly macrocephalic, but decided, after discreetly glancing at him several more times, that the effect was only caused by the man's baldness. McGarr, who was also bald, felt the need to examine his own appearance in a mirror, but contained the urge. The other man at the far table had white hair, the curls of which had been allowed to develop freely à la mode, a thick black moustache, and a sallow complexion. Both were very well dressed and were speaking what McGarr believed was Spanish. He could only hear a word or two from time to time.

After thick, black coffee, McGarr and his staff pushed on.

McGarr burst from the outbuilding with his handkerchief still held to his nose and walked quickly toward the car where his staff and Superintendent Scanlon were standing. It was true, he noted, that one could see in the distance the steep cliffs of the Great Blasket being slammed by the North Atlantic. It was cold here still, however, what with the breeze off the ocean, and the stone house of at least twenty-five rooms had a bleached appearance, as though too often cleansed by the brilliant sun, stiff breezes, and salt spray.

The man in the shed had been in his late sixties, McGarr supposed. He was tall, thin, in good shape, and from the marks of thrashing in the chicken droppings on the floor McGarr guessed he had been tied up and left there for some time before being murdered. The bullet itself did not pass through his head. The cord binding his hands was elasticized, like that used to secure parcels to the carriers of bicycles, but thicker.

To get out of the wind, McGarr opened the door to the Rover and, sitting in the front passenger seat, put down the lid to the glove compartment. On this he placed the contents of the man's pockets. His wallet said he was Edward Llewelyn John Hitchcock. He had a U.K. driver's license listing a London address in St. John's Wood, a national insurance card, Barclay's Bank, American Express, and Carte Blanche charge cards, a return stub on an Aer Lingus jet from Shannon to Heathrow, and membership cards to the East India, Bat, and Proscenium men's clubs. A compartment contained eighty-seven pounds cash. The wallet was initialed, black alligator, thin, and very efficient in appearance. Keys to a Jaguar sedan also fit in twin slits. Hitchcock had kept green ink in his Mt. Blanc fountain pen. On the back of his Rolex wristwatch, the dial of which was equipped with a device to determine times in other parts of the world, was the inscription "To C. from your Sis-ter," and under that, "Peace through Truth, London, 1973."

"Strange caption," McKeon mused, "even from one's sister."

The men were crowded around the open door of the Rover. "That's the first time I've known an inscription to stammer," said Harry Greaves.

"C. is what the chief of SIS, the British Secret Service, is called."

Scanlon raised his head and looked at the house again. "And there I thought he was on the Coal Board all along."

"Probably was—as a front," said McGarr.

Dick Delaney added, "That's the outfit that isn't required to account for its funds, and I mean the legal ones it gets from Parliament, not whatever the Chinese or Russians will pay for negotiable state secrets."

"How was the weather hereabouts last week, Terrence?"

"Cold, windy, and wet. Foggy at nights. We had a storm on Monday."

"Let's take a look at the house. Hitchcock was wearing only a thin cardigan and cotton clothes. The gunshot he suffered might have been a coup de grace for all we know."

After having crossed a wide and chilly veranda, they found the front door open. Spare was the word that occurred to McGarr as he looked about the parlor and dining room. He supposed that Hitchcock and his wife had bought the house "all found," and what they had found had either been quite meager or not suited to their tastes. Thus, the large parlor contained only a straight-back love seat and two chairs grouped around the fireplace. Intricate designs, all swirls and frills, had been carved into the heavy oak. These garish pieces seemed to require the vast emptiness of the room. Linen curtains, yellow with age, were drawn across three windows. They were brilliant now in the full sun.

The dining room was on the other side of the hallway. There a massive table of the same design as the furniture in the living room dominated the middle of the room. The backs of the twelve ornate chairs were as tall as McGarr. The only other item in the room was a matching and ponderous sideboard. The table had been set for one, and a meal of spring lamb with a pretty suprême of potatoes, carrots, brussels sprouts, and leeks had been half-consumed, as though whoever had killed Hitchcock had disturbed him in the midst of his dinner. A half-empty bottle of Hermitage Rouge, 1967, sat near the wine glass, which appeared to be, surprisingly, empty and clean. There was no sediment or stain of dried wine on the bottom. Certainly Hitchcock hadn't drunk from the bottle. McGarr picked up the cork, which lay directly above the knife, and squeezed it between thumb and forefinger. It was still moist and springy.

The kitchen was a mess that bore all the appearances of having had an amateur chef at work in it for, say, an afternoon. McGarr knew from his own brief forays into the world of haute cuisine that the hobbyist never thinks of washing or re-using a spatula, spoon, whisk, grater, garlic press, etc., in order to minimize his cleaning duties at the end of the preparation, but is usually at least one step behind the recipe and has to rush to keep from ruining the whole meal. Thus, as in this kitchen, eggshells are not dispatched immediately after use, knives lay about the tops of the tables and cutting boards, pots, and pans begin to mount up, until all kitchen surfaces are cluttered.

What struck McGarr, however, is why a man would go to such bother—a pâté in a fluted pastry shell (McGarr cut himself a slice: hare), vichyssoise, scalloped oysters—just to dine alone. One cooks for an audience, especially something as toothsome as the deep-dish gooseberry pie that was still on a rack in the open oven. Also, the trash, which was kept in a small bin behind curtains under a counter, had been spilled about the floor in that area. The bin itself was still upright, but somebody had reached in and extracted its contents, as though looking for something. Things were just not quite right inside this house, McGarr thought.

After having examined the rest of the house, which he found to be as spare and neat as the living room, McGarr returned to the kitchen, cut the gooseberry pie in seven generous pieces, and put on a pot of water for tea.

While the gas flame roared on the copper bottom of the kettle, he said to Hughie Ward, "Well, now—I want a thorough autopsy of Hitchcock's body. I believe that the bullet, given the point of entry at the base of the cranium and trajectory through the skull, might not have struck bone." He fished in his pocket and pulled out the cartridge casing Scanlon had found in the outbuilding under a crack in one of the wall sills. "We could be lucky. Many twenty-two-caliber handguns are special issues." McGarr had once put a dope smuggler away for life because of the man's preference for unusual weapons. "If it's intact, I want a complete analysis of the chamber markings and a set of photographs."

Ward copied these requests into his notebook.

The tea kettle began to whistle. McKeon warmed the ceramic pot, tossed out that water, added tea, and then poured the boiling water over it. "I wonder if the blighter imbibed anything stronger than wine."

Hands in raincoat pockets, the men were waiting for a go-ahead from McGarr to hunt up a bottle, which all of them knew such a house must contain.

But McGarr did not want anything in the dining room, bottles in particular, touched. "Fingerprints all around, Hughie. We'll put the teacups and pots on the veranda as we leave." He stood and walked back into the dining room. Suddenly the room grew dark and seemed gloomy. McGarr parted the curtains. The sky in western Ireland could change dramatically within minutes. Now it was freighted with storm clouds racing in off the ocean.

When he looked down at the table, the wine glass again caught his eye. Striking a wooden match, he held the flame near the exterior surface to see if he could detect the traces of fingerprints. There were several. He also noticed, however, a blue tint on the inside of the glass. He walked back into the kitchen.

In the shadows under the sink McGarr found a liquid that he knew would leave a blue film on a glass which was not thoroughly rinsed in hot water. "I want the inside of that wine glass in the dining room analyzed and also the surface of this soap container checked for fingerprints, although I don't think we'll find anything on that." McGarr was staring at a rubber glove that had been tossed carelessly into the cabinet. It was hanging from the S-curve of the sink pipe.

With his fountain pen he pried up the edge of the glove. The inside was wet.

McGarr opened the cupboards and with his handkerchief began taking plates off the stacks. Only the bottoms of the first of every size were wet. One whiskey and one wine glass also had been washed in liquid cleaner and imperfectly rinsed.

Ward had poured the tea.

McGarr drank off a cup.

If the killer had first dined with Hitchcock, thought McGarr, and, after having drugged or poisoned him, carted him out to the hen house where, sometime later, he finally dispatched the man, then he *would* have washed the dishes and put them away to expunge all trace of his having been there. "I also want a blood analysis. He doesn't look like he was a drinker, but this wine bottle bothers me. If the killer drugged his wine and then took the precaution of trying to wash away the drug from the glass *and* of killing Hitchcock sometime after the drug had worn off, then it could be he knows we can trace the drug to him. Let's take a look at the garbage."

Out at the trash bin, McGarr discovered that somebody had also rifled through the garbage. Within the small, wooden compound near the back door, refuse had been tossed on the ground and then kicked about, as though somebody in a rush or fit of pique had been trying to find something.

"What are you looking for, Chief?" asked Sinclair, who had followed him throughout his perusal of the house and its contents. Sinclair was a tall man who dressed nattily. He had spent over twenty years on the Sydney police force before returning home to work for McGarr.

"Wine bottle. I'd bet my brown derby nobody drank from that bottle on the table in the dining room."

They poked through the garbage but could find no other wine bottle.

McGarr turned and walked toward the shed. He pulled out his pocket torch and once again held his handkerchief to his nose. There, in the shadows and against the wall, Hitchcock still lay contorted either from the force of the shot into the base of his skull or from the momentary agony of his death throe.

McGarr was most interested, however, in the pattern of his movements through the dirt and chicken droppings on the shed floor before he was dispatched. After all, if the man indeed had been the chief of SIS, then perhaps he might have taken pains to provide at least one lead to his killers.

The shed was small and McGarr quickly covered every square inch. He then began turning over the dirt and offal on the floor wherever Hitchcock had crawled. Still nothing. Finally, McGarr searched the corpse once more, thinking that perhaps he might have missed something the first time. But he was disappointed, until, just as he was about to leave, it struck him that the only means a man who had been bound as thoroughly as Hitchcock had to conceal an object would be with his mouth. When McGarr squatted and, using his handkerchief, gently pried up Hitchcock's lips, he found something wedged between the back of his teeth. With a jerk, McGarr pulled it out. It was a cork. Shining the beam of the torch directly on it, he discovered a perforation in the center, the kind a pressure wine-bottle opener made. Whoever had killed Hitchcock had probably taken the drugged wine bottle with him, but, since Hitchcock, as host, must have opened it himself, he probably placed the cork in his shirt or cardigan pocket and later, when coming to in the shed, realized what was happening to him and pulled the cork out of the pocket with his teeth. Because of the way his wrists and ankles had been bound together, the pain must have been agonizing. Another possibility was that, feeling the first effects of the drugged wine and knowing that he would be killed, he had slipped the cork into his mouth before he had passed out.

Now there were several other policemen in the shed with McGarr. Sinclair said, "Probably drugged or poisoned the wine. That's how the killer or killers got him out to the shed."

"Drugged, more likely," said Ward. "He did a lot of moving in there. Also, there's probably only one killer."

Sinclair and Greaves looked up at Ward.

"Only one of each type of plate had a wet bottom."

"First honors for the lad with the little black notebook," said McGarr. He dropped the cork into a little plastic bag that Ward was holding. The chief inspector then donned his jacket and coat once more. Greaves shoveled the trash back into the bin.

At the car, fat drops of rain had begun to fall now, and the sky was a patchwork of tumbling dark clouds where the ocean storm met the warm air off the land.

# 2

Next morning, McGarr stepped into a phone booth and dialed Hugh Madigan's office. He was a London-based private detective and an old Dublin friend of McGarr's. After some small talk, McGarr said, "I've got an assignment for you which is a part of an official Garda investigation into the murder in Ireland of a U.K. citizen."

"Then, why call me? Not that I mind, Peter; it's just that the procedure seems extraordinary. Shouldn't you request assistance from Scotland Yard?"

"Well—let me give you the man's name. I haven't released it to the newspapers yet." McGarr considered briefly the cloak of red tape in which the British government could wrap his investigation. "I want a credit check and complete dossiers of him and his wife. I want to know if he had any personal enemies, who his friends were, and what, if anything, he has been doing since"—McGarr recalled the date on the back of the dead man's watch—"1973." The house on Dingle Bay held none of the accouterments—books, games, objets d'art—of a man of leisure, but looked more like a get-away-from-it-all place.

"Name?"

"Edward Llewelyn John Hitchcock."

"Not——"

"I thought nobody was really supposed to know who he was. His address is Sixty Avenue Road, St. John's Wood." The other end of the line was quiet. "Hugh?"

"I now work in this town, Peter. We're no longer two agency pals who are doing each other a good turn, now and again. This is my business, the sole support of my family. Have you informed the government about this?"

McGarr looked out at the crowds pushing by the phone booth: Pakistanis, Indians, and Orientals mostly, with some Caucasians here and there and probably half of them Irish. "I'm at Heathrow, just having arrived. When I hang up this phone, I'm headed straight for Scotland Yard."

Still the other end of the line was quiet.

"Think of all the extralegal assistance I've provided you in the past, Hugh. And in this case we're willing to pay."

"I'm not trying to extort a big fee, Peter; you know that. It's just that, if I know SIS, they'll swarm all over this case.

"The section chiefs went to the same schools, belong to the same clubs. They're more like a social subset than a ministry. They'll not want any news of the killing, any inquiries other than their own, and certainly none originating from another country, especially Ireland."

"But, you see, Hugh, the murder happened in Ireland. I've got the details. If they try to keep me from investigating here, I'll give them none of the facts of my investigation there. I might even release the whole bloody business to the most lurid of London dailies. It's as simple as that."

"It is? Don't count on it. These are snooty old boys, Peter. To them, red tape *is* all they have that resembles work. Your news will bring them together. They'll collect in some smart City club and consider the demise of poor Hitchcock. 'Dear C., poor C., he was right enough in his own curious way, what?' They'll then concoct some baroque argument to explain the murder or some means to obfuscate his personal history, as if that mattered. You know—it'll all be such fun considering who and why and—if you refuse to give them any details—how. Then the process of 'keeping the wretched business quiet' will occupy them for several days at least. To tell you the truth, I don't want to become involved with those idiots."

"If you act fast, we can have all the information before they even become aware of his death."

"Why don't you do it yourself?"

"You can answer all my questions in one morning on the phone.

You've got the contacts and know where to look. Nobody will think your inquiries are anything but routine. Once I open my mouth, Whitehall, the Yard, MI-5, maybe even the Home Guard will be put on notice."

Madigan sighed. "What's your first step?"

"The Yard, as I told you. I've got to tell them I'm here and ask for their cooperation. If they agree, I'll hand them my report without once mentioning that I know who Hitchcock was. Who knows —maybe we might blunder right along with a perfectly regular investigation."

"Don't expect that."

"Well, the most I'm hoping for is a chance to get to talk to his widow."

Madigan sighed again.

"And maybe talking to his former associates."

"Not a chance. Lookit, Peter—I don't know why you're being so assiduous about this thing. From the little I can remember about Hitchcock's reputation, he deserved all he got and more. These people are something less than professional murderers. They give the orders. When one of them gets hit, we're all better off for it."

An old woman, who throughout McGarr's phone call had been standing close to the booth, now turned and, using the heel of her palm, banged twice on the cabinet. The sheet metal roared.

"Hello—are you there, Peter? Peter!"

"Why, the old hag," said McGarr under his breath. She was wizened with age and her lips, now working over false teeth as she glared at McGarr, had spread her lipstick in a halo around her mouth. "Yes—do we have a deal?"

"You scared me," said Madigan. "For a moment I thought Hitchcock's associates might have proved more efficient than I thought."

"Is it a deal?"

"Well—all right. But I'm only going to give you one day. I can't put anybody else on this thing and I can't afford to waste more than a day on it."

"Waste? Think of it this way, Hugh—not only are you getting paid, and well, but you're also getting a chance to work for your own country."

"For once. It'll be the closest I've ever come to having a job back home."

The old woman hit the shell of the phone booth twice more and McGarr rang off. Stepping out, he said, "You ignorant old shrew—have you no manners?"

"In direct proportion to your consideration for others, Paddy. And bad cess to you." She stepped into the booth and rammed the door shut behind her.

McGarr took a taxi to Scotland Yard.

McGarr had always enjoyed London. Like Paris, it was a world center—bustling, cosmopolitan, vibrant—but the scale of London's buildings and streets was human, small townish and friendly. McGarr knew that for several centuries the town had been notorious for deplorable living conditions, poverty, and vice. And he knew of sections which even now were less than desirable to inhabit. But compared to the slums of most other large cities, London's low-income districts were showplaces. Trams, trains, buses were regular, clean, and safe. And the yardstick that mattered most to McGarr weighed heavily in favor of London—one encountered more men of goodwill here than in any city of its size that he had ever visited.

Today, the sky was mottled and the wind brisk. Like the beams of klieg lights, bright rays of sun broke through the cloud cover momentarily and passed up the gray streets, causing office workers in the financial district to doff their heavy coats and stroll after lunch. Still, the air was cold and damp in the shadows, and the city had not fully accepted the advent of spring.

New Scotland Yard, which is situated on a bank reclaimed from the Thames, had always seemed a cozy place to McGarr. Maybe it was its stolid, round turrets, or the air of quiet confidence that its personnel exuded, or its long history of precise police work, but at times, when McGarr could forget the repression which certain agents of Scotland Yard—many of them Irishmen themselves—had imposed upon his homeland, he almost wished he worked there. The diesel engine pinged and shuddered as McGarr paid the cabbie, who then geared off slowly down the cobblestone courtyard.

McGarr presented his credentials to the porter, but his luck wasn't holding. No sooner had he and a constable rounded a corner near the lift than McGarr met Ned Gallup, another former Interpol agent who was now chief constable to Assistant Commissioner C., this is to say, second-in-command of the Criminal Investigation Department. Being a friend, Gallup was the last man McGarr wanted to see, since his requests concerning the investigation of the Hitchcock murder would require a certain premeditated withholding of information.

"McGarr, old man—how do you do?" Gallup pumped McGarr's arm. Fat, rosy-cheeked, always suffused with energy and bonhomie, Gallup allowed his thick moustache to spread across his face in what McGarr knew to be the most ecstatic of his many smiles. "Gad— Ronny and I were just talking about you at dinner a few nights back, wondering how you were getting on in Dublin and so forth. Remember that little trattoria in Naples? Seafood it specialized in. Sat on the hill overlooking the harbor. Eel, octopus salad, squid, all sorts of unsightly roe dishes. It still amazes me how you could pack all that"—Gallup shuddered—"away. How's Noreen?"

"Well, quite well."

"Kids?"

"Not yet. How is Ronny and the rest of your brood?" Gallup had seven children and in jest McGarr had often called him a covert papist.

"Implacable, relentless, thriving." Gallup patted his stomach and chuckled. His eyebrows were so bushy one seldom saw his eyes. In all, he put McGarr in mind of a moustachioed Buddha—benign, beatific, blessing with every gesture the continuance of existence in its present form. "What brings you to this gloomy place, other than"—he checked a large, gold pocket watch and replaced it in a vest pocket—"to have lunch with me. I know of a small Armenian restaurant—patlijan moussaka, stuffed grape leaves, shish kabab cured in a marinade that is a family secret worth more than the business itself, curried prawns, stuffed spring lamb spit-roasted over hickory, coffee no different from the cafés of Istanbul, Damascan delights for dessert, *and* this is no ascetic Ankaran bistro, my man. They've got, of all things, a license to sell liquor on the premises!"

"Then I insist that the Republic of Ireland shall take you, Ronny, and your troops to dinner tonight."

"No, no, no—lunch on me, dinner on you—or, er, your government. That'll make me something of a fixture in the spot, what?" He beamed over McGarr's head, "You know, special tables, superior service, the pick of their wine cellar, and token aperitifs."

McGarr pushed the UP button of the lift. "Lunch is definitely out, Ned. I've got to get some business out of the way immediately."

"Well, then—how about my club? Escoffier's illegitimate grand-nephew wears the high hat there. British fare, of course, but entirely palatable. Entirely." He stepped into the elevator with McGarr. "What's it all about? IRA? Troublesome business that. I sometimes have nightmares the chief will detail me some of that mess, and, what with trying to keep the Mc's and O's straight and to understand the gibberish that passes for speech in the Six Counties, I wake in a sweat that requires several stiff whiskeys to quell." Again Gallup removed his watch and checked the time.

When the doors slid open on the fifth floor, the executive offices of CID, Gallup said, "Well, so, what luck!" He reached out and stopped McGarr. "Tell me about it."

McGarr sighed and looked up at the large man. Indeed, if his children were implacable and relentless, they owed the qualities to their father. McGarr smiled and shook his head. "I can't tell you, Ned. It's an official matter between me and the assistant commissioner. I'm operating on strict orders from my government to discuss this case with nobody but him. You'll understand later if he decides to tell you."

"There you are wrong." Gallup winked and bustled into a side room.

McGarr called after him, "I'll ring you about tea time."

McGarr presented himself at the receptionist's desk near the assistant commissioner's office. "Peter McGarr. I'd like to talk to the chief, if I may." McGarr handed her his card.

"May I ask the nature of your business?"

"It concerns the murder of a U.K. citizen in the Republic of Ireland."

A trim woman in her sixties, she immediately took the card into a room behind her desk. McGarr could hear her knocking on a door beyond.

Here again, McGarr noted, the homely, heavy office furniture, the old typewriters, the solid, useful, but stodgy decor of the building seemed to reinforce the undeniable competence of its denizens.

Moments later, the woman showed McGarr into the assistant commissioner's office, where a man was seated at the desk, a newspaper that concealed his face and chest fully opened before him. When the secretary had shut the door, a voice from behind the paper said, "What is it you want, MacGregor?"

"McGarr," said McGarr. "I'm investigating the murder of a British subject in Ireland. I would like to request permission to interview several British citizens, including the man's wife, as part of my investigation."

"Name of the victim?"

"Hitchcock, E. L. J."

"Address?"

"Sixty Avenue Road, St. John's Wood."

"Age?"

"Late sixties."

"Retired?" Still the paper had yet to descend.

McGarr noted something familiar about the voice. "I don't know as yet."

"You realize, of course, that a Yard officer will have to accompany you on these interviews."

"My government is prepared to pay all expenses incurred."

"Very well. Have Miss Cameron direct you to the office of Chief Constable Gallup. He'll be happy to accompany you."

"But——"

The man lowered his newspaper. It was Gallup himself. "But what?"

"But how——?"

"I'm the new assistant commissioner, Peter. Well—it's not quite official yet, you know, but I'm doing the job until the Board meets and passes on my nomination."

"What happened to Scruggs?"

Gallup's face sobered. "A contingency which we all must meet someday. He was a great policeman and one hell of a good fellow too. And while on serious topics, why are you so reluctant to accept my help?"

McGarr furrowed his brow. "No reason. I just didn't want to mix business with pleasure." He hated to withhold information from a friend, especially when that friend had just been named to such a prestigious position, but he decided then that his own investigation of the murder was as important to him as any secrecy the British government would want to impose concerning the murder of a former chief spy. Also, he had given Ned Gallup all that was required. If Gallup didn't recognize the name, that was his own look-out—seven kids, their friendship, and all else considered. "Shall we go now?"

"I'll get my hat, my mysterious friend." Gallup pulled himself out of the seat and made for the closet.

"It happened in Dingle," said McGarr, "at the man's vacation home. We found him in an outbuilding where . . ." McGarr began telling him every detail he had discovered in his investigation except for the inscription on the back of the wristwatch, and before they left the office McGarr put in a call to his own office in Ireland.

Hughie Ward came on the line. "As you surmised, Chief, the bullet did remain whole in Hitchcock's skull. And you could be right as well about the gun. The impression on the cartridge casing is odd. We've narrowed it down to J2S-P Baretta automatics, then certain types of twenty-two Walthers, Colts, three models of Harrington and Richardson stock, and an Iver Johnson kick-shell type. There are over a thousand guns like that registered in Britain and Ireland and that's probably only the tip of the iceberg."

"That's so satisfying."

"What?"

"Being right."

"The cord used to wrap his hands and feet can only be purchased in commercial lengths and is used mostly to strap down cargo in air transports. So much of it is sold that this line of investigation will doubtless prove unavailing, although Bernie is presently pursuing it."

In the background McGarr could hear somebody grumbling.

"Now, then—we turned up no fingerprints but Hitchcock's, the cleaning woman's, some other female latents which are probably his wife's. Whoever ate with him and drugged the wine must have worn gloves or kept in mind absolutely everything he touched and later wiped it down.

"The autopsy of the body shows nothing much new. The killer had, as we suspected, let the drug wear off so that the trace in Hitchcock's blood would be too slight to permit a complete analysis. Using those traces, however, Al McAndrew at the lab says it's some chemical he's sure he's never encountered before, and so, rather than ruin whatever amounts the cork contains, he's sent his preliminary disclosures over to Professor Cole of the Trinity College chemistry department. If she can't determine what the substance is, nobody can.

"How is it going over there, Chief? Have you questioned his wife yet?"

"Not yet. The Scotland Yard number is eight-seven-three-nine-two and I'll be at Hitchcock's Avenue Road address. I don't know the phone number but you can find it in the registry, if you need me."

After discussing the details of a pending court case and some routine office business, McGarr rang off.

A constable then drove Gallup and McGarr toward St. John's Wood.

The house of at least a dozen rooms sat, like its neighbors, right on the street. Its old brick had been painted white. A brass door knocker, door handle, kick, and nameplates gleamed with fresh polish. Window sashes, shutters, and wrought-iron street guards were black.

An elderly butler answered the door and, taking Gallup's card, directed them into a small sitting room furnished with comfortable wing-back chairs and a sofa. Leather-bound books lined two walls and a pale blue oriental rug, into which a green-and-yellow design had been worked, covered the floor. The butler lit the gas fire in the hearth.

Ten minutes later, a woman appeared in the door. Mrs. Hitchcock's facial features were what McGarr always imagined when upper-class English ladies were mentioned. Perhaps it was her slight smile, as though her thin lips were unable to cover fully her protrusive teeth, or her bent nose, high cheekbones, or the broad reach of her forehead, but the impression remained quite strong for McGarr. A woman past fifty who was wearing a high-necked, aquamarine dress, her hair neatly coiffured and tinted a delicate blond, she was the mistress of the mansion to McGarr, the vacationer in the Rolls speeding down to her holdings in Killarney, the lady under the parasol holding the fifty-pound ticket stubs in the grandstand at the Leopardstown race course. To admit that the face was somewhat equine would be to say she resembled a very pretty horse indeed. Her ankles were thin and she crossed them as she sat. "Would you care for some refreshment, gentlemen?"

"No, thank you, ma'am," said Gallup. "Our visit is official and a matter of some delicacy." He firmed his upper lip so that his moustache spread in a somber curl across his face. He was unable to look at her directly; his eyes searched the pattern of the carpet.

After a few moments, Gallup suddenly glanced up at her and said, "It is my sad duty to tell you that your husband is dead."

She neither blinked nor in any way altered her expression. "Where is he now?"

"In Dublin. We have to ask you to go there to make a positive identification."

"How did he die?"

"He was murdered with a gun."

Still, she hadn't blinked. She turned her head to McGarr. "Who is this man?"

"Peter McGarr, ma'am. Chief Inspector of Detectives, Special Branch, Dublin Castle Garda. I'd like to ask you a few questions, if I may."

She stood. "I must make a phone call first, if you'll excuse me please." On her first step, she faltered slightly, steadied herself on the doorjamb, and walked resolutely out into the foyer.

"She's a cool one, what?" Gallup said. "I wonder who she's calling, her barrister? Could she have done it herself?"

McGarr shook his head. The possibility that a woman might have killed Hitchcock had never really occurred to him, since the crime was most remarkable for its utter lack of passion, attention to detail, and swift execution once the incriminating evidence had been eliminated. McGarr did feel, however, very uncomfortable indeed, since he knew very well whom she was phoning—whoever was presently C. of SIS.

When she returned, she said from the doorway, "Chief Constable Gallup is wanted on the phone." She still held Gallup's card in her hand, and she didn't move when he squeezed by her. As the butler directed Gallup down the foyer to the telephone, she merely stared at McGarr. Her features were expressionless, completely devoid of feeling, as though she had long prepared herself for this eventuality, that this was a final working out of a scene she had played over and over in her mind.

"Peter!" Gallup said even before he got to the sitting room. "Pardon me, ma'am." He squeezed past her, taking one long stride onto the carpet and plunging his fists into his suitcoat pocket. "Why didn't you tell me who Mr. Hitchcock is, er——" he glanced at Mrs. Hitchcock.

"Was," she supplied.

McGarr decided then that he would have to feign innocence, if only to preserve his friendship with Gallup. "Well, who was he?"

"You mean you don't know?"

"A retired civil servant with the Coal Board, I believe, although I must admit that this house and the one in Dingle seem rather pretentious for even the most enviable Civil Service appointment."

"Edward had an inheritance," she supplied somewhat too readily. "My family has money."

"Is that why you didn't want me involved in this case?" Gallup demanded once more. "Because you knew you'd have to lie to me?"

McGarr sighed and looked at the gas fire in the grate. "I didn't lie to you. I told you the facts I discovered in my investigation. I'm sure Mrs. Hitchcock isn't interested in hearing us squabble."

She said, "Indeed I am not."

"Then perhaps I might ask you a very few questions concerning your husband, his reason for being at the house in Ireland, and the nature of his present involvements."

"No, you may not. Frankly, I don't know why he would have been in Ireland. For all I knew he was still in Great Britain. I had good reason never to question my husband about his activities. Constable

Gallup will explain the situation to you in the police car. Good day."
She turned and walked up the foyer.

"Ned—this is a murder investigation, not a housebreaking."
McGarr thought it wise to act like the hurt party now. "I didn't come
all the way over here to be brushed off by some"—he waved his
hand—"self-important widow. I want the facts and, damn it, I'm
going to get them. If not, then your department will see how quickly
cooperation on the IRA and the troubles in the North will cease."
This was a bluff. McGarr was a policeman, not a politician. He could
only recommend noncooperation and would never consider doing
so just because of one murder investigation that London chose to
quash.

The butler cleared his throat. He was standing in the foyer, holding both of their hats.

In the police car, Ned Gallup told McGarr who Hitchcock had
been and then directed the driver to take them to the Proscenium,
the men's club at which, rumor had it, most of the important SIS
business was worked out over pink gins. Present C. wanted to meet
them.

Gallup was now in a foul mood. "Two days on the job," he kept
saying. "Two days and what? A world-darkening blunder. How did
I not recognize the name?"

"We've worked with these people before on the Continent, Ned,
remember? They change procedures, contacts, controls, drops, et
cetera, monthly. All this is smoke and shadow, secrecy for the sake
of secrecy. You're hungry. If they feed us, you'll feel better." But
McGarr had begun to wonder why the old boys of SIS wanted to see
them. Present C. had only to call the commissioner of Scotland Yard
to get the whole thing kicked under the rug. And Dublin was sure
to honor a request for secrecy as well.

Thus, as the car weaved through noon-hour traffic along the
esplanade of Hyde Park, McGarr devised several explanations for
SIS curiosity: for some reason as yet unknown to McGarr, SIS had
sponsored the assassination of Hitchcock and now wanted to know
how much McGarr had uncovered; SIS had an inkling who might
have killed Hitchcock and wanted the facts to confirm this suspicion;
SIS had no idea of who had done this thing or why, and the murder

shocked and surprised them too. In spite of all the rumors he had heard about the sullen manipulation of agents in the field, how the section chiefs sat back in the Proscenium and wrote off operatives when their usefulness had passed, he was certain, again, that these were men of goodwill who would respond, after some prodding, to his need to know the truth. McGarr thought fleetingly of the inscription on the back of Hitchcock's watch. Certainly intelligence-gathering operations were, in some ways, important to the maintenance of world peace.

The Proscenium was on Broadway, not far from SIS headquarters. The black and canopied marquee was a bit too grand for the squat, granite building. The porter opened the rear door of the police car and said, "Colonel Cummings's man is awaiting you at the top of the stairs." Up a long flight of gleaming marble, a man dressed in tails and a stiff white tie was standing. He didn't appear even to look at Gallup and McGarr as they approached, but simply walked down the hallway which old wood and portraits of past club members made dark.

They passed reading and billiard rooms, a library, a bar, several offices, a large banquet hall, and were finally escorted into a small dining room which light gray walls and spanking linen tablecloths lit. Napkins were fanned in the water goblets, and tropical plants with wide and rubbery leaves framed French windows that offered a view of a miniature Augustan garden.

Four men had been conversing in front of one of these windows. Now they turned to Gallup and McGarr, and one of them, a middle-aged man, advanced with his hands clasped behind his back as though about to review troops at a dress parade. "Gallup, I take it, and . . . ah . . ."

"McGarr," said Gallup.

The man allowed his eyes, which were slightly glassy from drink, to run down McGarr's dark raincoat, his charcoal gray suit, and black bluchers. He then looked McGarr in the face and said to Gallup, "Does he have any identification?"

"Oh." Gallup pulled his arms out of his raincoat. "No need, no need. I worked for Peter when I was with Interpol. He's genuine."

Again the man considered McGarr briefly. "If you say so." He took Gallup by the arm and directed him toward the group of men who were still standing near the window. "Meet my associates. Edward Gallup, this is . . ."

McGarr asked one of the attendants where a public phone might be, walked out of the dining room and down the hall to the cloak-room, where he deposited his raincoat. He wanted to be able to retrieve it in case present C., this Cummings fellow, should prove even less of a man of goodwill than he had first shown himself to be.

In the public phone booth, he phoned the Trinity College, Dublin, chemistry department collect. When, at length, Dr. Cole came on the line, he asked, "What have you found, Patricia?"

"I'm guessing it's a ketobemidone compound, guessing because there was so very little of it on the top of that cork you sent me. Colorless, odorless, as tasteless as distilled water. It's very new, incredibly expensive because of a complicated cracking process, and totally unobtainable from any supply house since the price makes it commercially unfeasible as a substitute for any of the common anesthetics. If you want some, you've got to make it yourself and had better have a good lab and some skilled assistants. It's volatile and unstable at high temperatures."

"Good job, Pat. Thank you for the fast work." McGarr was about to hang up, but said, "Hold on, Doctor—would you please call my office and tell them I'm at this number in London. That way I'll save the citizens a few shillings." He gave her both numbers and rang off.

He then called Hugh Madigan, who said, "Hitchcock was on a pension. I estimate that if he was receiving half-pay he got five thousand pounds per year. He had a small inheritance, as well, of about five hundred or so. Her family used to have scads of money around the turn of the century, but lost it through mismanagement and the failure to diversify. They made saddles, tack, and riding boots. Some one of her brothers ran off to Rhodesia with the last of the company funds about five years ago, and the business collapsed. She, however, hasn't changed her habits, and still keeps a stable of show horses. One of her mares won the Derby last year. All things considered, it began to look like they had a lot of expenses and not much income, except for the Derby win which was a one-shot affair, so I did some further checking.

"I have a contact at the income tax office who discovered that Hitchcock had a full-time job as director of security for the ENI outfit's Scotland operation, you know, their exploration for oil off the coast. That's the Italian concern, I believe. What do the initials stand for, Peter?"

"*Ente Nazionali Idrocarburi.*"

"I often wondered why Italians are so enamored of initials. Now I can well see why. Where was I?

"Pays taxes on fifteen thousand, but with fringe benefits, et cetera, it's more like twenty. Even so, they live at the utter end of their tether, and their credit rating isn't much. I was beginning to think that now with the fellow dead she'd be having to cut her expenses drastically—both houses are mortgaged right up to the eaves—when I managed to come upon this interesting fact."

"Insurance?"

"Yes. Let me save the best part for last. He had a Civil Service standard policy which he had already borrowed against up to the eighty percent maximum, so that renders two thousand pounds. He had a private endowment plan of twenty thousand, had paid in about six, but had borrowed it back at five percent interest, so that yields about thirteen. Then there's a post office policy of under a thousand pounds. And then"—Madigan paused—"there's a relatively new—five years—straight term policy for one hundred twenty-five thousand pounds. The premium payments, given Hitchcock's life expectancy and his former occupation, were extraordinary, but the Dutch company that assumed the risk claims that the payments were current."

"Who's the beneficiary?"

"That's somewhat strange, that is. Even though he had a son of whom he was quite fond, everything in the big insurance policy goes to her."

"Son's name?"

"Edward Bernard David and resides in All Souls College, Oxford. Teaches mathematics, I believe. He's sure to inherit some of this estate."

"Well—that's just fine, Hugh. Is there anything else?"

"Yes. Who's handling this case? Gallup?"

"Right."

"Is it true he's going to be the new assistant commissioner of CID?"

"Yes."

"Why, then, don't the two of you meet me at the Carlton for drinks about tea time?"

"Don't you know him?"

"Not as well as I should, considering his new and exalted position."

"I'll try to bring him 'round and will call you if I can't."

"Don't bother about calling. Just be there yourself. We haven't hoisted a few jars since—I can't remember when."

McGarr surmised that Madigan, a functionalist, also had some Irish problem beyond his wish, which McGarr did not doubt in the least, to share a few drinks and reminisce about dear, dirty Dublin. "What do you know about the present C., Colonel Cummings?"

"That he's very good at his job, but not very well liked by his staff."

"Why so?"

"Runs the place on fear. Sacked a number of old-timers straightaway, put the rest into administrative limbos. Hasn't really done much field work himself—you know, a couple of years in Budapest where he specialized in blonds, beards, and bars, one year in Istanbul, and then he got a Washington assignment. Lacks humanity, they say, and a feel for what it's like being out on point all alone and cut off."

"Four-thirty?"

"Five—better, five-thirty." Madigan hung up.

Gallup was just completing his secondhand relation of the details pertaining to the Hitchcock murder when McGarr returned to the dining room.

Since the four men were sitting close to Cummings at the head of the table, which had been set for eight, McGarr had the choice of three seats. He chose the one at the other end of the table. This made a gap of two seats between him and the other men.

"And what do you know about this affair, McGarr?" asked Cummings. He had just finished a dish of thick oxtail soup and now gently stanched his lips with his napkin. Besides his obvious nastiness, there was something supercilious about his manner, gestures, and appearance. Somehow what little hair that remained on the sides of his head was a bit too neat and his skin seemed too fresh and talced, like that of a baby with an officious nanny. His gray eyes were sparkling now, as he reached for his wine glass.

"Only what I related to Assistant Commissioner Gallup, and he, no doubt, has conveyed to you."

"Assistant Commissioner?"

In the midst of raising his soup spoon to his lips, Gallup glanced at the other men and blushed.

"Some congratulations are in order, it seems." Cummings took the opportunity to taste his wine again.

Several of the men smiled to Gallup, but nobody said anything. It was quite obvious that Cummings had the floor and that, far from being a pleasant convocation over lunch, the meeting was to be an interrogation of McGarr.

"But certainly having seen poor C. in his last agony——"

One of the other men started, his head turned toward the window, and his hand began fumbling in his suit for a packet of cigarettes.

Cummings stared at him until he had the cigarette lit, then continued speaking to McGarr, "——you can tell us more particularly about—how do you people in the police phrase it?—the significant details?" Turning on the man with the cigarette, he said, "I really wish you would learn to quell that filthy habit, Stone. Having to smoke between courses is incontinent, as well as being quite disagreeable to the others of us at this table."

McGarr had tasted his soup, which he imagined must have taken a full day to prepare—sweating the thin oxtail slivers over a bed of carrots, leeks, and onions, covering it with an eight-hour bone stock, simmering for ten more hours, clarifying with chopped beef and further leeks, finely chopped, both ingredients whisked with raw egg white, then a brown roux and tomato purée for thickening, and sherry for taste—and found it delicious. He hardly heard Cummings say, "McGarr? Well—McGarr?"

McGarr took several additional spoonfuls of the soup and blotted his lips with the napkin. "No. I have nothing to add." He dipped his spoon in the soup once more.

Gallup had caught on to McGarr's tactic in dealing with Cummings. Being one of the men sitting closest to McGarr, he asked, "How do you manage to remain so thin, Peter? Your appetite has always been so unbounded."

"I concentrate on my comestibles, never rush through a meal, and always try to dine in pleasant company." McGarr smiled toward Cummings, who said, "Let's get the facts straight. Hitchcock was shot once in the back of the head. Small-caliber gun. His hands and feet had been trussed behind his . . ."

While Cummings catalogued the details of the crime and his associates pretended to listen to him attentively, one waiter removed McGarr's now empty soup service and another began serving *entrecôte mirabeau,* the cut between the bones of the ribs of beef which had been grilled, garnished with anchovy fillets, tarragon leaves, and stoned, blanched olives. It was served with anchovy butter. At the same time, the wine was changed from a pleasant Marsala to a hearty Clos Vougeot. Halfway through the dish, a waiter informed McGarr he had a telephone call in the lobby.

When McGarr returned to the table he pushed the plate aside and, interrupting Cummings, said, "Are all your operatives issued a ketobemidone knockout potion?"

"Of course not—those supplies are signed out only for special need and on a high-priority basis."

"How many of your agents carry twenty-two-caliber automatic handguns?"

"None. They're issued an effective weapon, the Walther nine millimeter. Each weapon is registered, as are the firing pin configurations and barrel markings. Look here——"

"Would it be possible to obtain a list of present and former SIS agents who had a grudge against Hitchcock and might want to kill him?"

"Certainly not. I don't know or care what the esprit may be in Irish organizations, but here in SIS the staff respect their commander. That some former agent, no matter how alienated, might try to murder Hitchcock is unthinkable." Cummings glanced around at his men. All were busily eating their steaks.

"Perhaps, then, you'd better begin thinking the unthinkable. The phone call I just received was from Dublin." McGarr stood. "Another man has been found in the same shed at the same house with a similar bullet hole in the back of his head. His name is C. B. H. Browne. Does that mean anything to you?"

Two men placed their napkins on their plates. Another slid back his chair and stood.

"I'd appreciate greatly your checking your records about the ketobemidone compound, the gun preference, and for disgruntled agents who might have threatened either one or both of these men. Also, I'd like to know right now if you have any idea of some foreign power which would benefit by the systematic execution of your former chiefs. Is this some sort of vendetta?"

Cummings shook his head. He was worried.

McGarr turned and started for the door.

"Where are you going?" Cummings demanded.

"Dingle, of course."

"Hold on—Gallup is going with you?"

Gallup looked up from his partially consumed steak.

"Well, aren't you?"

Gallup took a swallow of wine. "Well, I don't think so. I'm running CID now. That's an administrative assignment."

"Nonsense. I'll take care of all that," said Cummings. "I want *us* represented in this investigation." Cummings eyed McGarr once more.

As they hustled down the stairs of the Proscenium Club, Gallup said, "Blast his hide. Who the hell does he think he is?"

"A most important man in your government."

"But besides that."

"Isn't that enough?"

"I can't go traipsing all over the Irish outback like some rookie leg man. I've got supervisory duties to attend to. I've planned a reorganization. And then there's the new man I shall have to break into my old job!"

"But what if we crack the case and put a lid on the messy business right off?"

Gallup only looked out the window of the speeding police car at the busy London street.

"Anyhow, feel lucky that you won't have to work for Cummings but just this once."

"Only the idea that this killer, whoever he is, is working on a pattern cheers me at the moment."

At Heathrow, a Shannon-bound jet had been held up and was awaiting them. On the way down the aisle toward first class, McGarr ordered double whiskeys from a passing stewardess.

# 3

Midafternoon in late spring, the sprawling runways of poured concrete were bare. From above they looked like intersecting shuffleboards built for a giant. McGarr noted the clusters of buildings—light manufacturing and assembly plants, warehouses, and worker residence units—which now dotted the area near the terminus. As ever, the grass below was very green, the Shannon River silver, the ocean beyond a blue that merged to black offshore.

At the airport Garda post, McGarr and Gallup were unable to arrange for the use of a police car, since, as the lieutenant on duty told McGarr, "Of the three, two are in use, and one must remain at base in the event of an emergency."

McGarr looked the man straight in the eye and began smiling. He knew that the Shannon airport duty was considered to be among the softest in the country, since during the late fall, winter, and early spring very few problems arose. He wondered what sort of police business the other two automobiles could possibly be engaged in on a day like this. "This is an emergency of sorts. Ned Gallup, here," he gestured to the Englishman, although they had introduced themselves to the lieutenant a few minutes before, "is the assistant commissioner of CID, Scotland Yard. He has flown all the way over here to investigate a matter in Dingle. He's a busy man and must get back to his duties as soon as possible."

"That's no concern of mine," said the lieutenant. He was a wide man, young for an officer, with protrusive cheekbones that made his eyes seem sunken. His thick shock of black hair had been combed down but still bristled. "Orders are orders. The car stays put."

"I want the keys," said McGarr. He looked the man straight in the eye.

The prominent knobs on the lieutenant's cheeks flushed. "Well, you can't have them and that's *that.*"

Both of the Garda patrolmen who were in the small office turned to them. One was reading a newspaper and smoking a cigarette. His feet were on a desk. The other was pecking out a report on a typewriter.

McGarr turned to Gallup, "Would you wait in the car, please, Ned. I'd like to have a word with the lieutenant in private." The Cortina patrol car was visible through the window at the rear of the office.

"Well, goddammit!" the lieutenant shouted. "You so much as move and I'll place you under arrest!"

Gallup gave him a pained look and walked straight through the office and out to the car.

The two patrolmen were standing now, and one had walked toward McGarr, who turned to them and said, "My name is Peter McGarr and I'm chief inspector of detectives, Dublin Castle. Now, obviously your lieutenant doesn't believe me, but don't you make that mistake too." He pointed to one of the men. "Where are the other two police cars?"

The man looked at the lieutenant.

"Never mind about him," said McGarr. "Just tell me."

"Well," the man stammered, "one's at—at home with one of the boys. His wife has a doctor's appointment in Limerick. And the other is——"

"Son of a——" The lieutenant spun on his heels and took two large strides to the desk. He picked up the receiver of a phone and dialed *0.*

McGarr was still looking at the Garda patrolman. His small blue eyes demanded an answer.

"Well, the truth is only the lieutenant ever uses that one. It's new. It hasn't yet been run in."

"Where is it?" McGarr turned to the window. He could only see one car out there.

"Over in hangar *B.* We keep it there whenever the weather looks like it might be soft. One of the Aer Lingus boys gives her a touch with his polishing cloth now and again."

"Is this Dublin Castle?" the lieutenant barked into the phone. "Do you have a McGarr there? Put him on." He paused a moment. "Is this McGarr?"

McGarr knew the policeman must have reached McKeon, who dealt with all incoming queries when McGarr was away.

"This is Garda Lieutenant Mallon calling from Shannon airport. Does a McGarr work there? What's his position? I've got a joker here who says his name is McGarr. He claims he's chief inspector or something." McGarr had been on the job slightly over two years now. He conscientiously maintained a low image, which he believed best for efficient police work. He had had little to do with the regular Garda. Still and all, Mallon should have known who he was. "He's a little man, bald, about fifty." McGarr was still in his forties.

He distinctly heard McKeon say, "He's *the* chief inspector of detectives, special branch, and his other . . ." before Mallon tightened the receiver to his head. His other title was superintendent of the Garda Soichana, which made him the second most important law enforcement official in the country. Only the commissioner, who was two years from retirement, held higher rank, and McGarr had been hired into his present job on the agreement that the top post would be his when it came open. Of course, the Minister for Justice controlled all police matters, but his was an elective position.

From the length of time that Lieutenant Mallon listened, he must have been hearing most of this from McKeon. When Mallon turned to McGarr again, his face was drawn. The redness in his cheeks had spread. He handed the phone to McGarr. "Sergeant McKeon would like to speak with you."

McGarr took the receiver from him. "Do you mean Detective Sergeant McKeon?" he asked, smiling. McKeon's sergeancy was perhaps twenty years away from Mallon's present rank. "Bernie?"

"SIS, London, has been trying to get in touch with you for several hours now. They won't talk to anybody but you or Assistant Commissioner Gallup."

"Number?"

"No number, just an operator. Seventy-eight dash *H*. They do things official there. You'd think you were dealing with the Kremlin or the Pentagon."

"Many of the things they do involve both of those places. I sort of wish we could become a little more official over here as well." He glanced up at Mallon.

"If they call again, tell them to get in touch with Superintendent Scanlon in Dingle. That's where I'll be." McGarr hung up. He figured Cummings had been in no great rush to cooperate with him in his investigation of the Hitchcock murder and could well do with a little of the same treatment.

Turning around, McGarr said, "Would you two patrolmen mind leaving us alone for a moment?" He would never dress down an officer in front of his men. If he took away Mallon's pride, he could never expect the lieutenant to command the respect of his staff again.

When the men had shut the door behind them, McGarr asked Mallon, "How old are you, Lieutenant?"

"Thirty."

McGarr raised his eyebrows. "That's quite young to be a lieutenant. You must have done things right previously. University?"

"Cork."

"Honors?"

"Second, but high second in history."

"What do you think of this post?" McGarr meant the Shannon lieutenancy.

Mallon, flustered by the questions, confused that McGarr wasn't ripping into him, said, "Well—it's a—it's a job."

"But not much to do, right? No challenge. That's what the car is all about isn't it? That's at least a part of why you feel rather"— McGarr searched for the proper word—"nettled today? You think this is a dead end, that your career will be a concatenation of similarly boring assignments—Donegal, Roscommon, Wexford—little cattle towns or fishing villages with a paltry pension at the end of it all. Are you married?"

"Yes."

"Children?"

"Two. Boy and girl."

"How does your wife feel about this place?"

"Well"—Mallon was still looking down at his shoes—"it's not Cork City."

"Nor Dublin."

Mallon glanced up at McGarr. He breathed out and said, "No—nor Dublin."

"So, you're not happy here."

"No, I'm not."

"And, consequently, you're not happy being a Garda lieutenant."

Mallon breathed heavily again. "I shouldn't say this, but no, I'm not."

"And you've been considering quitting to try your hand at something else? Business? The law?"

Mallon nodded. "Yes—the law. Look, if you're going to sack me, I'll save you——"

McGarr reached up, grabbed the young man's shoulder. "Hold it, don't say anything stupid. Control yourself, man. If I acted the way you are acting now, certainly I would have sacked you ten minutes ago. I've got a temper, too, you know. Have a seat." It was not a request.

Mallon sat on the desk. Now he was McGarr's height.

"Now then," McGarr checked his watch. It was 4:15. "How would you like to come to work for me?"

Mallon, surprised, glanced up at him.

"Wait—let me tell you the advantages and the disadvantages of my offer. First, you'll be living in Dublin, I'll let you go to school part-time, and you'll certainly feel challenged. That brings me to the disadvantages, which are legion. That man you just talked to on the phone——"

"Detective Sergeant McKeon?"

McGarr noted that Mallon had understood the distinction. "——he is not a gentleman. He will think he owns you. He won't give a farthing for your home life or aspirations. You'll lose that monkey suit and your title. You'll be the new boy on the block, a raw inspector. The pay will be slightly less, the Dublin expenses grievous. Now then, do you want to think on it, discuss it with your wife?"

"Well, of course, I must——"

McGarr checked his watch once more. "You can do your thinking in the car while taking us down to Dingle. That way you can observe what a very small—the best—part of your job may be like, after you're with us for a while. I'll give you five minutes to call your wife. Tell her you won't be home until late tonight. At that time I'd like your decision." McGarr walked through the office. At the car he apologized to Gallup for the delay and altercation.

"No problem—it's a wonder any of them were awake." The vast parking lot was utterly devoid of automobiles.

When Mallon climbed behind the wheel, he asked, "Dingle?"

"No. Hangar *B* is our first stop. It'll probably be your last chance to drive that or any police car for a long time."

"You didn't——" Gallup asked McGarr.

McGarr put his finger to his lips.

A traffic light brought them to a halt just in front of the hangar. Stopped in a car across from them and traveling in the opposite direction was the very same black man with the broad forehead and close-set eyes who had been dining in the inn on the Shannon the day before. Next to him sat the other man. He was wearing a tan coat with a large fur collar. The car was a black Morris Marina and looked brand-new. Watching it pass by, McGarr noted that they were headed toward the terminus.

They drove southwest, nearly into the dwindling spring sun which, now that the days were growing longer, lingered well past supper. It was still weak, however, and cast upon the rock pastures and ubiquitous stone walls a pale, grainy light. For the second time in as many days McGarr was rushing down the banks of the Shannon. At this time of day, the salmon fishing boats were port bound, bucking the stiff tide and current upstream. Starboard running lights, bright green, winked as the boats pitched in the choppy whitecaps that a brisk wind now made. A supertanker droned twice, intending to overtake a pilot launch, and the other vessels scurried from its path. The monstrous craft, most of its hull submerged, wallowed up the estuary, pushing, it seemed to McGarr, half the Atlantic before its stubby prow.

Superintendent Terrence Scanlon was waiting for McGarr in front of Hitchcock's summer home on the tip of the Kerry peninsula. Hughie Ward and Liam O'Shaughnessy were inside the house.

After tea had been poured, Ward began his rundown. "The interior of the house is spotless, since we sealed the doors and windows because of the prior investigation. The outbuilding, too, was sealed, but that didn't seem to matter. Whoever they are, they hammered off the seal, then dumped Browne, who was unconscious—he's got a gash on his forehead—into the shed, and shot him once. His hands were bound with the same cargo cord."

Whoever they were, McGarr mused, they were very intent on making sure these two men with identical pasts had died in identical ways. "Have you checked the neighborhood?"

"No. We're only after just arriving ourselves," said O'Shaughnessy. "We called you the moment Terry called us. We had to drive."

"Then that's the first order of business."

"But most of the houses are vacant this time of year."

"But not all of them."

"No—not all."

"And laborers, field hands, shepherds, fishermen?"

"You could count them with either hand."

"Good. You take them, Terry. Liam and Hughie, you take the road to Dingle. After looking about for a while, Ned and I and Lieutenant Mallon will take the road around the head. Make sure you speak to everybody."

"What exactly are we looking for?" asked Scanlon. He, being the Dingle barracks commandant, was not used to McGarr's techniques.

"Anything out of the ordinary. If necessary, sit down, have a cup of tea. Certainly these two bodies didn't drop from the sky."

But, in fact, McGarr couldn't have been more wrong, for after having examined C. B. H. Browne's body and having quickly perused the immediate environs of the house, the three of them began canvassing the other dwellings in the area only to find a woman who had indeed noticed something strange earlier in the day.

Her bungalow was perched below the road and on the very face of the cliff of Slea Head. The walkway down to her front door had been chipped from the basalt itself, as had the foundation of the house. A long paned window in the main room, which served as a kitchen and living room, offered a view of the sunset over the western ocean.

Rolling clouds way out on the Atlantic were now a fiery pink that cast a red glow along the inner walls of the room. Over a peat fire, a black pot, hanging from an andiron, piped a small jet of steam. McGarr recognized the aroma immediately. It was lamb kidney stew with rashers. Also, he could smell fresh soda bread, the kind with caraway seeds and eggs. Sure enough, cooling on a low, stone-top table near the hearth was a large, circular loaf, its crown a glistening golden surface of baked yolks through which the currants protruded like so many eyes.

"Sit down. Where are ye all from?" the old lady asked. She shuffled over and switched off the early edition of the Telefis Eireann news. "Are ye from the 'far side'?" by which she meant England. "I should think so, considering your odd way of speaking and all. Would ye care for some tea?" She pronounced the last word "tay."

"No, thank you, ma'am," said Mallon, "we just——"

But McGarr, who was about to sit near the fire, reached over and slapped the Garda lieutenant's arm, then motioned toward the pot steaming over the fire. "But on second thought," continued Mallon, "it *was* weak tea, if you know what I mean."

"I do, I do," she said. "You mean you're hungry." She allowed the oilcloth she kept on top of the television to drop over the screen. "I always cover the contraption," she explained. "It's rented and not mine, and, what's more, I love it and could no more do without the thing than church." She shuffled toward the sideboard, her gait arthritic, half-walk, half-trot. She seemed ancient, perhaps in her eighties. Her white hair was bunned and she wore clear-frame bifocals, now yellow with age. McGarr could see at least two dress hems near the heavy black stockings that bound her thin legs. She also had on a sweater, checkerboard apron, and fluffy house slippers with bright green pom-poms on the toes. In spite of all her vestments, the room was snug.

McGarr stood and removed his jacket, saying, "The last thing we want to do, ma'am, is to put you to any bother, but the truth is that we were summoned rudely from our lunch and I have not eaten

peat-simmered lamb kidneys and rashers since my mother died."
He imagined that the old woman had not had company all winter.

She looked up from the tea canister on the sideboard. "And when
was that, dear boy?"

"I was quite young, ma'am."

"How old? I was a mother meself, and you can tell me."

"Ah—ten, I believe."

She shuffled over and put her hands on his shoulders, "And here
now thirty years later in Kate O'Connor's kitchen you'll eat them to
your heart's content." Lowering her voice, she said into his ear,
"Could you use a bit of the good stuff? I'd offer it to your man"—
she tilted her head to Mallon, who was in uniform—"but what I have
isn't exactly legal."

"Ah—to hell with legality and the law," said McGarr. "I think
that'd be smashin'. Just a sip, mind you." And before she could
shamble back to the sideboard, he added, "And you can offer the
others a drop too, since I believe"—he glanced out the window at
the ocean—"we're westwards of the law."

"I like you," she squeezed his shoulders and raised her head so
she could the better see McGarr through the bottom half of her
bifocals. "IRA?"

McGarr shook his head.

The bridge of her nose was thick, the end a rosy ball. Her eyebrows were still black. At one time, McGarr speculated, she had a
sort of dark, Spanish beauty one seldom saw any more. "There's
something wild about you, boy." She straightened up. "But don't
be too sure about being beyond the reach of the law." She turned
to Mallon. "No offense, darlin'." She patted his shoulder, too, and
returned to her work. "Because I believe they're patrolling the coast
in airships and regular." She handed Gallup an empty jam jar, then
one to Mallon, and finally McGarr, to whom she also reached a crock
that was nearly too heavy for her arm.

"How so?" McGarr poured a good amount into his container,
then handed the crock to Mallon.

"Heliochoppers," she confided past her hand. "They've nearly
flown two of them in through my windows lately."

Gallup poured some poteen into his jam jar and got up to look
out the window, where McGarr now stood.

The sun was a magenta crescent sliding rapidly into the far Atlantic. It made the distant water seem very blue. Directly below them waves slammed into the sheer cliff of Slea Head. Shadows and a ground fog rising from the Great Blasket were beginning to obscure that island.

"From which direction, ma'am, and when?"

"My name is Kathleen, son. That"—she pointed over her shoulder, as she placed four plates on the sideboard. "From off the water. Five days ago in the morning, say, half-eleven."

"North or south?"

"North, I believe. I heard the throbbing of its blades minutes before, every time the wind blew in my direction. I couldn't imagine who could be hammering spiles here and at this time of the year, so I climbed up to the road to look around. I saw its little light on top winking. The beating grew louder as it approached and nearly knocked me off me pins when it whisked over."

"Did you see it land?" Gallup asked.

"Gad—he has a beauty of a way of speaking, what? Are you English?"

"My great-grandmother was Irish."

She was bending to lift the black pot off the andiron. "Don't tell a soul. The way you talk nobody will ever suspect. No—in answer to your question, sir—I did not see it land."

"Did the noise stop soon after?" Mallon asked, somewhat sheepishly, looking to McGarr to see if he approved.

McGarr nodded and sipped from his cup.

"Now that you mention it, it did, son. But I've noticed in times past when, after a storm, the air force sends out several machines to look for shipwrecks, that the throbbing has a way of dying suddenly, so I took no notice, until last night."

McGarr finished his drink and made for the crock near the hearth.

She had begun to ladle the lamb kidneys and rasher stew onto the plates, on which thick slices of soda bread, lavishly buttered, now rested. The tea kettle was sitting right on the coals. "Last night, it was far different. It's at night a person hears things more distinct, what?"

"Of course, of course," McGarr said into the raised jar.

"The beating seemed to pick up once the thing was over the

house. I threw open the door to see if it had landed on the road above. It was frightful the racket it was making. What I then saw was lights in the heavens. They were twirling through the fog we had. Suddenly the throbbing stopped, then the light went off, then a little later the whirring sound ceased too. I shut the door to keep the dampness out, so I did.

"Then, while I was dozing over my darning, hours later, the thing started up again, made a great hullabaloo, and died out."

"Did you see which way it went?" Gallup asked.

"I was too tired to get up. I only know it did not go over the house or out to sea, because I looked out the window. I wanted to see its lights over the water, don't you know. Sit down now and eat while it's hot."

"Hadn't we ought to——"

McGarr knew Gallup wanted to buzz right back to Hitchcock's house and check the ground for evidence of the old woman's story, wanted to complete the on-site investigation and get back to London as soon as possible. "It's not shish kabab, patlijan moussaka, or stuffed grape leaves, Ned, but we have no Armenians on the western coast, and you'll be glad of it once you taste this stew."

Glumly, Gallup ate.

McGarr had thirds. Kathleen managed to dig up several bottles of stout. The peat sputtered in the fireplace, the waves beat against the cliffs, and the wind rattled the loose panes in her bay window.

With a cup of hot tea in one hand and a freshly lit Woodbine in the other, McGarr asked the old girl if he could use her phone, which was displayed prominently on a table by the door. It too was covered, but with a clear plastic sheath. "The calls are going to be to Dublin and London, Kathleen. I'll leave the money for it under the mat here." McGarr tapped the table.

"Will you have enough? All that distance won't strain the thing, I hope. Remember, it's new. I haven't really learned to use it myself as yet. My kids who live in America got it in for me. They call at Christmas and Easter and sound as though they're in the next room. It's luvelly what they can do now."

"Bernie?" McGarr said. "Peter here. I'd like you to send the pathologist's van down to pick up this corpse and some lab boys to cover the outbuilding carefully once more. Then I want you to dispatch Sinclair to the Air Ministry office to see if they have reports of helicopter movements in the past six days, especially over the western ocean and then from Slea Head eastwards. Maybe radar installations might pick up something like that."

"Too low," said Mallon, who was sipping his tea.

"Also, I want you to canvass all helicopter owners, pilots, and landing pads in the twenty-six counties. I'm sure I can get U.K. cooperation for the other helicopters in the general area."

Gallup nodded and took out a small black notebook and pen.

"Put as many men as you have to on this. I want to talk to anybody who has flown a helicopter over Kerry in the past week and a half." A correlation occurred to him at that moment. "Also, which of these persons might have recently purchased the elasticized cargo cord we've been investigating."

McKeon sighed.

"Or might soon. I assume whoever owns this helicopter will want to replace what's missing. The only other thing I can think of is the ketobemidone-base drug that Professor Cole found in Hitchcock's body. We better check Browne for that, although I'm assuming now the same person or persons who killed Hitchcock killed Browne."

"They certainly want it to look that way. Have you called London yet?"

"Cummings?"

"I don't know his name, he won't give it. But please get a hold of him, Peter. How is a man supposed to get any sleep around here with this horn going off every quarter hour?"

McGarr chuckled and said, "I'm presently at Dingle three ring seven," and put down the receiver. He picked it up again and asked the operator to connect him with London operator seventy-eight-H. While he was being connected, he glanced over at the old girl.

She was worried. McGarr surmised that she was a pensioner and would probably be hard pressed after the spread she had laid before the three policemen, yet being hospitable to the wayfarer was a Celtic tradition that most of the older people in the country honored. And McGarr was sure they had cheered her.

When the London number answered, he said, "Peter McGarr, Garda Soichana here."

"We were wondering when you'd call, McGarr. I had the exchange route all calls through to my home. I haven't had a chance to relax all evening." It was Cummings. "What have you discovered?"

"Gallup will fill you in."

"I beg your pardon," said Cummings indignantly. "I thought we were going to cooperate on this matter."

"So far," said McGarr, "it has been all give and no take. Have you gotten the information I asked you for this afternoon?"

"As a matter of fact, I have. But I must say I don't care for your thinking you have to extort it from me." In spite of his bluster, Cummings's tone had changed. In back of it all, McGarr thought he could detect a little fright. If the assassination of SIS C.'s was following a pattern, he was next.

"Well?" McGarr asked. "This call is costing me money." They were no longer speaking to each other over lunch at the Proscenium Club and McGarr wanted to make that very plain. Any continuing relationship had to be mutually beneficial.

"I've put together a list of our agents who have been issued the ketobemidone-base drug. We began using it only a year and two months ago so the list is not long.

"I then cross-referred this list with that of former, disgruntled agents of SIS. I came up with one man who is now an ENI employee. His name is Moses Foster. Do you know that Browne was also working for ENI?"

"What position?"

"Security, deputy director and second-in-command after Hitchcock." Cummings's tone was becoming self-satisfied once more. "This Foster is quite competent. He spent eleven years in Havana during the Cuban revolution and later through the many purges. Castro sent him to their embassy in Moscow and then Peking. After he narrowly escaped being exposed, we offered him a desk job in London. That galled him. He demanded a large amount of cash, not just his pension, but what he called 'combat pay for a Cold War hero,' all of it in one lump sum and immediately. When we told him that was impossible, he ran amok in our offices, put several senior fellows in hospital, nearly killed a policeman.

"In what I thought a surprising reversal some months later, Foster then accepted the post Browne—who was C. at the time the man was refused the lump sum payment—offered him with the security team at the ENI operations in Scotland. Browne felt he was the cause of Foster's problems, since Browne should have known better than to have tried to put Foster behind a desk. Well, Foster took the job about two years ago. When I saw Browne at the club from time to time, he said Foster was working out just fine."

McGarr asked, "Is he black?"

"Why, yes—he's Jamaican."

"About six feet, sixteen or seventeen stone, wide forehead, and close-set eyes?"

"Right again—how do you know this?"

"I'm not sure that I do. Are any other of your former agents currently employed by ENI?"

"I've checked that. None."

"What sort of operation is ENI running up in Scotland that it needs such high-caliber security?"

"Oil exploration is a cutthroat business, Mr. McGarr. A man who knows where the oil is well may make his life's fortune with that information. Hitchcock's, Browne's, and Foster's job was to see that that information stayed in the company. They were being very well paid for their services."

"Does Foster now become head of the security operations for ENI?"

"Yes."

"What about a former agent, a man about fifty with lots of curly white hair, a big, black moustache, and a sallow complexion? I should imagine he's handsome in a Mediterranean way."

"Nobody I can recall. I'll check, however. Any other details on him?"

"No—he was sitting in a car when I saw him. What about Browne? Was he married? Can we trace his movements before he arrived here in Ireland?"

"Not likely. He was a bachelor and necessarily rather secretive about his personal affairs. He employed an aged manservant. We've questioned him. He says Browne left for Scotland about a week ago, called twice to have certain letters read to him."

"Did you get a look at those?"

"Of course not. I didn't ask."

"Well, could you?"

"I could but I wouldn't. The poor man is dead."

"That's precisely the point. The poor man *is* dead, and we don't have a clue as to why."

"Well——"

"And then there's Mrs. Hitchcock. Do you know she stands to benefit from her husband's death to the tune of one hundred twenty-five thousand pounds? Could you arrange to have me talk to her?"

"I don't know, McGarr. Perhaps after a while, but right now she's——"

Suddenly McGarr's temper squalled. "Listen, Cummings—your feelings aren't important in this matter. Two men have been murdered in my country. All I know about them is that they worked together and at one time occupied your post. They were executed. If I were you, I'd be wondering if, perchance, these murders aren't following some bizarre pattern."

"I've thought about that."

"Then, can you get me an interview with Mrs. Hitchcock?"

"Well—not immediately, since her doctor has had to put her under heavy sedation."

McGarr doubted that. The woman he had met would require nothing like that.

"And when you do, I won't stand for any bullying or badgering of her, McGarr."

"I'm a slow learner," said McGarr. "I can remember nothing of the techniques you employed in the dining room of the Proscenium Club this afternoon." He hung up and asked Mallon for the Shannon Garda office number.

When it answered, McGarr said, "This is Peter McGarr again, do you remember me from this morning?" He was probably all the patrolmen had talked about since then. Their lieutenant was gone and no explanation, other than McGarr's altercation with him, could be given.

"Yessir."

"Do any of the rent-a-car franchises there have new, black Morris Marina two-door models for hire?"

"Yes sir, Ryans."

"Could you go over there and impound the one that a large black man was driving today? I think he's a Jamaican by the name of Moses Foster, although I could be wrong. There was another man with him —white, curly hair, black moustache, sallow complexion. He was wearing a tan coat with a tall fur collar. Both were well dressed."

He said to Mallon, "You'd better leave now. Scanlon will pick us up at the Hitchcock house. Find out, if you can, what flight they took. Do you have their descriptions?"

"Yes, I've been listening." Mallon thanked the old woman and left.

Gallup already had his coat on and his hat in his hand.

McGarr had returned to his jam jar of poteen.

"Hadn't we better . . . ?" said Gallup.

The phone began ringing.

Kathleen shambled over to it, saying, "Ah, there now you warmed it up for me and it's working. I wonder who that could be." She lifted off her glasses, put the receiver to her ear, and listened. "Where'd ye say? London? Then, 'tisn't for me, this call. I know no one there."

Already Gallup was rushing toward her with his hand out, "I'm from London, ma'am. Perhaps it's for me."

But it wasn't.

It was Hugh Madigan for McGarr. "Your man, McKeon, gave me this number, Peter."

"And you're at the Carlton, Hugh. Forgive me. We had to leave on a matter of some urgency."

"No problem. The reason I'm calling is that I happened to bump into an oil industry contact of mine here. Over dinner, for which I plan to charge you, he told me about a disputed oil claim in the Scottish offshore oil fields. It seems that a small, newly formed outfit called Tartan Oil Limited bought the exploration rights to a sliver of property which, because of inaccurate surveying by ENI engineers, is located between two of their big claims. Tartan immediately erected a derrick and began pumping. ENI claims Tartan has canted its well holes down into the ENI pools, since the geological configurations pretty much prove that there could not be any oil directly under the sliver of property. The matter is before the courts now, but if the determination goes against Tartan, they'll have to indemnify ENI for every barrel they've pumped so far. Tartan is an around-the-clock operation. The rig itself cost nearly five million pounds. If Tartan wins the fight, however, they can put up more rigs. The Tartan principals then would become very wealthy men indeed." Madigan seemed to think this story was fraught with significance. He had been drinking a good deal, McGarr could tell.

"But, I don't understand," said McGarr. "What does this have to do with me?"

"Didn't I mention that Hitchcock was a co-founder of this concern along with a chap named C. B. H. Browne?"

That knocked McGarr back. "No—no you didn't. Tell me, Hugh, did a fellow named Moses Foster work for them as well? He's a big black man, former SIS too. Pretty much of a rough customer."

"I wouldn't have the vaguest, but if you'll hold on———" Suddenly, McGarr could only hear the sounds of a bar crowd, a small band, and a chanteuse wailing a sultry nightclub number in decidedly American dialect. At least five minutes later, somebody demanded, "Is this McGarrity?"

"McGarr. Who's this?"

"Rod Drake of Exxon." He too was quite drunk. "How 'bout that nigger of yours—he pack a punch?" Drake had a heavy Texan drawl.

"Yes, I think so."

"Then, he works for ENI. Damn near handed me my head three weeks ago."

"Why so?"

"Got in an argument with him in a bar. Not much to do out there in Scotland but drink and fight and———" The bar crowd drowned out the last word. "He's got a thing about Cuba. Says it's a form of necessary totalitarianism."

"He does?" McGarr was surprised that this line of conversation could have come from a man like Foster who had spent years as a covert agent in several Communist countries including Cuba. Perhaps his recent troubles with SIS, McGarr thought, had changed his approach.

"Some happy horse manure about the citizen-worker. I asked him to step outside. That sidewinder grabbed me by the craw and chucked me down the gulch out back. Told me if he saw me again he'd break my back. He ain't seen me again."

Madigan came back on the line. "Isn't there a dandy little conflict of interest here, Peter? I say—working for one outfit's security section while your own company is pumping its reserves dry. We both know Hitchcock could have used the money."

"Could you do the same sort of background investigation of Browne too, Hugh? And Foster, if that's possible. And Tartan itself. Would you mind?"

"Now—no. I'm interested in this whole messy business, and I'm beginning to think I'm over in the States." When McGarr didn't say anything, Madigan completed the thought. "All the money I've spent today is green."

McGarr groaned and placed the receiver in its yoke. He took thirty pounds from his wallet and fitted the bills under the mat on the table. He had decided on the amount previously, thinking it enough to cover the food, drink, and phone calls. Now he wasn't quite sure and added ten more to be safe.

Gallup handed him his hat and coat. "Let's get up to the house and look around, then get me back to Shannon."

"Don't you want to call Cummings?"

"Not until I look around up there at the house. You know how he is—sticky on details."

"Perhaps I better tell you a few things as well," said McGarr, "but first——" McGarr turned back to the old woman. He wrapped his arm around her shoulder. "Thank you for the very fine dinner, as tasty—*tastier*—than I remember my mother's as being. I put a few quid under the mat there. Buy yourself something special with what's left."

"Isn't that nice of you, lad. What did you say your name was again?"

"McGarr, Peter McGarr."

"And I could tell from your conversation that you're a policeman."

"That I am."

"It shames me to think I asked you to commit a crime."

"It isn't the first time a pretty woman has."

"Nor, I hope for your sake, the last," said the old woman.

As they tramped down the road toward Hitchcock's vacation house, McGarr told Gallup what he had learned on the phone:

—that Browne, like Hitchcock, had worked for ENI.

—that the two former C.'s of SIS had hired a certain Jamaican, named Moses Foster, who had had access to SIS ketobemidone and was disgruntled with that agency. Because of Hitchcock's and Browne's deaths, Foster would become the security chief of the Scottish operation, a very well paying position.

—that Hitchcock and Browne had been involved in Tartan Limited, a company that was exploiting a discrepancy in the mapping of the ENI oil fields, information to which the two of them would have been privy.

—that McGarr may have seen Foster both at a Shannon inn two days ago and at the Shannon airport earlier in the day. Both times Foster had been with the same Latin-looking man.

It was this last bit of information that disturbed McGarr. "If, say, both Hitchcock and Browne had been ferried in by helicopter and Foster was involved in their deaths, then what was he doing in that car? Who is the other man?" McGarr noted the slight tang of salt spray and ozone off the wet rocks below the cliff. The sky overhead was cloudless, and the air, purified by winds of the Gulf Stream, was as clear as any he had ever breathed. Consequently, stars, layers deep, and the merest crescent of a moon lit their path.

At the house, the other policemen were clustered around the car.

McGarr looked at O'Shaughnessy, who shook his head. The others had found nothing. They all looked tired.

McGarr and Gallup walked to the end of the kitchen yard and climbed over a stile in the rock wall. Taking a pocket torch from his raincoat, McGarr searched two adjacent fields until, in a third, he found the grass flattened in a whorl and the tracks of helicopter landing bars in the soft earth. Also, he discovered very good impressions of two pairs of shoes, each person having debouched from sides of the craft. One set, he assumed, had been Browne's. They were huge. The feet of the other man were tiny, size seven or perhaps eight at most.

Staring down at the dark earth and dew glistening in the beam of the torch, Gallup said, "They probably needed that Foster fellow for muscle. Whoever owns feet that size is a near midget. He'd have trouble handling Browne even trussed."

McGarr asked Scanlon to take casts and ship a set to Dublin.

Far different from the afternoon was McGarr's reception now at the Shannon Garda office. Mallon was waiting at the counter with a sheaf of reports, and his two assistants were at their desks, heads bent over their work.

Mallon handed McGarr a sheet of paper and a carbon copy to Assistant Commissioner Gallup. He explained. "The black man rented the car under the name of Ignacio Garcia, when he arrived here a week ago from London. He used a British passport for identification. I've since checked it with the British. It's false.

"Since the other man didn't have to identify himself, I couldn't find his name, so I sent the Ignacio Garcia name to Detective Sergeant McKeon, who then conducted a computer search for the passenger lists of planes, ships, trains, and border crossings that the Garcia name might have appeared on. I figured that, unless he entered the country illegally, his name would have been logged and placed in the memory bank of the computer."

This computer process was new to Ireland and one of the many innovations which McGarr had made since becoming chief inspector. It allowed the police to keep tabs on visitors to the country.

"Here is the list." He handed another sheet to McGarr and a carbon to Gallup.

One name caught McGarr's eye. It was that of Enrico Rattei, the head of the ENI consortium. He turned to Gallup, who had also noticed it. McGarr, thinking back on the seven years he had lived in Italy while working for Interpol, could remember Rattei as looking very much like the man he had seen in the inn the day before and in the car here at the airport just a few hours ago.

Mallon continued, "The flight is from Birmingham via Dublin. I've circled the names of all the passengers who boarded at Dublin."

Rattei and "Garcia" had taken the flight from Birmingham.

"Check this name"—McGarr underlined the Rattei on the list—"and see where he went tonight. He departed from Shannon within the last six hours."

Mallon called over a Garda patrolman who set about the task.

"As far as we can determine, Garcia has not left the country, although a jet that was carrying an American basketball team to Russia stopped at the airport to refuel. They left with one more passenger than they had when they landed."

"How many blacks aboard?" asked Gallup.

"Nearly all of them."

"See if you can check with the airline about who the additional passenger was. When the plane lands in Russia, the airline telex should be able to tell us his name.

"Also, put a general alarm out for this Garcia bloke. He's six feet tall, seventeen stone, balding, speaks English with a Jamaican accent, no doubt. His other name may possibly be Foster. If it's not, we can hold him for possessing a false passport."

Mallon wrote these instructions on a small pad, then said, "Otherwise, this Garcia could have left on any of the small private planes that used the airport today. We've checked all fifty-three flight plans and passenger lists, but anybody wanting to smuggle him out of the country had only to put Garcia aboard without logging him on the list. We have no regular agency to check the veracity of private plane flight plans or passenger lists. They go and come as they please."

Mallon handed McGarr yet another sheet of paper. "This is my preliminary fingerprint report. Both occupants were wearing leather gloves."

Again McGarr and Gallup exchanged glances. Foster, if indeed the black man *were* Foster, would certainly wear gloves throughout any assignment such as the execution of Hitchcock and Browne. But McGarr wondered why Rattei hadn't, like Foster, used an alias. The latter, being a professional, should have insisted upon it.

McGarr's thoughts then ran to Hitchcock. He probably would have gone to great pains to prepare that dinner for Rattei. Officially, Rattei was his boss. Rattei was probably used to eating well. And Hitchcock might have felt some guilt regarding his involvement with Tartan Oil Limited.

At the end of the room, a Garda patrolman ripped a sheet from the autowriter of the telex, walked over, and handed it to Mallon, who read, "Rattei, Enrico: Shannon to Dublin to Birmingham, where he changed to Caledonian that flew him to Aberdeen."

"Back to the oil fields," said Gallup.

McGarr smiled. "Good job, Lieutenant." He then looked the young man in the eye. "Well?"

"I accept your offer."

"What did the wife say?"

"She said, 'Ah, Dublin!'"

"That's fine. Now then," McGarr turned to Liam O'Shaughnessy, "Lieutenant Mallon will report to you on"—it was Wednesday—"Monday next, Liam. He'll have our car with him." McGarr meant the one which O'Shaughnessy and Ward had driven out to Dingle. It was parked outside the office now. "That way he'll have transportation and Hughie won't have to lug us back to Dublin."

Ward was relieved. He allowed his shoulder to rest against the wall.

McGarr checked his watch. "Do you reckon we can catch a shuttle back to Dublin, Lieutenant?"

Mallon looked at the clock on the wall. "Within the hour."

"When's your plane, Ned?"

"Two hours," Gallup replied glumly.

"Then I'll stand us a round or two in the bar," said the chief inspector. "You too, Mallon. A celebration, what?"

Mallon smiled and ripped the top sheet off the scratch pad.

Sitting in a lounge booth on the second floor of the terminus, McGarr looked out on the expanse of concrete runway. The landing lights diminished into the distance until both lines seemed to merge. A plane taxied slowly past, its fuselage beacon spinning and tail lights winking.

McGarr sipped from the tumbler that contained fourteen-year-old Jameson's poured over crushed ice, and tried not to hypothesize about Foster's role in the Hitchcock and Browne murders. He knew such speculating was bad form in police work, but often, as now, he couldn't keep his imagination from speeding ahead of the facts.

Thus, he mused: Foster had discovered Hitchcock and Browne's involvement in Tartan Oil. Foster went to the Italian with the information. Rattei hired Foster, a man with a penchant for violence, to help him dispose of the two former C.'s of SIS. Rattei asked Hitchcock for a meeting. On holiday at the time, Hitchcock invited him down to Dingle. Foster waited in the car so Hitchcock wouldn't be suspicious. Rattei presented Hitchcock with a gift—a bottle of wine drugged with the supplies Foster had gotten when working for SIS. When Hitchcock passed out, Foster and Rattei dragged him out to the shed, waited for the drug to wear off, then killed him. That was six days ago. Rattei flew out of there in a helicopter.

Four days later, Rattei had Browne flown in, perhaps ostensibly for a meeting with him and Hitchcock, whose murder Browne could not have known about. They didn't fool around with Browne. They bashed in his head, dragged him into the vacation house, and murdered him.

One thing bothered McGarr about all of this—why a man in Rattei's position would resort to the murders even of corporate criminals like Hitchcock and Browne.

If McGarr's speculations were true, then the helicopter pilot with the small feet was crucial. His stake in the Hitchcock and Browne murders could not be as weighty as Rattei's or Foster's.

In order to distract his rampant fancy and learn more about Rattei, McGarr asked Gallup, "Wasn't Enrico Rattei the last classic example of a condottiere?" For Interpol, Gallup had specialized in corporate crime.

"With one exception," said Gallup. "He had his own private vision of the part which Italy should play in international affairs and strong views of internal policies."

The waitress had just delivered the second round of drinks, and McGarr couldn't keep himself from staring at her. But for a bump on the bridge of her nose, her face was beautiful. It was long, cheekbones and chin angular. She had brushed her black hair off her forehead. Her eyes were gray.

What pleased McGarr most, however, was her body. She was just slightly overripe. A big woman, he knew how she would feel against him—soft, maybe just a little too soft. And that would be good.

Embarrassed under his gaze, she hurried off.

Remembering himself, McGarr asked Gallup, "Didn't Rattei go along with Mussolini?"

"Of course. He despised private industry, thought it inefficient because competition was wasteful of the nation's collective energy and provided no mechanism for leadership and planning. In his Italy, he said, there would be no need for one hundred and eleven bicycle manufacturers. Italy would make one bicycle, the world's best. And so for planes, ships, cars, et cetera. And nearly everything that his state-owned companies made *was* the best at least in some way.

"I remember him on the Via Veneto, sitting at a sidewalk café like any other worldly Roman, having an aperitif and ogling the prostitutes, jibing with the pimps, familiar with the gangsters, dope peddlers, down-and-outs of every description. He remained cynically disdainful of bourgeois mores. For him, life was a circus. He was no different from the performers on the Via Veneto, except that his act was to make huge industries run profitably. A Roman to the core.

"And how about his skinning the international oil companies?"

"What was that about again?"

"The oil people had made a deal to pump Libyan oil. All of the companies had agreed to offering the Libyans no more than thirty percent of the profits. The Libyan government then had no choice. If they wanted their oil pumped, they had to agree to the thirty percent rate. They signed the deal and the companies began moving their equipment into Tripoli.

"Then Rattei heard about it. Some oil executive at a party bragged about how his company had negotiated the agreement and that it was signed and there now was nothing ENI could do about it. Next day, Rattei was in Libya where he offered that government fifty percent. The oil industry was stunned. They never dreamed he'd attack them by cutting what they thought was an inviolable profit margin. All the other Arab countries began demanding a fifty-fifty split.

"The television news interviewed him at his table in the café on the Via Veneto. He was smiling like a self-satisfied tiger. He said that if the privately owned oil companies couldn't compete with ENI, they would have to step aside, that he was going to reexamine his profit margins in other countries the next morning. If he could still break even with a split of less than fifty percent, he would take some more foreign drilling rights away from the oil cartels. He said he would in no way honor any agreements that were founded on price fixing and international capitalist exploitation. Three days later, a plane on which he was supposed to be riding blew up. A few weeks after that, some gunman shot at him in Paris."

Every time the waitress glanced over at their table, McGarr fixed her with his gaze.

Gallup continued. "Then there was the time he went on television to boast to the nation how ENI had discovered vast supplies of methane in Ferrandina, *and* right where private industry had prospected and found nothing. He began laughing again, and, I think, the entire Italian nation laughed along with him. Tall, good-looking, holding a ruler in his hand like a schoolteacher, he had taught the British and Dutch and Americans how competent Italians were. He wanted to give his countrymen a chance to gloat along with him."

"What's his background?"

"Working class. Father was a carabiniere, and Rattei ran ENI for the citizen-workers of the country. ENI led all commerce and industry in providing for worker comfort and dignity."

"Sounds like an interesting man."

"All that and more. Recently, in spite of his Fascist background, he has become the first Westerner to set up derricks in the Soviet Union. ENI is currently pumping Russian crude.

"That puts Rattei in Russia, Libya, Iran, Saudi Arabia, Venezuela, Scotland, and, I believe, he's currently negotiating a deal right here in Ireland somewhere out there"—Gallup gestured toward the windows—"off the western coast. Some investment bankers think he's overextended right now, that ENI profits, of which Italy itself absorbs most, don't justify all the exploration drilling he's doing, but others, who have backbone, have financed him so far. One thing is certain, however—he needs to show some results."

"You mean Tartan might be hurting him?"

"Maybe not in barrels-per-day pumped, but Tartan complicates the Scottish picture for ENI. I'm sure Tartan is a thorn in Rattei's side. I understand he floated further oil exploration loans based on his own purported estimates of ENI's Scottish holdings, which now he's got to make pay."

"Is he married?"

"No. They say he had a disappointing love affair when he was a student in university, and that ever since he has remained a great womanizer in the Don Juan mode—he makes no permanent commitments."

"Which university?"

"Siena, I believe. But he was born in Rome."

Because McGarr paid the tab, he was the last to leave the booth. "Are you married?" he asked the waitress, as he placed the money on the table.

"Widowed. And yourself?"

He cocked his head, but said nothing.

"Are you off to Dublin now, Inspector?" she asked. McGarr surmised that the story about Lieutenant Mallon had spread throughout the building. "That's a shame," she continued. "I was thinking it would be nice to have a drink and talk to you."

McGarr looked up at her face.

It was her turn to fix him in the gaze of her gray eyes. She smiled. Her cheeks were flushed.

McGarr walked toward the other policemen, who were waiting for him in the hall. He paused at the door and looked back at her.

She had her back to him, placing the empty glasses on the tray.

Passing by the international section, McGarr thought about popping into the duty-free shop and buying something for his wife. But he rejected this formal expiation. Somehow his guilt would sully the gift.

And of this he was glad, since, when the police car pulled up in front of his modest Victorian house in Rathmines, a suburb of Dublin, he saw the light go on upstairs in his bedroom. His wife, Noreen, who was nearly twenty years younger than he, had drawn McGarr a bath by the time he deposited his hat and coat on the rack in the hall and poured himself a short drink.

A small woman whose hair was a tight nest of copper curls, Noreen's body was so perfectly proportioned that all her movements seemed effortless. Her face, arms, and legs were delicately freckled. Knowing he was tired, she didn't ask him any questions, only smiled when she dried him with a large, fluffy towel, and took him to bed.

# 4

From the shore, the oil derricks seemed like toys in a child's dream, appearing now and then through the mist. Here the coast of Scotland was treeless. Gorse, thistle, saw grass and lichen clung to the rocks and fronted the stiff breezes off the North Sea, such as the one into which McGarr and O'Shaughnessy now squinted.

Both were standing at the windscreen of a launch that was charging through the choppy sea toward the ENI oil claim. They had dressed for the weather and seemed like Principal and Interest, two London bankers in search of a profitable deal, for not only did both wear black bowlers and charcoal gray overcoats, but also, standing side by side, their differing sizes made them seem like Investment and Yield in a vertical bar graph. O'Shaughnessy was 6'8", McGarr just 5'9". The latter, however, wore a bright red rose in his buttonhole. It was the first of the season, and he had plucked it from a bush outside his front door.

O'Shaughnessy, not attempting to speak over the roar of the diesel engines, nudged McGarr and pointed into the overcast sky off the port bow. There a helicopter had dipped below the clouds and now skimmed over the water, passing by the launch in a rush. Earlier, they had seen several others. In a telephone call, Gallup had said that the job of checking on helicopter owners and pilots would be nearly impossible, but McGarr had scoffed at his attitude and had insisted on the continuing search. If they could find the helicopter pilot with the tiny feet, McGarr was sure they could learn the facts of the murders. The launch pitched and yawed, as McGarr and O'Shaughnessy stepped into the elevator of the oil rig.

*"Buona sera,"* said McGarr to a man who approached them when

they had reached the work platform of the derrick. Here everybody wore yellow safety helmets.

The man held two in his hands which he gave to McGarr and O'Shaughnessy. *"Sera,"* he said. *"Se e lecito, potrei sapere chi e lèi?"*

*"Me chiamo Pietro McGarr. Io sono il* chief inspector *di la polizía, Dublino, Irlanda. Questo e il Signor Liam O'Shaughnessy, mio coòrte. E possíbile parlare con Signor Rattei?"*

*"Certo.* Follow me," he said in English.

As they walked toward a collection of low buildings near the center of the drilling platform, McGarr asked him, "Are you the security officer here?"

*"Si,"* the man replied laconically. He, too, was small. He wore a heavy sweater and the left side of his face presented a walleye to the policemen. McGarr could see O'Shaughnessy checking the man's feet, which were quite small.

On two corners helicopters were chained to the platform. One was a large freight-carrying affair with twin jet engines along the fuselage. The other was a small two-seater. The drilling shaft of the well was spinning very fast. Everywhere, it seemed, large diesel engines, painted the same bright yellow as the hard hats, were roaring. One was raising the hook of a crane. Another was turning a dynamo for electrical power. Others drove forklift trucks and mechanical mules.

Once inside the metal building, however, the din ceased with an abruption that made McGarr's ears ring. A pneumatic valve sealed the door. Thick insulation made the interior toasty. The security man waited while McGarr and O'Shaughnessy doffed their hats and coats, then showed them into a lounge area, one wall of which was a magazine rack. Periodicals in all the European languages bristled from it. On the other side of the room was a tea station. Hot water in Silex pitchers bubbled on the stove top. The large table in the center of the room was obviously used for conferences. The ashtrays were brimming with snuffed cigarette butts. Thus, the air was stale. McGarr stopped the security man before he could sugar their teas. "Signor Rattei will see you shortly," he said and left the room.

"I hear the pay out on one of these things is phenomenal," said O'Shaughnessy, easing himself against the table.

McGarr had sat in a low chair near the magazine rack. "It would

have to be. Just think—you're Bolognese, used to urban living at its
pleasantest. You take a job out here to make yourself a stake, say,
for a little business. The money is great, but you work fourteen
straight days with nothing but the magazine rack for solace, then get
three days off in some Scottish fishing village where the women wear
knickers and bathe twice a year. I don't know"—McGarr reached
out and fanned the pages of a magazine—"life is too short to go
through it like a drudge."

O'Shaughnessy looked into his teacup. "The pot and the kettle."
He took a sip, then added, "Tell me what two intelligent human
beings from another part of the world are doing out in this godfor-
saken place?"

"Exactly my sentiments, gentlemen," said a man who was standing in the doorway of the lounge. He too wore a hard hat and a
yellow down jacket that made his arms look puffy. "I'm Enrico
Rattei. What can I do for you?"

McGarr stood.

O'Shaughnessy extended his hand and introduced them.

Rattei was a tall man whose looks were rugged but not unhand-
some in a southern Italian manner—his complexion was swarthy
and rough, nose angular, eyes dark and clear. His moustache was,
like the man in the car, black and full, crimping around the corners
of his mouth. His smile was full, however, and he seemed genuinely
pleased to meet them. He removed the hard hat. His full head of
gray curls, almost white, made him identical with the person McGarr
had seen in the inn on the Shannon and in the car with the black
man.

"We're investigating two murders."

"Where?" Rattei was rubbing his hands together. "Here? Not
here. In Dublin?" He walked toward the tea station and poured
himself a cup of thick, black coffee.

"In—rather, near—Dingle."

Rattei added several sugar cubes to his coffee. "I've been there,"
he said. "One of the men who works for me——" He stopped
stirring and looked up at McGarr. "Not Hitchcock."

"*And* Browne," said O'Shaughnessy.

Both he and McGarr were staring at Rattei.

"How?" He seemed shocked.

"Bullets in the backs of their heads."

Rattei walked over and closed the conference room doors. "Maybe we had better step into my uffizio," he said, then corrected, "off-fiss," as though his thoughts were preoccupied. He was wearing a navy blue V-neck sweater over a yellow shirt. His pants were uniform khaki; his heavy-duty shoes had steel toes. He wore no jewelry, not even a wristwatch. Evidently, when he was working, McGarr mused, he left the Via Veneto in Rome.

The interior of the small office was similarly businesslike. What with the desk and at least six filing cabinets—geological charts stacked on top and nearly to the ceiling—there was hardly room for McGarr and two big men like O'Shaughnessy and Rattei. Yet, the latter shut that door too. At his desk, he opened the top drawer and took out a tin of mints. He offered them to the two policemen, then placed one on his tongue. McGarr concluded from this and the absence of ashtrays in the office that, unlike most Romans, Rattei didn't smoke. He certainly was an uncharacteristic refugee from the Via Veneto.

"But why?" Rattei asked. His brow was furrowed, eyes worried. "Could it have been because of their former——" He glanced over at the other two.

O'Shaughnessy said, "We know who Hitchcock and Browne had been before coming to work for you. We've cleared this investigation with the British government. It's possible, but not likely, in view of our investigation. What I mean is that no other power would have ordered them murdered. They were retired, and that sort of thing just isn't done to heads of a department."

Throughout the interview O'Shaughnessy was to do most of the talking. They had planned it that way, so McGarr could assess the effects of their questions on Rattei.

"Well then, who—why?"

O'Shaughnessy reached into his suit coat and drew out a small black notebook. The Garda superintendent was so large that he had to have his clothes tailored to him. Today he was wearing a light gray suit, double-breasted, that fit him perfectly. He had shaved his red face so closely it shone. His nose was straight, eyes light blue.

His sandy hair had begun to gray at the tips. He was sixty-one. "May I ask where you were yesterday, Signor Rattei?"

"Certainly. Here. All day. Why this question, if you don't mind?"

"Because a man who resembled you was seen at Shannon airport."

"Well"—Rattei flicked his wrist—"there are many men who look like me. But the fact is, I didn't leave the rig. We're having some—er, difficulties that I want to oversee personally. If you like, you can question the personnel. I could be mistaken, but I don't believe any of our craft left the rig yesterday."

"Did you have any deliveries?"

"Of course, throughout the day."

"And at night?"

"No, certainly not. It gets—how do you say?—sacked——"

"Socked," McGarr supplied.

"That's right—socked in here at night."

Rattei picked up the receiver on his desk and said, *"Prego. Abbiamo ricevuto noi alcuni consegni questa mattína? Alcuni genti—operàio o visitatóre?"* When he put down the phone, he said, "This morning the sea was too rough. One helicopter pilot is on leave. The other is in hospital at Aberdeen. You are the only two visitors today, or, for that matter, forever. Nobody but ENI personnel has ever set foot on this installation."

"We would like your permission to check all of this," McGarr said.

"Certainly, Signor——"

"McGarr," McGarr supplied.

"And——" Rattei glanced at O'Shaughnessy.

"O'Shaughnessy."

"O'——" Rattei began copying their names onto the top sheet of his blotter, which McGarr had noticed and wanted to scan earlier. It was covered with jottings.

O'Shaughnessy handed Rattei his card.

McGarr placed one of his on the desk too.

"Irish names," Rattei explained, somewhat embarrassed, "are probably like Italian names to Irishmen. Impossible to spell."

"Tartan Limited," said O'Shaughnessy. "What can you tell us about that outfit?"

*"Ladri, rapinatore, predone!"*

"Have you ever had that company investigated?"

"It is a Panamanian concern, which means the principals do not have to reveal their identities. In any case, I am too busy to deal with these *scarafaggie*. I have lawyers for such characters."

"Hitchcock and Browne were the co-owners of Tartan Limited."

Rattei snapped his head to O'Shaughnessy. His eyes flashed. "That's a lie. I don't believe you. Have you any proof? Why couldn't my lawyers discover this?"

"They probably did," said McGarr. "But the names meant nothing to them. Your lawyers, I take it, are not involved in the everyday operation of your company."

Rattei nodded. He paused, then said, "I don't understand."

"Neither do we," said O'Shaughnessy. With one long finger he flipped a page in his notebook. "Now—Moses Foster, what can you tell us about him?"

"Foster?"

"He works for you."

"Really? Here?"

O'Shaughnessy nodded.

Rattei reached over and opened a file cabinet which he thumbed through. He drew out a file. "So he does." He placed it on his desk and opened it. "Ah, yes, the black man. Browne hired him. An African, isn't he?"

"Jamaican."

"That's right." Rattei flipped through the file, then handed it to O'Shaughnessy. "I can't tell you any more than what you see here. I've met the man once, seen him on this and our other Scottish rigs on other occasions, but I can only afford to spend a small amount of my time up here. You must realize that ENI is——"

O'Shaughnessy said, "Yes—we understand. Do you know that he now becomes chief of ENI security here in Scotland?"

"Obviously—he's next in line."

"Do you have confidence in him?"

"Now, if what you tell me about Browne and Hitchcock is true, I don't know. Could he be involved with this Tartan as well?"

"We don't as yet know."

"When you do, could you tell me?"

O'Shaughnessy looked at McGarr, who nodded.

"I'd appreciate it, but, in light of these disclosures, I should imagine the entire security operation should be examined. I often wondered how this Tartan could have discovered our surveying error. I always thought the engineers themselves were involved in this thing. I dismissed the lot of them outright."

"Seven days ago, where were you?"

"London."

"Where did you stay?"

"I didn't. I stopped there only to have dinner with a friend."

"Name?"

"Can I trust you to be discreet?"

"Yes."

"Her name is Cummings. Her husband is presently——" He looked up to find both O'Shaughnessy and McGarr staring at him. "——but you probably already know who he is. Her name was Enna Ricasoli before she married that——" Rattei reached for another mint and placed it on his tongue. "——person." He looked out the narrow double window into the rough water of the North Sea. "I knew her when I was a student in university."

"Siena?" McGarr asked.

Rattei nodded. "Her name, as you probably know, is that of one of the original noble families of Tuscany. We attended lectures together and became friends. It's been the same ever since. Whenever my schedule allows me to visit London, we dine together."

"Does her husband know about this?"

"I don't know. I never asked her. I should imagine so—it's been going on for some time."

McGarr cleared his throat. "You're a powerful man, Signor Rattei. Your personal history is more or less public knowledge. Is this the woman people speak about as being the reason you never married?"

Rattei looked away. "I don't care to speculate about that."

"Well then—do you love Mrs. Cummings?" asked O'Shaughnessy.

"Nor that either. You're getting too personal, gentlemen. I didn't murder Hitchcock or Browne. And I don't know who did." He stood. "What's more, I must get on with my work."

"One more question," McGarr said. "How much does Tartan hurt you?"

"With a dozen rigs they could pump this cistern dry. But they are enjoined now from erecting others until our countersuit is settled. And then—I don't know if you realize the dynamics of the problem —they had to run their pipe under our claim. See that portable rig?" Rattei pointed out the window in back of him. "It has been placed there solely for the purpose of finding the Tartan well pipe and smashing it. Did you notice any crude in the water when you came in, gentlemen?"

The policemen shook their heads.

"That's because ENI is so good at its job that yesterday we cut their pipe and pieced our own into it. Eventually a permanent well will be erected there."

McGarr asked, "But what about ENI's international financial position? Aren't you overextended?"

Rattei smirked. "I've read that too in some financial journals. But that's why those men must spend their time writing about men like me. They're rabbits, afraid to take chances."

"Unlike the men who founded Tartan. Certainly they weren't afraid to take chances."

"I think you know how I feel about them."

"But in a large sense Tartan complicates your financial picture. You floated loans for further oil exploitation based on your purported success here."

Rattei sighed, opened the desk drawer, and took out the pastille box again. "Signor McGarr, the oil industry is booming. ENI is opening more new wellheads than any other single entity in the world. If one half of these produce even moderately, ENI will dominate the oil picture in twenty years."

"But if——"

"No 'but ifs.' I have no time for 'but ifs.' I personally examined all the research reports, and then made my decisions based on forty years of unequaled success in this industry. Fifty percent of the wellheads is my minimum estimate. It can go no lower." Rattei said that with a conviction that would convince most investment bankers, McGarr believed.

"Now then," said Rattei, "would you like to speak to my men and this Foster?" He picked up the phone. "Afterwards, would you please ask Foster to get in touch with me immediately. He should be at our docks in Aberdeen."

But when after five minutes of ringing Rattei got no answer, he called his job-site chief into the office. Also an Italian, he said he had not been able to reach Hitchcock for the past week and a half, Browne for several days, and had never, in fact, spoken to Foster.

Rattei shrugged. He was disgusted.

As McGarr and O'Shaughnessy put on their overcoats, they could hear Rattei and his job chief discussing their security arrangements. In a rush of Italian, Rattei was saying, "No wonder those bastards knew about that error. They weren't doing a thing around here but looking for a way to bilk us. I want you to get that Foster in here as soon as you can find him, Maurizio. And have a severance check ready. I don't care if he's guilty of corporate theft or not. He had something to do with those——" Rattei couldn't find an adequate descriptive term. "——and that's enough for me. Get rid of him."

For over two hours, the policemen checked Rattei's explanation of his whereabouts on the days of the murders. McGarr's Italian passed through a formal, rusty stage, and finally became colloquial again. They could not find one man who appeared to be telling anything but the truth. All corroborated Rattei's story.

They reached the docks of Aberdeen at nightfall. The ENI office was dark; and the watchman, after much convincing, finally called Rattei's office on the oil derrick, received permission, and allowed the Irishmen to search Hitchcock's and Browne's offices. They discovered each to be as neat and as free from personal effects as one would expect of two former C.'s of SIS.

In fact, a film of dust covered the top of Foster's desk.

McGarr picked up the phone and called Hugh Madigan in London.

"Peter! Where in hell have you been? I've been calling Dublin and half of Scotland trying to get in touch with you."

McGarr said nothing. Madigan really never expected dialogue when he had something to disclose. "My contact in the Panamanian embassy got in touch with a certain record keeper in her country.

Guess who else is listed as a Tartan officer?"

"Cummings."

The line remained silent for a moment. "You knew?" Madigan was deflated.

"No—just a lucky guess. I figure Hitchcock, Browne, and Cummings were all part of the same set. When they needed money to launch a venture that might have proved lucrative, they would have kept it among themselves. It's common knowledge that Cummings is quite wealthy."

"Do you think, then, that ENI ordered their murders or that Cummings is next?"

Shaking his pack of Woodbines, McGarr placed his lips on the pack and drew out a cigarette. He flicked open the top of his lighter and lit it, holding the flame to the end of the cigarette. The smoke was sweet, relaxing. It was his first cigarette of the day. He was trying to cut down. The office was very quiet. McGarr could hear the slosh of water below them, underneath the docks. "Perhaps Cummings is also a target. It's been made obvious that Foster is either the actual killer or an accomplice. It's been made equally clear that Rattei had plenty of, let's say, 'overt' motives to murder Hitchcock and Browne. But why would Rattei have been so careless about traveling with Foster, about being seen with him in public and even by me? Could he have wanted to kill them himself so badly that he couldn't think of anything else? The crimes themselves were utterly devoid of passion, more *colpi di grazia*"—he used the Italian term instead of the French—"than murders."

The Garda superintendent nodded once.

"And Rattei could be a consummate actor. Today he seemed so shocked, so completely surprised about the Tartan details." McGarr was trying to remember something Gallup had told him about Rattei having appeared on television, smiling like a contented tiger. "And now it appears he has two motives to murder Cummings. *That* bothers me."

"Why two?" Madigan asked.

"It's complicated," said McGarr, not wanting to breach the trust Rattei had asked him to observe. "Lookit, Hugh—could you contact Ned Gallup at CID and tell him everything you know? That way he can provide Cummings with immediate security. This Foster fellow is certainly effective. If Cummings is Foster's next target, he'll need some protection."

"Will do," said Madigan.

McGarr imagined that giving Madigan the opportunity of calling Gallup with this information would be worth more to Madigan than a thousand formal introductions to the assistant commissioner of CID.

"And another thing," said McGarr, knowing the time was ripe to ask for a favor. "Could you put a few feelers out about Rattei? You know, personal things, what he's like as a human being, his passions, vices if any, his hobbies and preoccupations."

"I wasn't the only one who has been making inquiries about Tartan in Panama."

"Really?"

"Lawyers in London by the name of Loescher, Dull, and Griggs made a query three weeks ago."

"Could you find out who they represent?"

"For a fee."

"Of course." McGarr rang off.

"Hadn't we better call Cummings himself?" asked O'Shaughnessy.

McGarr remembered that he had used operator 78-$H$ and surmised that in the case of emergency she could connect the proper party with the C. of SIS. A half-hour later, during which time both of them ransacked the office for a drink with no success, the phone rang. It was Cummings.

When McGarr told him his life was in imminent danger, Cummings scoffed, "That's the nature of my profession, Mr. McGarr." But plainly he was concerned.

"Well, the nature of mine is that of apprehending whoever killed Hitchcock and Browne. And for either of two reasons or both, I believe that you are the killer's next target."

"That's rubbish—who would want to kill me and why?"

"I can explain it to you in detail."

"Not now, you can't. I've got a dinner engagement."

"Where?" McGarr wanted the information in case Gallup was too late in reaching Cummings.

"Is that really any of your business?" Cummings was trying to act superior again, unafraid, on top of it all.

McGarr knew, however, the stance was feigned. He sighed. "Let me tell you a thing or two, Mr. C. of SIS. I really wish it weren't. Everything I've seen in this case leads me to believe that you are being set up. Enrico Rattei—do you know him?"

Cummings paused. "Yes. What do you mean being 'set up'?"

"You are being set up to be murdered. Why would Rattei want to kill you?"

"Well—all this is absolutely out of place over the telephone and I've got to rush, but I suppose it's common knowledge in certain circles that, when I married Enna, Enrico Rattei vowed he would kill me if I ever dared return to Italy."

"And, have you ever?"

"No, but I plan to soon. I don't think I've told you, but I'm being named ambassador to Italy tomorrow. One of my first official acts there will be to represent our country—excuse me—the United Kingdom at the Palio. Which reminds me. I've got to hang up. The dinner engagement I spoke of is at the Italian embassy. They want to welcome me and all that. I must go."

"One more question," said McGarr. "How long ago did you know you were going to be named ambassador?"

"At least six months. It was then that the ministry began screening candidates to succeed me in my present post. Satisfied?"

"One more."

"McGarr!"

"How's your investment in Tartan Limited working out?"

"In what?"

"Tartan Limited. You know—the Panamanian outfit."

"Really now, you're beginning to become difficult."

"The oil company. The one that's operating in Scotland."

Cummings sighed. "For official purposes, all my money—that is, the money my father left me and the money I received as dowry from Enna's family—was placed in a blind trust some twenty-eight years ago. The only business that I concern myself with is that which might interfere with the operations of the British government in foreign countries."

"But unofficially, did you know that you are listed as an officer of Tartan Limited?"

"Of course. It's a splendid investment. My lawyer told me about it."

"Did you know that Hitchcock and Browne were the controlling officers?"

"No—they couldn't be. They work for ENI. My lawyer would have told me if they were."

"Does your lawyer belong to your club?"

"Certainly. He's an old school chum."

"May I have his name?"

"It's Croft. Sir Sellwyn Gerrard Montague Croft."

"How long will you be at the Italian embassy?"

"I don't know. Hours, I suspect—cocktails, dinner, and entertainment after that. Why?"

"I'm going to stop 'round."

"*What?*"

"I won't embarrass you, don't worry."

"You had better not. And I don't want any talk about Browne, Hitchcock, or Tartan Limited, do you understand?" Cummings hung up.

"What's worse," O'Shaughnessy asked, standing, "a little embarrassment or a little lead?"

"Taken in the proper amounts, it only dulls the brain." McGarr called a cab that took them to the airport.

There, waiting for a plane to Heathrow, McGarr called Noreen, who had been staying at the Carlton since morning. Earlier in the day, McGarr believed that he would be busy in London for some time, at least until the Hitchcock and Browne murder investigations were solved or met some new impasse. Now, however, he wasn't so sure. The Palio was only three days away. Besides getting a line on Foster's whereabouts, McGarr believed Cummings was his only immediate lead, that is, if Foster tried to murder him. Also, McGarr firmly believed that Foster wasn't alone in all of this, that he was just working for a payoff and no doubt a very large one indeed, some figure only a man like Rattei could afford. Thus, McGarr asked Noreen to put on her most formal gown and meet him at the Italian embassy in two hours. Noreen's precise and diminutive beauty would make McGarr inconspicuous. He wouldn't even be seen.

Next, he called Bernie McKeon in Dublin and asked him to assign
a detail of men to tail Rattei. He said they'd require the use of a
helicopter, automobiles, and a sizable amount of expense money.

Lastly, McGarr called the Irish embassy in London and arranged
to have a limousine pick up Noreen at the Carlton and another one
meet them at the airport. At the speeds McGarr planned to have the
car move, they would require diplomatic immunity. Also, admission
to the Italian embassy was probably no more than having arrived in
a large, official automobile.

And McGarr was right. The semicircular drive was lined with
Rollses and Bentleys, Cadillacs, an antique Lamborghini, Lancias,
and Citroens. Noreen popped out of a Mercedes and met McGarr
in front of the building.

And McGarr was indeed correct about Noreen as well. She was
wearing the satin dinner dress that had cost McGarr nearly a whole
month's salary when they had gone to Paris on holiday the year
before. In a small country like Ireland, the second-ranking police
official was often invited to state affairs. The dark blue dress comple-
mented Noreen's copper hair; the cut emphasized her posture and
precise features. In all, she seemed to be a creature from a more
refined age, when beauty was a delicate arrangement of proportion.
On her chest she wore three strands of pearls. The effect was stunning. Immediately, Cummings himself engaged her in conversation.

The dinner had just ended, and cigars and cognac were being
served in the salon of the embassy. There, a small orchestra had
begun playing a Scarlatti concerto.

McGarr and O'Shaughnessy gave their coats to a butler, and the
two men weaved their way through the guests to explain their presence to the Irish ambassador.

Moments later, a woman approached the three men.

"Enna," said John Frances, the Irish ambassador to England, "I
don't believe you've met Peter McGarr, Ireland's premier sleuth,
and his Watson, Liam O'Shaughnessy."

The Garda superintendent blushed.

"I'm certainly pleased to make your acquaintance, Chief Inspector," Mrs. Cummings said in a voice that was low, at once throaty

but soft, and just slightly accented. "My husband has told me much about you and your associate. Your competence astounds him. Scotland Yard, it seems, now has some competition at last." It had been Enna Ricasoli Cummings's face that the masters of the Sienese school had been trying to paint, McGarr imagined. Perfectly oval with a long, thin nose and dark eyes, she looked like a Matteo di Giovanni Madonna to him. He had often accompanied his own wife to Siena in pursuit of her hobby, art history. McGarr could imagine the young Enrico Rattei, having lived among the hundreds of Duccio, Simone Martini, Andrea Vanni, Sodoma, Sanno di Pietro, Bartolo di Fredi, and Lorenzetti Madonnas during the nine years in which he pursued his dottoria in economics, suddenly looking upon the youngest daughter of the revered Ricasoli family and loving her with a passion that his country's culture reinforced.

McGarr said, "I'd prefer to think that we of Dublin Castle offer Scotland Yard skilled cooperation. And, speaking of cooperation, this morning, while investigating a crime in Scotland, I received a good measure of cooperation from Enrico Rattei. I believe he's a friend of yours."

She lowered her eyes. Her eyelids seemed tanned, or at least a deeper brown than her olive complexion. "Yes, Enrico and I are close friends."

"I think he's in love with you," said McGarr. He knew such a statement was rude, but he wanted to see how she'd react.

That pained John Frances. He looked away and shifted his weight.

She smiled. Her eyes flashed at McGarr. They were brown, almost black, and appeared depthless. "Yes. I think he is." A tall woman, she was wearing a lilac dress. The material was sheer and had been fitted with great care to her thin but angular frame. But it was her eyes that were most interesting to McGarr. They conveyed an overwhelming sense of serenity. She was indeed a woman a man could kill for. "You're so direct, Mr. McGarr."

"It's necessary in my profession."

"Which one is that?" asked a man who had just joined the group. "Police work, isn't it? In Rome and Paris and now back home to Dublin." He held out his hand. "I'm Francesco Battagliatti." He was a man even smaller than McGarr. His light brown hair was close-cropped and bristled. He wore heavy metallic-frame glasses that shone.

"The politician." McGarr shook his hand.

"Political leader, party chairman are more pleasant expressions." Battagliatti meant the Communist party in Italy.

Although this was the first time McGarr had ever met the man, he knew something about his past. Having lived in Tuscany for a time, McGarr had watched Battagliatti build the Communist party from a ragtag band of resistance fighters during World War II into the regnant political party of that province and the second most powerful force in Italian national politics.

Having been a Communist ideologue during his university days —Siena also, McGarr believed—Battagliatti had had to flee Mussolini's Italy. Rumor had it Battagliatti had participated in some of the most dreadful acts of Russia's Comintern, and, when he returned to Italy as the American troops were advancing up the Tyrrhenian Peninsula, he proved to be the most capable of the guerrilla generals who stalled the German exit to the north.

Battagliatti always appeared in public dressed in a double-breasted gray suit. He had an amiable chuckle and a sharp wit, but his charm was that of an intellectual. One was left with the impression that his mind was icily rational. "Do we have criminals in our midst?" he asked McGarr.

The chief inspector thought he'd test the man's vaunted intelligence. "The criminal lurks in everybody's personality, signor. He is never really absent from our deliberations."

Battagliatti smiled and sipped from a snifter. "I trust you speak for yourself, Mr. McGarr. In spite of the innumerable occasions on which I have searched my own persona, I have never revealed a criminal element." All the while he spoke, he was staring at Enna Cummings and not once did he look at McGarr. His eyes were sparkling and, although his smile was probably a permanent affectation of his personality, McGarr judged that at this moment it conveyed a genuine emotion.

Whenever she looked at him, she too smiled, yet in no way did she seem to be coy.

McGarr said, "Come now—each of us contains numerous possibilities within himself. We all have the seeds of greatness and banality in us. Robber, shaman, murderer, saint—we're power obsessed at one moment, recluses at the next. Have you never imagined yourself a mobster, Signor Battagliatti, or a *borghése* in Milano, a *fannullóne* on the breakwater in Catania, a troubador journeying to Rome for the Christmas holidays?"

"Never," said the politician. "At all times, I am, sadly, Battagliatti." He pronounced his name histrionically, gesturing his hand with a slight movement of the wrist. "A man with the same emotions as those which had surfaced in his pitiable personality when he was still a foolish student, young and in love. Most of those other personae whom you've named have never darkened his demeanor. And you didn't mention unrequited lover." He glanced once more at Enna Cummings.

"Stop it, Francesco. You're boring Chief Inspector McGarr. I'm sure that the set of personalities he deals with daily are much more colorful than those he'll find in this room."

"Not so," said McGarr.

Noreen and Cummings now joined the group. The contrasting beauty of the two women—one diminutive with red hair and fine, white skin; the other tall and dark—created a most pleasant tension.

McGarr continued. "It's just that we're less adventuresome than those we choose to call criminals. Society and its values have made too deep an impression upon us. We've quelled the grosser elements in our personalities. But we lose something all the same, don't you think?"

"Ah, yes," Battagliatti said, "the freedom to loot and pillage. The license to kill and maim. But then again, Mr. McGarr, it's easy for you to talk, since you *have* the license to kill."

McGarr smiled. A waiter presented O'Shaughnessy and him snifters of brandy. Taking a glass off the tray, he said, "Within limits, of course—those set by society."

"But what about the man who has led an exemplary life for, say, fifty-five years? Suddenly, he slays his mother-in-law. Surely, his is not a 'criminal' personality."

"Which is exactly my point. The balance of his personality has gone awry, the harmony has been broken momentarily. A psychologist, a sociologist, a——"

"Policeman?" Battagliatti suggested.

"——anybody with compassion and a little common sense," said McGarr, "can discover the why and the how of the imbalance. It's a simple paroxysm that the criminal is going through, that's all."

"And not likely to happen again?"

"If those conditions that led to this 'journey to the end of one aspect of his personality' no longer obtain, then it might not happen again."

"Then you don't believe in capital punishment."

"Of course not. How could I, if I believe what I've just said?" McGarr smiled once more.

"But surely you do."

McGarr shook his head. "Having to deal with 'criminal' personalities on a daily basis has made me envious of their freedom. What I've just said was a 'journey to the end of the thespian element in my personality,' and no more."

"*Toccato!*" said Battagliatti. "Beware of the policeman with wit. He may understand the deviations of a man's personality and not despise him, thereby diminishing the value of the criminal's emotional paroxysm. Crime then becomes a nasty little joke that the criminal has played on himself."

"But we must never lose sight of the victim," said McGarr. "What part does he play in the crime?"

"Some would say"—Battagliatti allowed a little, perhaps again his professional, smile to crease his smooth features—"the victim invites the crime, that some imbalance obtains in his personality that begs for an untoward act to be done to him. Some would say so, wouldn't they, Chief Inspector?" He turned back to McGarr.

"Some would, but not I. And then, of course, we would have to examine the motives of the some who would say that."

"*Toccato ancora,*" Enna Cummings said. "It's a good thing you're not a criminal, Francesco, or Signor McGarr would have you incarcerated in no time at all.

"Have you met . . ." She then began introducing Noreen and McGarr and O'Shaughnessy to the other persons around them.

Throughout it all, however, McGarr's thoughts were preoccupied. All of these people seemed to be old Italian friends of Enna Ricasoli Cummings, either being from Siena itself or having attended university with her, and they were all quite successful persons in their own rights.

For instance, besides Battagliatti, McGarr was introduced to Oscar Zingiale. He had formed the IRI *(Istitúto per la Ricostruzione Industriale)* during the depression and had almost single-handedly pulled Italy out of economic straits more dire than those most other Western nations experienced. Under IRI he created the Italian coal and steel industry, RAI, which was the state-owned radio and television network in Italy, Alitalia, and Finmare, the shipbuilding concern based in Genoa.

His companies were archrivals of those that Enrico Rattei had created, but when McGarr asked Zingiale about his competitor, he answered, "In fact, we're dear friends, *when* we can put business matters aside, which is seldom. I saw him last at the Palio two years ago. That's where we met, you know."

"At the Palio?"

"No—in Siena, at university. We roomed together, both as poor as church mice."

"And look at you now," said Battagliatti, who had been standing next to McGarr all the time. "Two bloated capitalisti."

Zingiale laughed. "Sometimes I don't believe we attended the same university. You think too much in categories, Francesco. *One* bloated capitalista," he pointed to himself. He was a bald, rotund man, with a heavy gold watch chain on his belly. "Rattei is a"—he moved closer to the two men and whispered—"Fascist. That's an unpopular word nowadays, and one not to be said lightly."

"But when the Fascists ruled, what were you, Oscar?"

Zingiale shrugged. "A Fascist, what else?"

"Then a capitalist is merely a chameleon." Battagliatti's eyes flashed.

Zingiale smiled benignly. "If he's successful, he's a *bloated* chameleon."

"What about Fascists?" McGarr asked Battagliatti. "How do you think of them?"

"As any other intelligent man does, as individuals."

*"There,"* said Zingiale, "he's learning, he's maturing."

"Take Enrico Rattei, for an instance," McGarr suggested.

Battagliatti paused, sipped from his snifter, and said, "I admire him very much. I am also one of his friends from university."

McGarr wouldn't swear to it, but he thought he saw Zingiale's features glower a bit at that remark.

Then there was Remigio Agnollo, the Turin carmaker. His family, like the Ricasolis, had always had money. He too joined the group and was introduced to McGarr.

After him, McGarr met Umberto Pavini, the historian, and Maria Garzanti, a rotund, chesty woman who was a leading soprano with the Metropolitan Opera in New York. They and some others, whose names McGarr didn't recognize, gradually added themselves to the circle of people standing near Enna Ricasoli Cummings.

And perhaps it was the orchestra, which had begun to play the stately air from Bach's Concerto for Strings in D Major, or the ambience of the drawing room, which was furnished with reproductions of Quattrocento Florentine craftsmen, or the heat of his palms, which had freed the delicate yet heady aroma of the Luccan brandy in his snifter, that made McGarr wonder what it had been like to be young and at the university in Siena during the late twenties with this group of gifted and intelligent people, how it must have seemed that an interloper, Cummings, had plucked the rose of their coterie from their midst. McGarr now understood Rattei's purported threat somewhat better. And he wondered how much Cummings himself figured in his recent appointment as ambassador to Italy. Friends as powerful as his wife's might certainly be capable of engineering such an appointment.

The cigars were Nicaraguan, the wrapper leaf *colorado maduro,* the smoke a light blue, the taste sharp—pleasingly bitter, mellowing. McGarr was beginning to enjoy this assignment. "A good drink, a pleasant smoke, and scintillating company," he observed to O'Shaughnessy.

The Garda superintendent's light blue eyes were merry as he surveyed the guests from his eminence.

And that was not all he saw, for when the Cummingses, now surrounded by bobbies, and the McGarrs and O'Shaughnessy left the Italian embassy, pausing on the veranda to bid their final adieus to their host and hostess, the tall policeman, looking over the heads of the other departing guests, saw Foster. He was standing in the shadow of a doorway across the street. There was nothing he could do but pull on McGarr's sleeve and gesture in the direction of the wide black man. The walkway down was crowded with people, the semicircular drive now blocked by waiting limousines.

With Cummings and his wife pausing on the top stair of the embassy, however, Foster might have had a perfect shot at him. The distance was, say, seventy-five yards through an iron fence, the driveway gates of which were open. In the confusion which was sure to follow such an assassination, Foster's escape would have been assured.

McGarr wondered why Foster let the opportunity slip.

His thoughts ceased, however, when Noreen grasped his hand in the dark of the back seat of the Bentley. As he had expected, the moment Cummings approached his limousine and the policemen became free to chase after Foster, if they chose, a small car pulled up in front of the building across the street, Foster hopped in, and it pulled away. The rear lights of the vehicle had been disconnected so that the license number was obscured in the darkness. In any case, the car had most probably been stolen.

Their rooms at the Carlton were at once as sumptuous and ugly as only a decorator with a perfect understanding of upper-middle-class British taste could devise. Individually, all the items in the room—a squat dresser made from fine-grained Honduran mahogany polished to a mirror sheen; an imitation rococo mirror that matched a mantelpiece on which several twentieth-century casts of Victorian reproductions of eighteenth-century ceramic figurines in sickly pastels had been placed—were so gauche as to be nearly laughable, but in all the room looked solid, and that, after all, was the effect intended.

McGarr phoned the lobby and learned that the kitchen had not yet closed. To test its fare, he ordered the soup du jour. When that turned out to be a pleasant *potage velouté aux huitres,* they ordered *salade Niçoise, moules à la marinière,* and a bottle of very dry Schloss Johannisberger. If the soup had been lackluster, McGarr would have ordered meat.

Noreen slipped into a beige dressing gown, and they ate leisurely.

Much later, McGarr found himself awake, wishing the soup had been lackluster. He got out of bed and went out into the other room of the suite. There he read the newspapers, English and Irish, until dawn.

He then woke Noreen. They were to accompany Cummings, who had a final briefing in Whitehall that morning, to Heathrow, Milan, and Florence aboard airplanes, and to Siena aboard a train.

Cummings's wife and most of the other Italians who had been present at the embassy party had left aboard an IRI jet the night before. They were to be special guests of the Ricasoli family in their palazzo in the Piazza del Campo, where the Palio was run.

Before they left the hotel, McGarr received a call from Gallup. "Just did a little checking on Rattei, if only to keep my own information up to date, Peter. ENI's financial situation is a lot tighter than I imagined. His Scottish drilling has turned out to be sixty-five percent more costly than his engineers estimated. He had floated other loans based on prospective Scottish returns. When he needed additional funds to cover the increased costs, he had to hunt high and low and finally managed to convince the Russians to underwrite several heavy short-term, high-interest loans as a part of that deal."

"So?"

"So he *has* to win that court case against Tartan and there are no two ways about it. If the decision goes against him, Tartan can claim triple damages and erect more wells with the proceeds."

"Which gives Rattei a motive."

"Especially Rattei, I'd say. He's—proud. You know, hyperbolically so."

McGarr thanked Gallup, and Noreen and he left for the airport.

In a final call to Dublin from Heathrow, McGarr learned that a man had been taken off the plane that had carried the American basketball team the moment it had touched down in Moscow. Also, British customs reported that a Moses Foster had passed through Heathrow the day before. His passport documented a three-week stay in Russia.

Also, during the night Enrico Rattei had left on a small ENI jet. The flight plan listed Florence as his destination.

# 5

Like many Italian cities, Siena owed its train station to Mussolini. The style was Fascist modern, a sprawling granite structure with sweeping windows and a flat roof.

As McGarr had expected, all the other passengers detrained at once. They rushed toward the central exit.

The crowd was motley. In spite of slicked-down hair and Sunday clothes, the *contadini* couldn't disguise their sunburned faces. Their wives' leg muscles bulged in new hosiery. They carried string sacks filled with country gifts for Siena relatives—cheeses, a goose, rounds of sausage, *fiasci* of new wine.

Dapper Florentines, by contrast, had draped their precisely tailored jackets on their shoulders. Men and women alike wore stylish sunglasses that wrapped around their faces. Used to city streets, their step was smooth, even jaunty, and they were most impatient at the door.

When the crowd had cleared, Hughie Ward, dressed as a Jesuit, left his compartment and walked down the platform as far as the engine of the train, checking the cars for other passengers. Liam O'Shaughnessy made straight for the lobby, where he informed the waiting carabinieri that Cummings had arrived and then surveyed the bar. He returned shortly, walking very fast. Signaling to Ward, he ducked his head under the door of the train compartment and said to McGarr, "May I speak to you a moment, Peter?"

Seven carabinieri, dressed in knee-cut boots of black leather to match thick waist and shoulder belts, had approached the train. Their white summer suits with red piping and white motorcycle helmets made them look very militant. Their sergeant piped on a shrill whistle and the carabinieri formed a wedge in front of the open train compartment door.

Near the platform newspaper stand, McGarr saw two men watching the train. Nobody but Englishmen would wear shell cordovans in Italy in July.

When Ward had reached them, O'Shaughnessy said, "He's there. In the bar."

McGarr was puzzled.

"The nigger—Foster, I mean."

"Are you sure?"

"Come see for yourself."

There, sitting at a table which at once placed his back to the wall and allowed him to watch the long bar and table area, was Foster. McGarr opened his pocket secretary and checked an SIS photo Cummings had given him. "You're right, Liam."

"Shall we collar him? I don't think he's seen us as yet." They were standing in back of the cigarette counter, looking between two cardboard displays. "You know—the carabinieri could lock him up for the duration of the Palio."

McGarr thought for a moment. Given Foster's experience in covert operations, he would not have exposed himself like this unless he was sure of his position. Either Rattei or some other powerful figure was behind him, and the Italian police would not be able to hold him for long. Also, McGarr himself was not on indefinite holiday with Cummings; he was merely following a hunch, the expense of which he would have to justify to the commissioner of police and soon. McGarr had a week at most in Italy. If something were going to happen, he'd prefer that it be soon. "What do you think?" He glanced up at the tall Garda superintendent.

"Did you see those two fellows near the newsstand?"

McGarr nodded.

"They were speaking English like Englishmen when I passed," said Ward.

"I think they should take care of their own man themselves," said O'Shaughnessy. He meant Cummings.

McGarr looked at Ward, if only to let him believe that he had a part in their deliberations.

Ward said, "We're investigating two murders, not protecting

Cummings's life. Those carabinieri on the platform look capable enough to me. And then, we wouldn't stand a ghost of a chance to extradite him. We've got no real evidence against him, and he's got a passport that says he was in Russia when the murders were committed."

"They're the best," McGarr admitted. He glanced back out at the train and thought briefly of Cummings. In spite of his occasional observance of class distinctions, he really wasn't a bad sort. Certainly, he didn't deserve to die. "Come on," said McGarr, "I'll buy you a drink."

They pushed into the bar, and McGarr ordered three white wines. He stopped the waiter, who was passing, and told him to take another of whatever Foster was drinking to him. He placed a thousand-lire bill on the tray. *"Immediataménte, per favore."*

*"Mille grazie, signor."* The waiter turned to the bar and placed the order.

When the waiter had placed the *grappa* in front of Foster and had explained from whom it had been sent, McGarr turned to him.

Like a large black house cat smiling down into a saucer of milk, Foster lifted the thin glass and knocked the *grappa* back. It was vile stuff with a range of ketones—hallucinogens, other alcohol impurities that were poisons if taken in the proper amounts—that researchers knew nothing about. Not once did he look directly at the three policemen. He just stared down at the glass, which his fingers twisted on the tabletop.

Now free of the worry of guarding Cummings, McGarr felt very tired when he got to the Excelsior Hotel near the park and the Medici *fortezza.* Italian beds are much too soft. McGarr and Noreen did not awake until the sun had passed over the hotel and shone directly through the chinks in the heavy window blind.

This McGarr raised and looked out over Siena. Down below him was the city's Stadio, in the distance the Duomo and Campanile with its horizontal green stripes of Prato marble imposed on white Carrara. Farther still was the Mangia Tower of the town hall, which dominated the cityscape. It rose over the brown roofs to a height of a hundred meters and shimmered in the heat, which McGarr knew would become oppressive by the time the Palio began at 3:00

that afternoon. He checked his watch. It was 1:45.

Below him, two Sienese, with red, green, and white bandanas wrapped about their shoulders, were talking.

One said, "To be honest, I wish our *contrada* had another symbol."

"That's heresy. Don't talk nonsense."

"Whenever we win, we're forced to eat goose. I detest goose. I ask you, is this the sort of weather in which it is appropriate to eat goose? It's downright unhealthy to eat goose in this weather."

"We're not going to win anyhow, and you know it," said the other.

"Some other symbol—the giraffe, the dragon, the caterpillar, the owl, the forest, the panther, the eagle—would be better than ours. Then we could eat something light like veal. Goose? The grease disgusts me."

"Don't talk so much, you're making me hot. We're not going to win, everybody knows that."

"You shouldn't say such a thing, somebody might hear you." The man looked up at the hotel, and McGarr stepped away from the window.

McGarr, Noreen, Liam O'Shaughnessy, and Bernie McKeon walked from the hotel toward the Piazzo del Campo where the Palio was staged. Noreen wore a spanking linen suit with a wide-brimmed hat to match. People turned to watch her go by. Hers was not the sort of beauty that an Italian saw every day. The men wore short-sleeve shirts and light pants. McGarr and McKeon had on sandals and vented, soft caps. They looked like twins. Liam O'Shaughnessy wore a boater with a paisley band and woven shoes. It was quite obvious they were *stranieri*.

The Sienese loved their city somewhat more than the automobile and had closed many of the city-center streets to traffic. Thus, the Irishmen had a pleasant stroll through the Palio crowd. They passed along the Piazza Matteotti onto the Via Pianigiani and then onto the Banchi di Sopra.

Here, many people were standing in the shadow that the tall Palazzo Salimbeni made. The palace, which McGarr favored above all Siena's others, now housed the Monte dei Paschi di Siena, the oldest banking institution in Italy. The narrow arcades of the first and third floors balanced elegant three-mullioned windows on the second floor. A cornice with small arches ran along the roofline. A Sienese arch—a pointed arch containing a lower rounded one— capped the doorway. The entire facade of the structure was gray marble.

Farther down the narrow and winding Banchi di Sopra, all the clothing shops, bookstores, art galleries, cafés, and smoke shops were crowded. McGarr's fluent Italian and skill with thousand-lire notes got them a table for four in the back of the Ristorante Guido on Vicolo P. Pettinaio. As they sat, McGarr could hear the crowd in the Piazza del Campo cheering the horses of their *contrade* as the *provacia,* or final, of four tests of the Palio horses was run. The other three had been held earlier that week.

For an aperitif, they drank a special fennel-base liqueur which the waiter, whom the maître d' had apprised of McGarr's benevolence, recommended. It was a house specialty, made for them in the country, he said. Tangy and tart, the liqueur pleased the Irishmen so much that they placed themselves in the waiter's care for the duration of their repast.

He then placed hot bread and two *fiasci* of full-bodied Chianti on the table. Antipasto was a selection of Tuscan sausages—*finocchina, chingiale, salsiccia di fegato,* and the blood sausage that was a Sienese specialty. The pasta course was *gnocchi verdi,* tiny green dumplings made with spinach and cottage cheese and served with melted butter and grated cheese. Finally, the waiter brought out the entree with enormous pride. As McGarr had expected, it was another Sienese dish, *buristo suino.* It was a rich pork casserole flavored with raisins and pine nuts. A platter heaped with *copate* (wafers made of honey and nuts), *riciarelli* (sweet, diamond-shaped almond biscuits), and fruit was served with pots of bitter espresso and glasses of plum brandy. One dipped the cookies in the brandy before biting.

It was Bernie McKeon's first heavy meal in Italy, and he hadn't, like the others, merely tasted a little of everything. Now he was slightly green. Looking from the cool depths of the Ristorante Guido out onto the bright, granite-block street of the Banchi di

Sopra, he said, "I can't predict what's going to happen to me when I hit that street. I might collapse."

McGarr poured him a glass of chilled *acqua minerale* and the sergeant felt somewhat better.

They had timed it just right. Their diplomatic passes allowed them to weave through the crowd until they reached the entrance to the Palazzo Ricasoli.

There, McGarr stopped suddenly and turned around. He had thought for a moment he had recognized somebody behind him. It was a woman who had looked surprisingly like Hitchcock's wife, the person McGarr had met briefly in the sitting room of the house in St. John's Wood. Thin, with high cheekbones and a crooked nose, this woman in the crowd turned her back to McGarr and began to walk away. They were only twenty feet or so apart from each other, but the gap quickly filled with revelers. McGarr had, however, gotten a glimpse of her ankle, which was very thin. Also, like Mrs. Hitchcock's, the woman's hair was blondish, having been tinted from gray in a manner that would not seem artificial.

On a wide balcony of the Palazzo Ricasoli, the view of the Piazza del Campo was spectacular. After shaking hands with essentially the same guests who had been present at the party in the Italian embassy in London, McGarr looked out over the expanse of the piazza. It was a great mass of people bounded by the race track, which ran the circumference of the piazza. On this, Sienese clay had been placed and large barriers had been erected to keep the horses, which were ridden bareback, from charging into the crowd.

The Piazza del Campo itself is one of the sublime creations of Italy's Risorgimento. The Sienese made use of the existing landscape—the bases of the three intersecting hills on which Siena itself is built—and constructed the piazza in the shape of an inverted shell. In 1347, they paved the piazza with bricks laid in a herringbone pattern, divided into nine sections by means of longitudinal strips of white marble.

Directly opposite the town hall is the Gaia fountain, built in the early fifteenth century. Its proportions clearly herald the coming Renaissance styles, but it is the town hall and Mangia Tower that

dominate the piazza and give it its visual strength. These are undoubtedly the most elegant examples of Tuscan gothic architecture.

McGarr admired most the balance of delicate three-mullioned
windows on the middle floors of the building with Sienese archways
on the ground floor and the crenellated roofline. This building was
grand, surveying the expanse of the piazza that now contained close
to one hundred thousand people, or so Il Conde, Enna Ricasoli's
aged father, now told him. Built beginning in 1288 of red brick, now
a light brown, the town hall had been designed to conform to the
shell-like configurations of the square so that its three wings faced,
like a triptych, different directions. The Mangia Tower to its right
rose into a gray stone and crenellated belfry that matched the stone
first floor of the town hall. In all, the piazza was exquisite.

McGarr and Noreen had spent two spring holidays in Siena some
years before. Then, during the afternoons, they would sip Campari
and bitters in the sun at one of the sidewalk cafés, read, and watch
the *genti* pass by.

But the bell in the campanile of the Mangia Tower had begun its
solemn tolling, and the crowd quieted until the first marcher had
entered the piazza. Then, like a wave that broke across the length
of the piazza, the roar of the crowd hit the Palazzo Ricasoli and
reverberated around the curve of buildings. The balcony seemed to
quake under McGarr's feet. Suddenly, it was very hot.

Cummings was standing to McGarr's left and slightly in front of
him. His wife was wearing a light blue dress with a wide skirt. In the
direct sunlight her black hair was lustrous. In the heat and noise she
seemed sublimely tranquil.

The procession, which preceded the horse race, had entered the
piazza now. Mace bearers, trumpeters, grooms, and standard bearers streamed onto the raceway, all dressed in the colorful medieval
costumes of each of the seventeen sections of the city. Some *contrade*
offered bands, others jugglers and acrobats, but the standard bearer
of each tossed his bright flag into the air, caught it, and twirled it
with consummate skill. Finally, an ornate cart drawn by four white
oxen rolled into the piazza. It carried the prize that awaited the
*contrada* of the victorious horse—the Pallium, which was a pennant
picture of the Virgin. "What's the cart called again?" McGarr asked
his wife.

The din was nearly palpable now, and she hadn't heard him. He repeated the question in a louder voice.

Enna Cummings moved toward them to explain.

"*Il Carròccio,*" Noreen said.

"Ah—so you speak Italian, Signora McGarr?" Mrs. Cummings asked.

"*Ma sì,*" said Noreen. And, in Italian she added, "Would it be too much to say it's the most beautiful of the European languages?" After university in Ireland, she had studied in Perugia and Florence.

"Perhaps. At least any Frenchman would dispute the contention. But how nice—there are so few English who have bothered to learn Italian."

Neither Noreen nor McGarr bothered to remind her that they were not English.

A waiter was offering a tray of iced gin drinks to the guests on the Ricasoli balcony.

McGarr had stationed McKeon on one corner of the balcony, Liam O'Shaughnessy on the other. At least a dozen carabinieri were clustered around the guests. In the windows above the balcony other carabinieri and the two British SIS agents scanned the crowd with binoculars.

The horses were led into the piazza and *La Mossa,* or the procedure which started the Palio, began. The ten horses and their bareback riders were herded between two thick ropes that spanned the raceway. The horses bucked and wheeled, charged into each other, and even tried to jump the barriers. They were large animals, every one of them, but frightened by the hubbub and lathery in the heat. An atmosphere of near frenzy pervaded the square.

Suddenly, one rope was dropped; the crowd, as one voice, roared; and the horses charged down the raceway, quickly attaining a pace that was too great for the quick turns of the roughly circular course. At the first turn, an advancing horse lost its footing, fell, and, skidding, knocked the two front runners down. Two of the jockeys did not move after they hit the clay. The other jumped to his feet and scrambled over the barricade not a moment too soon, for another horse and rider slammed into the padding right where he had climbed. The three riderless horses regained their feet and followed the other seven around the track. Medical personnel dragged the injured jockeys off the raceway.

The crowd was wild, the leading *contrada* supporters cheering and shouting, those from the fallen horses wailing.

McGarr sipped from the gin drink and scanned the crowd. Overhead, a jet was passing so high up its vapor trail was brilliant in the afternoon sun. McGarr wondered if anybody aboard could possibly know he was passing over this mad vortex of people and horses, this brief, impassioned bareback scramble through one of the world's most exquisite architectural monuments. How quintessentially Italian it all was—the pomp of the parade, the beauty of the costumes and setting, the race itself with its possibilities for fortune and honor. And then the most important social unit to the Italians, the family, was present as well, for that was what a *contrada* was, one great extended family stretching backward in time to the foundation of the city as a Roman military outpost, and forward with all the little children whom McGarr had seen marching in their *contrada* costumes during the parade. How many of those kids would leave this city after participating in this tradition and growing up in these streets, he wondered. Few, if any, and they'd feel like exiles in Milan or Turin or Stuttgart or New York.

Two laps were gone and only five riders left. The women of the Wave *contrada,* whose sign was the dolphin, seemed hysterical as they screamed directly below the Ricasoli balcony. Their horse had a long lead.

McGarr glanced up from them to look at the plane again and saw Foster.

He was standing on a roof where the piazza began to curve away from the Palazzo Ricasoli. Not one of the carabinieri could have spotted him from there. He was wearing a yellow dashiki and looked like a clashing, pagan icon on the rooftop. Also, he was pointing something.

McGarr neither had a chance to move nor did he hear anything but the crowd.

Cummings merely turned to him. It seemed at first that he had a brilliant red sixpence on his forehead. His eyes seemed to be focused on McGarr. They were the lightest blue, like the shade of his wife's dress. He opened his mouth as though he would say something.

His legs collapsed.

The horse from the Wave *contrada* blundered across the finish line.

The jet had disappeared in the blinding sun.

McGarr had to pull hard to make Enna Cummings release her husband.

But he was dead.

McGarr stood and looked up at Foster. He was sitting on top of the roof. The rifle was no longer visible. He was grinning down at the spectacle of the Palio below.

The carabinieri all had their guns out now. They were confused, didn't know where to look, and probably wouldn't have shot at Foster if they had because of the crowd.

McGarr left the balcony, O'Shaughnessy and McKeon following him.

From under his cassock, Hughie Ward handed them 9-mm Walther automatics.

McGarr got a sergeant to direct him to the back of the building. As he had surmised, the rear porches nearly connected with those of the neighboring palazzo. They climbed the stone railing and stepped around the divider. Now, several carabinieri and the two SIS men were following them. The last thing McGarr wanted was a gun fight. He had come to Italy because he had believed Foster would follow Cummings. He did not want to be denied the opportunity of talking to him.

O'Shaughnessy, using a hand brace, boosted McGarr onto the steep roof that semicircular ceramic tiles covered. None of them was secured to the building, but merely layered, leading edge overlapping the next to the peak of the roof. If McGarr fell or slipped or pushed off on them too rapidly, they might all, like an avalanche, cascade down the roof and over the edge. And McGarr had always feared heights of this magnitude. The building was tall. It was at least fifty meters to the cobblestone courtyard below. He could see Foster up there, silhouetted in the sun. McGarr was having trouble holding the gun and easing himself over the tiles.

The band of the Wave *contrada* had begun playing now.

If Foster chose, he could turn and blow McGarr right off the roof before the chief inspector could steady himself, aim, and fire his hand gun.

But Foster remained in place.

McGarr was making a racket too. The tiles clattered on each other. They were almost too hot to touch. McGarr was wringing wet and could hear his heart beating in his ears.

When he got his hand on the pinnacle, he pointed the Walther at Foster and said, "Drop the rifle behind you and remove that yellow thing slowly."

Foster complied. The rifle, a collapsible single shot, the stock of which was merely thin steel tubes ending in a narrow butt, skidded down the tiles, where Liam O'Shaughnessy, reaching up, caught it. Foster's body was massive and slick, covered with a fine film of perspiration. A small-caliber automatic was fitted into a shoulder holster.

"The same with the pistol. Undo the holster and let it drop in back of you."

A brief gust of wind lifted the dashiki off the roof, and it floated, tumbling then catching, down into the Palio crowd on the piazza side of the building.

When Foster had done this, only then did McGarr allow himself to wonder why he hadn't tried to escape. Only McGarr had seen him. He could have gotten off the roof, down the stairs, and into the crowd. He had timed the attack to coincide with the end of the race when the noise was loudest. With contacts—and McGarr was sure he had powerful ones—he could have slipped away completely.

"All right—down we go. You first."

Foster turned to him. "You have no jurisdiction here, Irish mon." His accent was decidedly Jamaican. "I will surrender to the Italian police alone." His forehead was very wide, eyes narrow and a strange yellow color. One front tooth was gold-capped. He was easily twice McGarr's girth. The ruby in the pinkie ring on his left hand was the size of a marble.

"The place is lousy with them. See for yourself."

Foster turned to look behind him. His neck was a knot of sinew and hard muscle.

A carabiniere had trained a riot gun on him, the sort that shot a slug that would rip a man in two.

"In any case, you killed Hitchcock and Browne. We'll have you back in Ireland soon."

The Jamaican only smiled at McGarr and, agile as a cat, scrambled down the tiles before McGarr could even begin to ease himself off the pinnacle of the roof. By the time McGarr had reached the back porch of the building, the carabinieri had whisked Foster away.

McGarr was wringing wet.

McKeon was shaking his head. "Jesus—I never thought of looking up there."

"You would have broken your neck if you had tried," said McGarr.

"But Christ—the poor bugger. Did you get a look at his wife?"

McGarr wrapped his arm around McKeon's shoulder. "Let me tell you something, Bernie: I saw Foster, I saw him aim the gun and pull the trigger. It all happened so fast nobody could have stopped him. Foster is a professional. There's really no way of protecting somebody from a man like that. He wasn't sitting on the top of that roof. You saw yourself how he managed to scramble down it without dislodging a tile. He waited until the race was at its most interesting stage, then popped up, and squeezed off a round."

"Well, how did you see him?"

"I was daydreaming. Gin-induced."

McGarr led his men back into the Palazzo Ricasoli.

None of the policemen would talk to each other. They all felt like failures. In particular, the British SIS men didn't know what to do with themselves.

McGarr invited them over to the Excelsior for a drink. Both promptly got very drunk. One wrote out his resignation on hotel stationery. McGarr said he'd mail it for him in the morning, then ripped it up.

He could hardly fall asleep himself, however, wondering about Foster. Twice he called carabinieri headquarters to try to observe their interrogation of Foster, but couldn't get through to Carlo Falchi, the commandant, an old acquaintance of his.

Noreen was still shocked and ashen. McGarr could tell she was reassessing the idea of accompanying him on his police business. He wondered if she knew that they had seen Foster earlier in the day and had decided not to tell any of the other police agencies.

McGarr called Dublin. Dick Delaney had nothing new to report on the helicopter aspect of the investigation.

A cool breeze was blowing off the hills beyond the city, and McGarr thought for a moment he could smell the vineyards and olive groves and the cypress trees along the roadsides on the hilltops. But mostly, he believed he could smell the red Tuscan earth, a clay soil that the plow blade turned over in thick ribbons.

# 6

Carlo Falchi was wroth. The carabinieri commandant was sitting behind his desk, taking successive quick sips from a large cup of espresso.

In McGarr's cup the pungent, black liquid was far too hot for him to drink.

The aroma of hot *caffè nero,* into which sugar had been stirred, pervaded the office, as did the delicate odor of hot brioche, a half-dozen of which lay on a caddy to McGarr's right. He broke one open. Its light brown crust yielded moist dough, butter-rich. McGarr wondered briefly how Sienese pastry compared with Parisian. The latter city prepared more complicated sweets, that much was certain, but the Sienese did some things incomparably well. Their dolces, like this brioche, were sublime. McGarr reached for another.

"To think of their attitude, that's what galls me most," said Falchi. "What do they think we do up here all the time, sleep? Romans!" Falchi had finished his espresso. He set the cup down on his desk with a crack and pressed a button several times.

McGarr could hear it ringing in an outer office.

Hours after Cummings's death, some big shots in the carabinieri, accompanied by the Minister for Justice, had arrived and relieved Falchi of the investigation.

"They ought to draw an international border at Arezzo and demand passports to be shown so that we can monitor this invasion of *cretini* from the south." Falchi could see out into the parking lot of the Duomo. The cathedral was crowded with tourists.

A large bus began off-loading some sightseers, many of whom were blond. The back of the bus had a white, circular disk on which had been painted the letters *D K*. Falchi got out of his seat and stared at the young blond girls who were shielding their eyes with their hands to see the facade of the church. A few of them were snapping pictures. All were very pale.

"Ah—*biondine!* Not your common Roman bottle blonds, mind you, but real Nordic fair women. Right now, I could leave all my cares with such a woman." Falchi was a thickset man with gruff good looks. None of his features was regular, but taken together his aspect was pleasing. And he was an inveterate womanizer. When they were both working in Rome for Interpol, he had once told McGarr that he was a big man who had so much love in him that it was his duty to spread it around, that the moment he believed he was stinting his wife of her just share of his love, he would stop his philandering immediately.

A carabiniere entered the room, picked up Falchi's empty saucer and cup, and reached for the tray of brioches as though he would remove that too.

McGarr showed him his palm. *"Con vostro permesso, per favore."*

Falchi spun around. His moustache looked like a straight black bar across his upper lip. The chest of his white summer uniform was a melange of ribbons and medals. McGarr had heard they were handed out yearly to officers of a certain rank regardless of their performance. "Ah—forget those things. How can you think of eating at a time like this, Peter? Take a walk with me. I'll buy you a hundred, a thousand brioches." Falchi grabbed his hat.

McGarr stood and placed three brioches in his left hand. This was insurance against the histrionic element which he knew to be present in Falchi's personality.

Walking across the parking lot to the Duomo, McGarr asked, "Do you think there's a chance they'll let me talk to Foster?"

Falchi shook his head and muttered, *"Bastardi!"*

The morning was again too glorious and presaged a sultry afternoon.

"First turn of the race, the horse of my *contrada* falls on his ass. Then the ambassador I'm supposed to protect, one meek little man, gets shot in the head in the midst of twenty-five of my best, hand-picked men. So—I make a spectacular arrest"—McGarr nearly choked on the brioche—"get the suspect back to the office, search his room, find certain evidence incriminating another——"

"Who?" McGarr asked. His mouth was filled with brioche.

"What?" Falchi looked down at McGarr. "Ugh—I knew you liked those things so I ordered them, but I forgot you'd have to eat them in front of me."

Now they were on the steps of the cathedral. Two gypsy children with rings in their ears came running up to them with their hands outstretched.

McGarr caught a glimpse of their father stepping behind a pillar. He had not yet taught them to recognize and avoid certain uniforms.

"Beat it, you little brats, or I'll run you in." Falchi was in a foul mood.

"Who?" McGarr insisted.

Falchi stopped. He turned to McGarr. "What—do you want me to make a second fatal blunder in as many days?"

"How so?"

Falchi began walking again. They were inside the cathedral. Compared with outside, it was dark and almost cold.

"I tell you and suddenly the news is all over Europe. And then that Roman riffraff will have me investigating a leak in my own office. No—they'll probably insist on handling the investigation themselves. At least that way I'll never be found out." And then, as though realizing that McGarr was probably tiring of his mood, he asked, "Do you know Enrico Rattei?"

McGarr nodded.

"He was arrested last night. Of course, bail was set and he's out now, but, nevertheless, with his arrest this case takes on the utmost importance. It's one thing to slay a British ambassador. It's quite another to arrest a *condottiere d'industria* of Rattei's magnitude."

They were walking toward the cathedral pulpit, around which the Danish girls were grouped while a Sienese guide struggled to explain the history of Nicola Pisano's masterpiece to them in English.

"Foster had a telegram in his possession from Rattei. It said,

'Luck, B-nine, one, eight, nine, seven, M. P. S.,' which turned out to be a Monte dei Paschi di Siena bank account somebody—and a teller swears it was Rattei himself; he's identified him twice—set up for Foster."

McGarr stopped. The whole affair—this information, Foster's not escaping into the Palio crowd, and all the facts McGarr had gathered in the other two murder investigations—seemed too obvious. And if Rattei were being framed, whoever was doing it could afford to waste twenty-five thousand pounds, a handy sum by any yardstick. "Has Foster made a statement yet?"

"Not yet. Tell me honestly, Peter—what do you know about this Foster? What are your"—he waved his hand—"musings about his involvement in this thing? And Rattei's? What are *all* the facts?"

McGarr didn't hesitate to tell Falchi. If Foster and Rattei were co-plotters in these murders, then he'd need all the help he could muster to get them back to Ireland after they were tried in Italy. "Foster's a former spy whom SIS did dirty. You know—low pension, low-pay desk job. He grew to hate the Service. He's probably always been slightly psychotic. It takes a special sort of person to kill for hire. And the malaise could have surfaced with his inactivity. Perhaps he jumped at the first chance to get free of the Service that was offered him, ironically by Hitchcock and Browne. Perhaps he then discovered how they were involved in the Tartan Oil venture and went with the news to Rattei. Perhaps they then discovered a mutual loathing for Hitchcock, Browne, Cummings, and the sort of, you know, aristocratic Englishmen they were. Perhaps they simply plotted to kill the three of them and were so all-consumed with that passion they neglected so many blatantly incriminating details. Perhaps and perhaps and perhaps. I'd give anything to talk to Foster or Rattei."

"So would I," Falchi said bleakly.

"Where do you suppose he is?"

"Who?"

"Rattei."

"In Chiusdino. He's got a big villa down there. It's beautiful—set in the wooded hills and surrounded by vineyards."

"Think he'd see me?"

Falchi hunched his shoulders, but his eyes were still following the blond Danish women. "I don't know. Perhaps. He's probably surrounded by packs of Roman lawyers. Those leeches would have moved in at the first hint of trouble and scandal. They're even more merciless than certain carabinieri high officials from that dunghill."

"Chiusdino?" McGarr asked. "I rather like that little town."

"No—Rome. Rome!" Falchi turned to McGarr. "Lookit, I'll make a deal with you. I'll try to get to Foster *after* the pompous bastards from the south are through with him. I won't let up on him night and day until he confesses to something. When he does, you'll be the first to know. That's a promise, and I'll tell you all the details.

"You, in the meantime, will keep me informed of all your shenanigans." He said the last word in English. "Like that Irish touch?"

It was an English touch, but McGarr didn't correct him.

"What about the murders in Ireland?"

McGarr said, "He'll say nothing about those. We still have a death penalty in my country, Carlo, and he knows we've only got the barest case against him. He's a professional and made quite sure of that himself. My bet is that there were two payments, either from Rattei himself or from somebody else."

"Who must be terribly wealthy."

McGarr nodded. "To reward him for framing Rattei or for keeping his mouth shut if Rattei was his co-conspirator." Just then something else occurred to McGarr. "Could it be that Rattei, out of some warped sense of manly pride, wants to show the world he has actually carried out his threat on Cummings's life?"

That stopped Falchi. "Could be. He's like that, you know. Fiercely proud. Then, what about the murders in Ireland?"

"Could be Foster was working on his own hook. Could be the Tartan Oil deal offended Rattei's heightened sense of manly pride as well—you know, that they should be working for him and using their inside information to fill their own pockets too."

"Ah, yes—it could be many things. We'll have to work hard, I fear. But, first, a little *divertiménto.*" Falchi turned to the women and said in an English as fluent as McGarr's Italian, "The dispute regarding this pulpit involves the question of who actually is responsible for it. We know this, that Nicola Pisano carved a pulpit in the cathedral at Pisa eight years after this one was finished. Now, Pisano's at Pisa is octagonal in shape instead of hexagonal like this one, and, above all, the movement of the figures is denser and more complex here.

"I believe Pisano's pupil, the justly famous Arnolfo di Cambio, is responsible for this undeniable masterpiece. And isn't it that, ladies? Arnolfo di Cambio, of course, is also responsible for such other trifles as the original design of the Cathedral of Santa Maria of the Flowers, that is to say, Tuscany's other duomo in Firenze, and the Signoria Palace, Tuscany's other town hall. But what you see before you is truly the master's *ne plus ultra.* Buildings are the concern of masons and joiners; sculpture is a thing of the spirit."

The Danish women were wide-eyed.

The Italian guide had walked away in disgust. Evidently, Falchi horned in like this often, whenever, McGarr supposed, the crowd contained blonds.

When he rang up the Excelsior, McGarr found that Noreen was still upset. "I can't seem to put it out of my mind, Peter."

"Well, why don't you do something different, something interesting. I know—why don't you take Bernie and Hughie to Florence for the day? Rent a car, show them what the place is like. Go to the galleries, eat at Il Latini." It was McGarr's favorite restaurant in that city. When the owner had visited Ireland a year before, he had stayed at McGarr's house in Rathmines. One of the man's sons was studying philosophy at Trinity. "All right." She seemed cheered already. "Bernie told me this morning that you should call his room. He's heard from Madigan in London."

McGarr jiggled the yoke of the phone and asked the hotel switchboard operator to ring McKeon's rooms.

McKeon said, "Madigan got a line on Rattei. It's nothing he can prove, mind you, but scuttlebutt has it Rattei has been visiting a certain house that specializes in sweet assignations for only extremely well-heeled gents and the escorts they have chosen for themselves. It's merely the place that's offered, you see. I've got the address here someplace. Ah, yes—Thirty-eight West Road, Surrey. Now, the interesting part is that he only ever has been seen there with one woman, and she is tall, dark, and exquisite."

McGarr thanked McKeon and hung up. He had never imagined that Rattei, given his fiery personality, could have maintained a platonic twenty-year love affair.

It was a short walk from the café in which he had made the phone calls on Via Diacceto, through the Piazza Independenzia, to the Via di Citta, the Piazza del Campo, and the Ricasoli residence. McGarr enjoyed these narrow, winding streets. There were no cars. People were forced to stop and talk to each other.

In the Piazza del Campo, workers were beginning to take down the viewing stands.

Liam O'Shaughnessy met him at the door of the Palazzo Ricasoli. Several carabinieri were also stationed there.

"What's up?" McGarr asked him.

"A couple of things. First, Battagliatti arrived early. After him came a limousine a block long, something old like a Bugatti. It was Rattei. And he was a different man from the one we interviewed on the oil derrick. First, he was dressed in a spanking blue suit with a silver gray silk tie and a shirt the same color but with blue polka dots to match. And his shoes—get this!—*they* were silver as well. Cripes, the value of the rings on his fingers was more than five years of my take-home pay.

"Then he got into a shouting match with Battagliatti in the foyer of the palazzo, and one of the maids later told me the signora refused to see him. I could hear him bellowing at her down here— how she couldn't deny him now, how he knew she loved him and he was tired of waiting and would give her only one week to decide. Well, he worked himself up into such a state he threw a punch at one of Battagliatti's henchmen when he left. That's the one over there with the shiner. Rattei's in good shape. That gorilla went down like he got hit by a hammer." O'Shaughnessy had nodded his head in the direction of a squat but muscular young man who was leaning against the fender of a grey Lancia touring car that had a small red flag flying from a standard on the other side. The man was dabbing at his left eye with a wet bar towel from the café across the piazza.

"But Battagliatti has been with her all morning. It seems she'll see only him. To tell you the truth, I don't care much for him. He reminds me of a weasel. He's far too taken with this whole business for my money. Doesn't he have a job?"

"No," said McGarr. "He's a politician."

They started up the stairs.

"Hasn't anybody else tried to see her?"

"Sure—the whole gang we met at the embassy in London, but Battagliatti won't have any of it. Says she's indisposed and will see them when Cummings is laid out or at the funeral. He won't even talk to me. Orders me around like I was some guard dog. I've been thinking I'm going to tell him where to get off the tram next time."

"Go ahead. You've got my O.K. But don't put your hands on him. Remember—people fight with their mouths in this country, and they've got a law that claps the first person to use his hands, regardless of the cause, in the can." Through McGarr's mind flashed the thought that in Ireland his people were fighting with bombs, random shootings, and ambushes, and he felt very sad.

O'Shaughnessy said, "And here's another stopper for you. Cummings is going to have a church funeral. He was a Catholic!"

"So?"

"So, I thought all those"—O'Shaughnessy cleared his throat slightly—"in London were Protestants."

"It's easy to start thinking like that where we're from. Too easy. The way I understand it, there are some pretty powerful English Roman Catholics. Their families never became Protestant."

"More power to them," said O'Shaughnessy. He was a man who was what he was, and nothing could change him from that.

McGarr, on the other hand, could never quite forget the part the Church had played during the Famine and its continuing attempt to keep Ireland isolated, provincial, and "preserved" as "The Holy Isle." Otherwise, McGarr too was what he was. He had been born a Catholic into a family that was only nominally so. His father had only gone to church because the pubs weren't open during those hours. Just to make conversation as they continued up the stairs, he said, "Hell—Alexander Pope was a Catholic."

"He probably would have to be with a name like that." O'Shaughnessy was in no sense a learned man, although he was quite acute in most matters.

McGarr opened the door of the foyer to the Ricasoli apartments, and there stood Battagliatti, right in front of them, smiling. McGarr couldn't see his eyes because his glasses mirrored the light from the doorway below. McGarr wondered if Battagliatti had heard them talking. The old hallway made voices echo.

"Signor McGarr, how nice to see you again. I caught a glimpse of you crossing the piazza." He offered his hand. It was limp when McGarr took it. "I suppose you've come to see Enna. I'm sorry, she's indisposed at the moment. I know you can understand that she wants to cooperate with you and the other police in whose jurisdiction you are presently operating, but, let us remember, she was married to the man for over thirty years, and, what with the violence and all, the accident has been quite traumatic for her. In fact, the family doctor has prescribed a heavy sedative, and I believe that she has at last fallen asleep." Battagliatti was standing in the doorway, blocking any farther advance.

McGarr said, "You know Superintendent O'Shaughnessy, don't you, Mr. Chairman," and made it necessary for Battagliatti to offer O'Shaughnessy his hand, as he had to McGarr. Thus, McGarr stepped by his right side. The little man twisted his neck around to watch McGarr, who said, "Actually, I think at this time you'd be more helpful to me, sir. May I be frank with you?" McGarr looked directly at Battagliatti.

"Why yes, of course."

"Where can we talk?" McGarr hooked his arm through Battagliatti's and began walking him down the hall. He opened several doors, until he found a small, vacant sitting room.

As they were about to step in, a maid appeared in the foyer. She was carrying a small tray with a cup and saucer, teapot, and accessories on it.

"Don't go in there!" Battagliatti hissed at her. "How many times must I tell you she's resting?"

"But she—— I——" The maid was flustered. She was young, dark, and somewhat too well built.

"Do as I say or I'll have you fired."

She flushed and scurried back into the kitchen.

McGarr noted that Battagliatti's attitude seemed strange for a Communist.

When McGarr got Battagliatti seated, he pulled a desk chair over so that he could talk to him confidentially, as it were, in whispers. McGarr then glanced at O'Shaughnessy, who stood behind Battagliatti and leaned against the wall. They had used this technique dozens of times before to intimidate suspects.

Battagliatti twisted around to see where O'Shaughnessy was. The towering Garda superintendent looked down at the little man as though he could eat him. And Battagliatti's features, although handsome, were too diminutive for a man. Thus, he appeared doll-like, and, now that he was aging, like one that a craftsman with a perverse wit had designed. His hair was flecked with gray. He began to say, "I see no reason for this——"

McGarr placed his hand on his sleeve and, looking at the door, said, "Enrico Rattei's been arrested for the murder of Colin Cummings. Accessory, I mean." He turned only his eyes to Battagliatti. These gestures, McGarr well knew, were histrionic but designedly so. It gave another dimension to their discussion.

There was something curious about this little man, as though the whole experience here in the Ricasoli apartments—the murder, its aftermath, his present stewardship of Enna Ricasoli's affairs—was heightened for him, who had done so much in his life and now controlled a province and had a say in the national political life of Italy. "But no! That's impossible," said Battagliatti. He adjusted his metal-frame glasses. "I just saw him an hour ago."

"He's been released, of course. They'll never keep a powerful man like him in the jug. Especially when he's got powerful political friends like you, signor."

Battagliatti's eyes wavered a bit hearing that. He then said, "This must be some sort of mistake. That row between Cummings and him was a silly schoolboy gesture, absurd and romantic. Enrico Rattei is a man of the world. He wouldn't do something like this."

"Love is a most absurd emotion, Mr. Chairman. Did you know that Rattei had been seeing Enna Ricasoli in London on a regular basis?"

Again Battagliatti twisted around to look at O'Shaughnessy.

"That maybe ENI's involvement in the Scottish oil fields was just an excuse for him to be in London often?"

Did McGarr then see Battagliatti flush? Certainly his nostrils dilated, and he straightened his tie.

"Some say they were lovers, you know, in a carnal sense. I have here an address." McGarr began to reach for his pocket secretary. "It's a place in London that wealthy men sometimes use when they've got company and want to remain discreet. Of course, they've got to pay a great deal for the privacy."

"That's a lie!" Battagliatti blurted out, then twisted around to O'Shaughnessy once more. "Can't he sit down?"

"No, no," McGarr went on in the same even tone. "This place exists *por una relazióne amorosa.*"

And then the discussion switched into Italian. "That's an insult to the poor woman—wife of a murdered husband!—who is resting in the other room. That's an affront to this noble family, to Siena, to—— And, what's more, the whole idea is incredible. Enna Ricasoli is a lady, in every sense." He straightened the lapels of his gray jacket.

"She never told her husband she went out with Rattei."

"That's because her husband was a boor."

McGarr furrowed his brow.

"That's right, a social imbecile."

McGarr held out his palms, *"Ma, signor! Il uòmo poveretto!"*

"The poor man doesn't need any lies told about him. He was a cretin and, what's more, he was an Englishman. You two have no love for the English, I trust." Yet again, he began to twist around to O'Shaughnessy.

"I try not to think in categories," said McGarr. "Do you know if Enrico Rattei is licensed to fly a helicopter?"

"No. We're both very busy men. I wouldn't know that."

"Are you?"

"Am I what?"

"Licensed to fly a helicopter?"

"I leave such things up to lesser mortals."

Once more, this statement implied an attitude that seemed strange for a Communist.

"What size are Rattei's feet? Do you know?"

McGarr glanced down at Battagliatti's feet. His shoes were narrow and tiny, like a woman's, like those that had made the impressions in the soft earth behind the Hitchcock summer residence in Dingle.

Battagliatti started chuckling, "What is this—some sort of a game? Am I supposed to know that?"

"Not really." McGarr stood. "I know you want to help your friend."

As though relieved, Battagliatti stood and turned so that O'Shaughnessy was no longer behind him. "And that I shall. I am a man who is not without a certain amount of influence in Siena," he said, smiling wryly, "and I shall see that this entire, unfortunate matter is cleared up quickly." He held out his hand to McGarr. "Thank you for coming to me with this information, Signor McGarr.

"And you too, Signor O'———"

O'Shaughnessy merely grasped the man's hand and stared at him. Indeed, alongside the Garda superintendent, Battagliatti did appear doll-like.

Down in the piazza, McGarr and O'Shaughnessy turned into Al Mangia Ristorante and ordered two glasses of Elban white wine. Tasting his, which had a coppery color and just the slightest tang of salt air, McGarr looked at O'Shaughnessy. McGarr didn't need to say, "Stay with him, Liam. Make yourself conspicuous. If he asks why you're following him, say it's for his own protection. Who knows, Rattei might try to have all Enna Cummings's friends killed, too."

"Where will you be? Remember my Italian is weak."

"Right now, I'm going to make several phone calls." McGarr slapped a fifty-thousand-lire note on the bar and told the barman to hold it until he finished his calls, one long distance to London.

O'Shaughnessy finished his glass, bought a newspaper, and sat at a sidewalk table from which he had a full view of the door to the Palazzo Ricasoli. Battagliatti would not slip out the back. He had too much pride for that.

Over one hour and two glasses of white wine later, McGarr managed to reach Carlo Falchi. He had had to insist that Falchi's carabinieri secretary give him a list of possible phone numbers at which he might reach the commandant. On the seventh try, Falchi answered. "You call at an inopportune moment. I'm in conference with the Danish professoressa from the tour bus. We're discussing a matter of great intercultural urgency," said Falchi, "namely, the rehabilitation of a carabinieri commandant's manly pride."

"But your secretary told me this was the number of your barber."

Falchi sighed, "What is a poor romantic man to do—ice maidens, all of them. Not one had anything but sangfroid. I wonder why they come to Siena, what they expect to learn without meeting her people?"

McGarr could hear a male voice sniggering in the background. He guessed it was Falchi's barber.

"How did Rattei get along with Francesco Battagliatti?"

Falchi snorted into the phone. "He didn't. He doesn't. Who do you think encouraged Mussolini to exile Battagliatti during the thirties? They've been feuding since they were students at university. Never in public, mind you, but it's one of the well-known oddities of the Italian political scene that every student of our government must learn. On national occasions, when they meet on the platform, they're scrupulously polite to each other, but behind the scenes they've been knifing each other in the back for decades. If the Communists ever become a part of a coalition government in Rome, one condition will certainly be the removal of Rattei from ENI and maybe even the dissolution of that organization. Nothing would give Battagliatti greater pleasure and nothing would hurt Rattei more."

"But the Christian Democrats aren't likely to invite the Communists into a coalition."

"No, but the Christian Democrats are no longer as strong as they once were. Other coalitions are becoming increasingly possible."

McGarr then could hear Falchi asking his barber to be most discreet about what he was overhearing.

The barber then replied that a patron should trust his barber even more than his confessor, since the operations the former conducted were so much the more vital, the neck being connected to the head, as opposed to what the priest did for the soul, which was insubstantial and could not grow a beard. "What's more," the barber added, "I speak no English whatsoever, since those words seem to foul the chin with spittle, which is unsightly and therefore bad for business."

"Could Enna Ricasoli Cummings be the cause of their original squabble?"

"Very likely. Rattei is—how shall I term it?—hot-blooded. And that woman! She's still a goddess, even today."

"But would she be attracted to a man like Battagliatti?"

"There is no accounting for taste. He makes up for his size in other ways. He's one of the most powerful men in Italy today."

"But he doesn't exactly act like a Communist."

"Because communism in Italy is more of a conversational stance, an ideology, than a firm belief. A few days ago I visited some university students who are so poor they live in a basement that doesn't have a single window. They publish a weekly Communist broadside —you know, scurrilous rhetorical attacks on anybody with money or power or both, and it's usually the Americans who come in for the most abuse. They had failed to register for a mailing license. While I talked to them, one of their other roommates returned from having been home in Piacenza over the weekend. He promptly unpacked his bags and showed me two new, flashy suits, a pair of shoes, and a clock radio that his family had given him. And these kids are about as hard-core Marxist as you can get in this country. They call themselves something special, you know, *Cinese*——"

"Maoists."

"That's it."

Liam O'Shaughnessy entered the restaurant and walked rapidly toward McGarr.

"Do you know if Battagliatti can fly a helicopter?"

"No. I do know he can fly an airplane, though. He was in the Russian Air Force from 'thirty-nine until he showed up back here in 'forty-four. He got a commendation from Stalin for his exploits. He's been trying to bury that information for years. It seems he's ashamed of his association with Stalin."

"You mean, he's got blood on his hands?"

"Some say so, but it all happened so many years ago and in Russia."

"But, would you say he's a man who could kill, if he had to?"

"He definitely gives that impression, doesn't he? He's got a mind like a steel trap. I don't think he'd let anybody get in the way of what he wanted. Why all the questions about him? Surely you don't think——"

O'Shaughnessy put his hand on McGarr's shoulder. "Battagliatti's bodyguards are readying his car in front of the palazzo. Looks like he's going someplace."

"Where would Battagliatti be going today?" McGarr asked Falchi.

McGarr then could hear Falchi asking the same question of his barber, but in Italian.

"Piombino. The Communists are having a rally there about ten o'clock."

More talk in the background.

"Yes, ten. When Battagliatti attends, they're always right on schedule. Are you going there? What's this all about anyhow? You'll keep me informed of any . . . developments, won't you? By the way, you're certainly not planning to leave town without coming to dinner? Remember, I haven't yet had the very great pleasure of speaking to your wife again." Falchi chuckled libidinously.

The barber, who had claimed to know no English, was also laughing in the background now. He said, "Cuckoo, cuckoo!" in a high voice.

McGarr hung up. He mused that it must be exhausting to be an aging Italian male. Sex preoccupied so much of every day, awake or asleep. They seemed loath to let the subject rest.

He called the Excelsior Hotel and left the message that he and Liam would be in Piombino at least until midnight. He also asked McKeon to contact British Customs and Immigration to learn how long Battagliatti had been in England last.

He then called London and after only a short while managed to reach Hugh Madigan. "Anything new?"

"McKeon get in touch with you about the Rattei development?"

"Yes."

"Well—here's another thing that just turned up. The lawyers— Loescher, Dull, and Griggs, Forty Parliament Square—who are the ones that queried the Panamanian government, represent somebody who is Italian and in oil. How's that strike you, Peter?"

"Like a very nice piece of detective work."

McGarr could tell Madigan was gloating. "It's going to cost you, my friend."

McGarr didn't respond.

"Well," Madigan demanded, "nothing more?"

"Like what?"

"You mean you're not going to put that together for me? Remember I'm stuck in this office most of the day working on business and, you know, other dreary things."

"Such as your accounts receivable, no doubt."

"This is the first real piece of police work I've had in a year."

"Anytime you want bracing police work twenty-four hours a day, I can offer you a job in Dublin for what I would estimate as one-third your present earnings."

"This is a two-way street, you know, Peter."

"I'm well acquainted with it, Hugh. It's got a big pound sterling marker on the street lamp."

"It's not that and you know it. I've got kids and we're settled here."

McGarr, one of whose fondest wishes was to have Madigan working for Special Branch, asked, "But does it feel like home there in London, Hugh?"

Madigan said, "I don't know why I talk to you."

"Business," said McGarr. "It's only business and very good at that. Think about it, though, Hugh. Talk to Maisie about it too. Tell her I'll fight for every farthing I can. The government will build you a house, say, in Rathfarnum. I can promise you every assignment that interests you. There's hospitalization, retirement, all the things you've got to pay for yourself. There's a very fine place for you here."

"In Siena?"

"Ah—g'wan wid ya now," McGarr said in Dublinese, and rang off.

The drive from Siena toward Piombino via Chiusdino was pleasant. They passed through valleys of planted fields, climbed hills the slopes of which became cow pastures, then vineyards, then olive groves. In mountainous terrain, the undergrowth was thick and appeared thorny and *Risèrva di Caccia* signs were ubiquitous.

The farmhouses they passed were all of a type. Faced with stucco, the living quarters were on the second floor with barn, stable, and kitchen—stoves and ovens—on the ground floor. The walls of these houses had been extended to form a courtyard. Larger farms had other stables, granaries, tool sheds, garages, and assorted outbuildings running off this to form a neat compound on the land. In color, the walls of the houses were raw sienna, or yellowish brown, while the ceramic roof tiles, which had been fired, were burnt sienna or reddish brown. Most shutters were green.

And every farmhouse had poultry in the yard. There were chickens, geese, ducks, domesticated pheasant, and even turkeys, which, McGarr mused, were one of the best gifts the New World had given the Old. And somehow, barnyard fowl, which had been allowed to grub beneath olive trees and along the rows of the vineyards, had a distinctive and piquantly fresh taste. It was, of course, the cooks of Catherine de' Medici who, bringing their foodstuffs and ideas for preparation from Florence to Paris, had laid the groundwork for the development of Parisian haute cuisine, than which, McGarr would be the first to admit, there was no gastronomy finer. But in the roasting of a plain barnyard chicken—*póllo arrosto* or *coq au vin*—so many elements were of importance: the diet of the chicken, its age (it must be young), but mostly its preparation. The care with which this simple dish was prepared was, to McGarr's way of thinking, one very accurate measure of a civilization's cuisine.

But, checking his watch and finding it to be 4:00 P.M., McGarr decided to delay dinner until the usual Italian hour, 8:00 or so, and, after asking directions in an *alimentari* in Chiusdino, they pushed on toward Massa Maritima. On the road, they were told, they couldn't miss Rattei's villa.

And surely the prospect of the villa set on a hilltop with a serpentine drive lined by ancient cypresses was magnificent. But rather than leave the hillside in park as, McGarr supposed, the original inhabitant had intended, Rattei had much of it under extensive and modern—the massive concrete vineyard pillars dotted the hillside —grape cultivation, with pasturage for sheep and goats where the terrain was rocky.

After a forty-minute wait in the gatehouse that had been heavily bombarded and rebuilt recently, McGarr and O'Shaughnessy were admitted to the grounds. McGarr imagined that because of Rattei's politics, the local peasantry had taken liberties with his property during the chaos that followed Mussolini's defeats and absconder.

After all, Rattei was an interloper from Rome and couldn't have enjoyed a squirearchical relationship with the neighboring *contadini*.

The villa itself was set on raised ground surrounded by extensive and towering ramparts, which the Fiat rent-a-car entered over a drawbridge. The interior courtyard was a garden of sculptured yews and a plethora of bright flowers that thrived with abandon in this warm, sunny clime. The gravel drive surrounded this and led to the house, which was pentagonal in shape and constructed of the ubiquitous Sienese brick that had aged to a delicate fawn color. Here and there—along the crenellated roofline, around one entire two-mullioned window that was bearing, as one would expect, a Sienese arch —McGarr noted the brick and mortar were new. The house too, he supposed, had been ravaged.

They were led down dark, cool corridors, the walls of which were draped with unicorn tapestries that delighted McGarr, especially the one in which the white unicorn reared up in a much-flowered green field which hunters on horseback and baying hounds surrounded. Head and body of a handsome horse, hind legs of a stag, and tail of a lion, it seemed a doomed figure, too beautiful and rare. And too proud.

A servant had to call McGarr twice to get him into the reception room. There Rattei and O'Shaughnessy awaited him.

Rattei was seated in a towering chair placed at the middle of a massive oaken table. His back was to the window, across which drapes had been drawn, so that two fat candles roughly at either end of the table supplied the only light in the room. He wore only a dark blue silk dressing gown and slippers to match.

"What is it you want, Mr. McGarr? You've interrupted my siesta." He spoke in English.

McGarr switched to Italian. "Such a lovely place you've got here, Signor Rattei. My wife would certainly enjoy taking a peek at your tapestries sometime."

Rattei sighed. "Certainly you haven't come all the way from Ireland to admire my holdings or discuss your wife's interests. She is, of course, welcome to examine my possessions anytime. As are you. Would you care for a little wine, an aperitif, whiskey?"

"Wine, please. I trust it's your own," said McGarr, sinking into another chair only slightly less ornate, although tastefully so, than that in which Rattei sat.

O'Shaughnessy took another one.

The servant left the room.

McGarr continued, "It's always so reassuring to talk to a man who can offer you something which his very own land has produced."

Again Rattei sighed. He looked trapped, as though the prospect of a long interview with McGarr displeased him greatly, yet he said in a pleasant manner, "It seems every time I talk to you it is in a setting more distant from your jurisdiction."

McGarr replied, "Ireland is a wet, foul place. We have no wine."

The waiter poured McGarr and O'Shaughnessy goblets, which he handed them. The tray also contained a plate of cheese and sausage slices.

"Not much sun, and certainly no women as beautiful as Enna Cummings."

Rattei motioned to the servant, who placed a goblet in front of him and poured some wine. The servant then left the room and closed the door. Rattei then said, "The Italian police released me because I proved to them: one, I was not in Italy when that person placed the money in the Monte dei Paschi; two, that the money did not come from my personal funds or those of my business concerns. I don't ever need to carry large amounts of cash with me. My word is binding, everybody knows that. Also, my company is state-owned. The auditors are scrupulous about every penny."

The wine was an Italian ideal—it had a hearty red body but was not saccharine, it was musky without an aftertaste. Yet for all of that, it was light and McGarr could still taste the grapes. "Those who corroborated your whereabouts were doubtless the same men we talked to that day aboard the oil rig."

"Of course—mine is not a noble name, signor. I must work for all of this." He indicated the room.

"Which makes your men love you all the more."

"I only hope they love me."

"So much so they'd even lie for you?"

"I will never ask them to do that."

"But they would."

"Certainly." Rattei sipped from his glass. In the shadows that the candles made he looked his age, which was fifty-eight. It was more his body that belied the years. "But then they would feel a certain contempt for me. I had used them badly, inexcusably."

"But this crisis would have passed. There are always new friendships to be formed, greater loves to be joined." McGarr smiled slightly. "Your wine is excellent."

"Have some sausage. It's a special recipe and not Tuscan." Rattei pushed the plate toward McGarr, who rose slightly to take a few slices.

Rattei said, "I am not a chameleon, signor."

"No—I think of you more as a unicorn."

Rattei cocked his head a bit. His ears pulled back. McGarr had struck a nerve. Rattei said, "I disagree. I am nothing more than a man."

"Who, like other men, has weaknesses."

Rattei looked up at McGarr inquiringly.

"Proud, forthright men don't go to bed with other men's wives and, if they do, certainly they don't make it a nearly thirty-year preoccupation."

Rattei's nostrils flared. He tossed off the wine in his glass and stood. He turned his back to them. "Perhaps you had better leave."

McGarr wasn't about to move. "Proud, forthright men—gentlemen—would not be able to support a situation in which they were forced to take their beloved to a—how shall I phrase it?—a place for amorous adventure."

Rattei spun around. "Get out! Paolo!" he shouted at the closed door.

McGarr said, "Did you ask Paolo and the others who work for you and love you to keep that little secret for you too? To lie for you if they were asked where you were on the nineteenth and twenty-sixth of June when you were not on the oil rig but rather in Ireland with Moses Foster slaying first Hitchcock, then Browne, and planning all along to kill the husband of the woman you love, whose own truly aristocratic sense of fidelity and pride was such she couldn't tolerate divorce or who perhaps, all along, never loved you? I've got the address of that place right here."

The doors of the room burst open and three men rushed in.

McGarr opened his notebook. "Shall I read you the address of that house in London? Perhaps Paolo will tell us how you trade on your relationships right now, how you can get people to believe in you and then get them to lie for you." McGarr twisted around in the chair. "Paolo—has Signor Rattei ever been to Thirty-eight West Road, Surrey? That's in London, England, of course."

Paolo glanced at Rattei, who said, "You're not needed, Paolo. I was mistaken."

Slowly, suspiciously, he and the others left the room. Paolo was a very small man with a sallow complexion and coal-black eyes. The other two men, being tall and bulky, emphasized his diminutive stature. Paolo shut the door behind him.

Rattei poured himself another glass of wine. "Where did you get that information? I'll pay you for it. How much do you want?"

"Twenty-five thousand pounds should be adequate." McGarr stood and poured O'Shaughnessy and himself more wine. "*If* you can assure me the money is by no means traceable to you or your businesses."

McGarr then changed his tone to one of quiet compassion for this man who was now indeed like some unicorn hemmed in by hounds and hunters. "Signor Rattei—you lied to us that day out on the oil rig. You said you had dinner with a friend in London. We now know that wasn't the whole truth. You said you didn't know Hitchcock and Browne were involved with Tartan, and yet I've found out that you instructed your lawyers to query the Panamanian authorities three days before Hitchcock's death about the principal officers of Tartan; you knew Foster much better than you let on when handing us his folder and saying he was African and not Jamaican; and ENI's financial picture is extremely precarious right now, much worse than you pretended. Tartan is hurting you and your court case against them is weak. If they win, then the portable rig you erected to cut into their drill hole will allow them to sue you for triple damages. Also, as you told us yourself, they'll be able to pump that cistern dry."

But Rattei said, "You seem to know so much about me. What do you know about Cummings, eh? I know I'm no saint. But that son of a bitch of an Englishman was a rotter to the core. Yes—I'll admit

it to you—I slept with Enna and not long after he married her too.
Do you know that he was bisexual? He discovered *that* shortly *after*
he married Enna. She, you see, didn't really please him totally. But
he, being a Catholic"—Rattei spit out that last word—"wouldn't
give her a divorce, and she, being a Ricasoli"—he treated the name
similarly—"wouldn't have sued for one anyhow. And then he was
content to remain married to her for twenty-seven years while he
knew—mind you, he *knew!*—I slept with his wife every chance I
got." Rattei drank off the wine. "I should have killed him way back
when I sorely wanted to."

McGarr wondered if that was a tacit admission in the present
situation and poured Rattei some more wine.

"For me the situation was at once intolerable and unavoidable. I
could do nothing about it, yet I loved her. He called me her Roman
gigolo, told me not to be 'ethnic' when I shouted at him on the
phone, told others who told me that it didn't matter how much
money I made, I was a peasant who could never get the dirt from
under my fingernails.

"You know, we all have vainglorious ideas of what we want to be
in life. Somebody has said that a man is happiest when he realizes
his childhood ambitions. Look at me—I have everything I always
wanted as a child, but for twenty-seven years I've secretly been
miserable. That's given me strength too, since in an ultimate way I
felt I had nothing to lose and thus have been able to take risks that
would make other men cringe."

O'Shaughnessy said, "Like the risk of killing not only Cummings
but the others like him—Hitchcock and Browne—who had also
treated you like a peasant only to try to steal from you too?"

Rattei shook his head. "No—I'm not sorry either of them are
dead, and I'm overjoyed that Cummings died in the manner he did.
It makes me believe that indeed justice obtains here on earth. But,
no—I did not kill them. *And,* I did not kill Cummings, although I
feel cheated that I've been denied the pleasure."

McGarr thought for a moment. "If what you tell us is true, aren't
you even curious about why Foster killed Cummings and the others
and tried to implicate you?"

"Yes. In a dispassionate way. Any man in a position like mine has made many enemies and most of them are undeserved. The rich hate me because I'm an upstart and have kept them from continuing to swindle the poor. The poor hate me because I'm no longer one of them. And the people in the middle hate me because they hate everybody including themselves and I'm more visible than most. And there you have it—not a very uplifting tale, eh?"

"What happens if Foster breaks down and confesses to your involvement?" O'Shaughnessy asked.

Rattei didn't even glance up. He was looking down into his wine glass. "Why even think of that? Nothing will happen. It's his word against mine. I'll go to court. My face will be in all the papers more than usual. People will gossip. Another facet will be added to that 'infamous diamond in the rough,' and I'll be acquitted for lack of evidence. The Italian people will return me to my endeavors. They wouldn't have it any other way."

McGarr said, "And *with* Enna Ricasoli."

Rattei smiled, "Hopefully, signor. Hopefully. You see, whoever hatched this plot has convinced Enna of my guilt and alienated her from my affections."

O'Shaughnessy asked, "But don't you feel two ways about this lady, that she caused much of the difficulty herself?"

He shook his head. "All of us are given certain talents, desires, and expectations, and the person who can achieve the most of them while hurting the fewest number of others least is best. Lord knows I've hurt my share. I'm not about to blame Enna for wanting certain things for herself and trying, although failing, to get them."

McGarr stood and thanked Rattei for the interview. On their way out, McGarr stopped at the unicorn tapestry. It seemed more complex to him, as though he had missed something when first viewing it earlier.

By the time they reached Massa Maratima, a pink sun had begun to sink into the Mediterranean and made the western slopes of the steep, hardwood hills a tan color that McGarr had always thought was imagination in Tuscan landscape painting.

O'Shaughnessy was saying, "We haven't reached the bottom of that fellow yet. He's a deep one. *And* tricky."

McGarr again thought of the description of Rattei as a self-satisfied tiger. "I keep getting the feeling we've selected all the right rocks—the smoking gun, the disgruntled killer, the bank draft, Rattei's description in all of the proper places at the proper times—but we're missing the lever to prise up the big boulder."

Suddenly, McGarr's stomach reminded him of its presence. He checked his watch, 7:40—plenty of time to have dinner in Massa Maratima and still make Battagliatti's rally at Piombino at 10:00. McGarr then remembered the *póllo arrosto* he'd contemplated in Chiusdino.

After many inquiries, they finally found a farmhouse *locando* which was reputed to have excellent chicken. It was one big room with oilcloth on the tables, linoleum on the floor, but with a fine view of the plain and the Mediterranean beyond.

Sipping a hearty, rawish red wine, they chatted with the old lady who was the cook. Her grandchildren, when they were present, waited the tables. They were working in Germany for the summer, and she allowed the two policemen to sit at the family table in the kitchen.

Her stove was antediluvian, a great iron monster with claw feet and cast-iron scrollwork along its top. The cooking surface, wood-fired, was cherry red in places, but capable of a slow simmer in others. The old woman said she had grown up with that stove. In spite of the heat, she wore a black dress buttoned to the neck and a spotless white apron. The kitchen too was free from the debris of food preparation. Like most accomplished chefs, she cleaned as she cooked, and McGarr made note of every detail.

She cut the fresh young chicken into six parts. She then heated some butter and olive oil in an earthenware pot, diced some onions and a lean breast of pork, and tossed that in. When these had browned, she put in the chicken, a thinly sliced garlic clove, an herb bouquet, and the special ingredient, *tartufi bianchi,* a delicate white truffle that grows in Tuscany from late autumn to early spring. On a hot part of her stove, she sautéed this mixture until golden, then removed the lid and skimmed off the fat. She poured some brandy over the chicken, ignited it, and then poured on a pint or so of red wine. They talked for twenty minutes. The old woman could not place *Irlanda* but imagined, looking at O'Shaughnessy, that the air must be healthful there.

She then removed the chicken to a platter, thickened the sauce with chicken blood, a beaten chicken liver, and a little more brandy. This she poured over the bird.

Two hours later, McGarr and O'Shaughnessy were in Piombino, a city whose economy was based on iron, steel, petroleum processing, and general maritime commerce. In former times, iron had been brought in by ship from Elba, which lay about twelve miles offshore. Now, however, the ore was transported from wherever it could be obtained, and the iron and steel mills shared the shoreline with petroleum cracking plants. Taking a walk to the harbor to kill time, McGarr and O'Shaughnessy found the water ocher from the sluices of the steel mills. Over this, dead fish formed an unsightly scum. Still, the Mediterranean beyond was azure, but McGarr wondered for how long.

# 7

The rally began with two big bass drums. They were rolled into the square. Behind them Communist party members marched, red armbands prominent on their right sleeves. The front line carried large red flags. Most of the crowd were factory workers, the men dressed in cheap suits, the women in dresses that were slightly dowdy.

Each report of the drums seemed to sidle McGarr's chair. A shiver ran up his spine, and he thought for a moment he would sneeze. The atmosphere was festive, the night balmy, and the skies clear. Kids coursed over the sidewalks, pushcart vendors sold ice cream, cotton candy, and red balloons. Shopkeepers came out onto their stoops to watch, and carabinieri directed traffic away from the square.

As was usual in affairs of this type, several speakers harangued the crowd on local issues—wages, low-income housing, public transportation, and schools—for the first forty minutes, and then Battagliatti, the little David of Italian politics, rose to speak about national concerns. Like other gifted public speakers, he appealed to the emotions of the crowd, not to its intellect.

They, he said, who did the world's work, alone suffered the world's miseries. Big landowners, big businessmen, big bureaucrats, and "others" were fat and happy living off the backs of the workers and peasants. The tables needed turning; that's what they were about. Battagliatti never once alluded to big labor or big politicians.

Specifically, he would never think of allowing his party to join any coalition government that included the Christian Democrats, the predominant political entity in Italy since World War II. They were the compromisers, they had no values. "What puts money in their pockets is the only ideal they embrace. And that, comrades, is the same corrupt approach which takes the money you made out of your paycheck at the end of the week and gives it to all those"—Battagliatti waved a hand—"all those middlemen, which is another word for——"

"Leeches!" the crowd roared. The bass drums boomed.

"——in the name of law. That's the sort of legislation the Christian Democrats have passed."

Standing on a platform behind a podium, Battagliatti's slight frame looked solid. McGarr imagined that this particular double-breasted gray suit was heavily padded.

"Never, never, *never* will we truckle to conciliate with those low-lifes! Remember, this is a class conflict in which we are engaged, you and I. And we must approach those political hacks who have misled their followers over the years with the same disdain that they have shown your efforts—the good work of the Italian laborers and peasants—since they bartered away our property and wealth for power after the last war."

Battagliatti did not mention that the Christian Democrats had not once offered the Communists a role in any of their governments, and probably would step down from power rather than do so. Years before, McGarr had heard Battagliatti say that never, never, *never* would elected Communist officials take part in any corrupt, bourgeois legislative assembly, yet they now were there. Conditions had changed, Battagliatti had said, and Italy needed the moral leadership of the proletariat in the Chamber of Deputies. Politics was, after all, the art of the possible.

Battagliatti then heaped on the shibboleths, building his declamation into a crescendo of catch phrases that had the crowd roaring, the drum booming. He left the stage amidst thunderous applause, returned, harangued them for several more moments, then quickly walked toward his car.

The crowd was hoarse and breathless.

McGarr was waiting beside the Lancia sedan, which was a rather chic automobile for a Communist leader.

"Ah, Signor McGarr," Battagliatti said in English, extending his hand. "I saw you and your compatriot among our comrades just now. I didn't realize you were interested in Italian politics, nor was I aware that the Communist point of view has any chance of success in your country."

"Ah, we tried a form of communism in my country about a thousand years ago. It only led to the British invasion and a nine-hundred-year occupation. One such lesson is enough for an eternity. But with a gifted speaker and organizer such as yourself, sir, sure and we'd all be chanting 'never, never, *never*' in no time at all, at all. But, it's not that I came to see you about." McGarr was standing right in front of the car door that Battagliatti had planned to enter. "It's about your friend, Enrico Rattei."

Battagliatti seemed to turn to see if any of his assistants had heard or understood McGarr. Standing out in the open, like this, their voices had not carried.

"I was wondering, could you tell me a little bit about the gent? People seem loath to talk about him now that he's been clapped in the can, and the police tell me this is an internal matter. I'm making little progress in the completion of my investigation. And I've got to write a report, I do." They were still speaking English, which allowed McGarr to phrase his questions with a self-conscious ingenuousness that Battagliatti might doubt. Only a native speaker whose people had been infantilized in the recent past could accomplish this.

Battagliatti breathed heavily. His smile crumpled somewhat. "How can I help you?"

"He went to university with you, right? Can you tell me, had he a happy home life?"

"His father was a Carabiniere, a Fascist." Battagliatti tried to say this last word without contempt but failed. "His mother died when he was quite young."

"Therefore, his father's influence was all the greater upon him."

"I suppose so, but he was—*is*—very much his own man in everything he does."

"How does he feel about blacks? I mean, like that Foster fellow we collared?"

"I'm sure I don't know. There were Africans at university with us when we were students. None of them was friendly with him, I don't think, nor with me either, for that matter, although I bear Negroes no ill will."

"Haven't you and Rattei been pretty much at odds over the years? I ask only because I'm trying to assess the man's personality. Whereas the police have got him dead to rights in this country, in all candor, the evidence we have against him in Ireland is strictly circumstantial."

Battagliatti tried to look surprised. Overacting, he dropped his narrow jaw. "Why—what is it that Enrico is supposed to have done in your country, Chief Inspector?"

"Only a couple other murders, as a cover, against the real object of his mania, Cummings himself. He was going to make it seem like Foster, a dissatisfied former agent of SIS, systematically knocked off all the former chiefs."

Battagliatti nodded his head. "I see, I see. But, he didn't succeed, did he, Signor McGarr? You and your associate here were too smart for him." He glanced up at O'Shaughnessy and smiled, then said to McGarr, "Yes, we've always had what I call an agonistic relationship —one based on competition."

"For Enna Ricasoli?"

"Yes and no. You must remember that her legal name *is* Cummings. The Englishman removed her from our contention years ago."

"But both of you continued to see her on a regular basis."

"Yes, *see* her." Battagliatti was no longer smiling. He was probably remembering his conversation with McGarr in Siena earlier in the day.

"Were you jealous?"

"Of whom? Of Rattei or Cummings or of any other male who looked upon her?"

"Excuse me, I meant to ask if Rattei was jealous. After all, *he* is the subject of our investigation." It was McGarr's turn to smile at Battagliatti.

"Of course he was. Anybody will tell you that Enrico Rattei has never been the master of his own emotions. And they will also tell

you that he was devastated when she chose to marry Cummings. He
wouldn't eat. He lost weight. He even left school for a time, although he couldn't afford to."

"Was she in love with Cummings?"

"I don't know. How can I know how she felt? Frankly, if I could
have made her love me, I would have done so. Any man would."

"Had she many suitors?"

"Has the sky many stars?"

"Who was her favorite?"

"In some ways, almost everybody. She has the knack of singling
out what's best in a person and developing it."

"And with you it was your wit, your quick mind."

Battagliatti looked away.

"And with Rattei it was his good looks, his good-heartedness, his
desire to help the little guys—workers, peasants—and——"

"I have that desire too! What the hell do you think *this*"—he
swept his hand to mean the political rally—"is all about?"

"——*and* his passion. In particular, his passion for her."

"Enna was afraid of him. He wanted to own, possess, crush her.
She told me so herself."

"So she fled to Cummings. He was a way out of her relationship
with Rattei, with you and the others, a way of extricating herself
even from the country."

Battagliatti removed his glasses. "Look, Chief Inspector, I'm
tired. Enna was young, emotionally immature. Rattei, with his low-
er-class talk of the worker's state and the need for order and harmony, frightened her."

"But didn't you—don't you—have your own conception of those
things?"

"Yes, but the difference was I was perceptive enough to keep
myself from talking about things that would frighten away a shel-
tered young woman from a noble background. Rattei was always
raving like a wild man. And then, when Cummings arrived with his
Oxonian charm, his ease of manner, he seemed so stable, mature,
part of her own class, which he was. All of us, Rattei, Zingiale,
Pavoni, and the rest were so busy squabbling over her amongst
ourselves, the Englishman stole her right away. We hadn't really a

chance. We—rather Rattei—had created a climate that forced her to flee from us." He reached for the door handle. "I really must excuse myself, Chief Inspector. I'm exhausted what with the events of yesterday and all. I've got a busy schedule tomorrow."

"One more question." McGarr opened the door for Battagliatti. "Didn't Rattei force you to flee Italy for over thirteen years?"

Battagliatti sat in the car, then flashed a seemingly genuine and full smile at McGarr. "That's just one of his victories in our *agon*, McGarr. It's a Greek word. You should look it up. Then, perhaps, you'll understand more completely our relationship, Rattei's and mine."

Slowly the car pulled through the crowd.

At a discreet distance McGarr and O'Shaughnessy followed.

The newspapers had said Battagliatti was speaking to merchant mariners in Livorno next morning, students at the university in Pisa the next afternoon.

McGarr planned to dog Battagliatti until he lost his aplomb.

The rally was on the docks of Livorno, in a warehouse alongside a barge canal. Mostly coastwise tankers plied that water and, now that the tide had fallen, the pilings that contained the banks were black with sludge. The sky was overcast, and it wasn't only the cool breeze off the Mediterranean that kept McGarr and O'Shaughnessy in the car. A clutch of party members, red stars pinned to their lapels, had clustered around the door of the corrugated metal building. They allowed only merchant mariners, dock workers, Italian policemen, and journalists inside. McGarr, wondering if Battagliatti had had anything to do with their exclusion, parked their car in front of the party chairman's Lancia.

While the building on occasion filled with shouts and cheers, McGarr ambled down the canal bank to a road, where in a tobacco shop he phoned Carlo Falchi, the carabinieri commandant in Siena, who said, "Foster has just confessed, implicating Rattei in everything."

McGarr said, "You just happened to volunteer to grill him all day long after your Roman co-workers were exhausted."

"*Esattaménte.*"

"You just happened to know what to ask him so that he cracked."

"The technique was Irish, of that much I am sure." Falchi was beside himself, having succeeded in extracting a confession from Foster after the big-shot Roman carabinieri had failed. "It was a highly detailed confession. He told of meetings he had had with Rattei, what Rattei wore, what he said. He remembered the names of restaurants, descriptions of waiters, the numbers of taxicabs they had taken, dates, times, places, everything. It appears that we've got Il Condottiere Rattei now. The sheer mass of the evidence is overwhelming."

"Have you picked up Rattei yet?"

"It's only just happened. We haven't got through to Chiusdino yet. In any case, it's early still. You must realize Italian hours differ from those of less civilized countries. Anyhow, I doubt that Rattei has gone anywhere."

At that very moment McGarr was conceiving of a very good place for Rattei to go and it was not jail, where McGarr's access to him would be constrained. In an official way, McGarr wasn't at all concerned about the Cummings murder. If Rattei had been an accomplice in the murders of Hitchcock and Browne—and McGarr still had not made up his mind about that—McGarr would bend every effort to get the Italian back to Ireland and justice, including a little official duplicity.

Falchi was saying, "We've begun to check Rattei's whereabouts on each occasion Foster said he met him. It all seems to dovetail."

"A work of art," said McGarr, his tone too wry for Falchi.

"Thank you. I don't mind saying I deserve the compliment." He was gloating.

"What, exactly, did he say?"

"When he discovered that his two superiors in the ENI security department were involved in a rival company, let's see—I've got the name someplace here——"

"Tartan," McGarr supplied.

"That's it. Then he, Foster, went to Rattei."

Here, McGarr thought, was an apparent discrepancy, since McGarr already knew Rattei, through his lawyers, had checked with the Panamanian government. Rattei could merely have been checking Foster's story, however.

Falchi continued, "In conversation, they discovered how much the both of them hated this certain type of Englishman. Foster, because of his prior involvement in the British Secret Service—do you know about that, Pietro?——"

"Yes."

"——hated all three of his former commanders, a certain Hitchcock, a Browne, and then Cummings himself; and Rattei hated the first two because of their having stolen those secrets from ENI and Cummings because he had married Enna Ricasoli."

"Then Foster told him that Cummings too was one of the major investors in Tartan."

"Of course."

"And Rattei's temper flared."

"Right again. He became a madman. They worked each other up to a fever pitch and planned the assassinations of the three of them. Rattei himself was to murder the first two in Ireland, and Foster was to take care of Cummings. Foster chose to do this in Italy, because Rattei, who knew Cummings was to become the British ambassador to the country, had connections here and knew how to work things so that if Foster were caught he'd receive a light sentence."

"And that makes such an interesting defense, doesn't it?" McGarr mused. "You know, the big man with big money entrapping the little and black man who is down on his luck. Did you ask him why he didn't try to escape?"

"Yes. He described it as a momentary lapse of consciousness, as though this dementia which had led him to kill Cummings had passed with the man's life. He felt—sorry."

"I see," said McGarr. "That much alone could form the basis of a plea of temporary insanity. In all, Foster has set himself up."

"Twelve years, I estimate," said Falchi. "With good behavior, he'll serve seven. If he's contrite enough, you'll never get him extradited to Ireland. Also, under Italian law, he might even get to keep the money that Rattei was supposed to have paid him. And the bank will pay him interest too."

"And what about Battagliatti?"

"Oh, yes. He's not a licensed helicopter pilot anywhere in Europe."

"But you told me he was a pilot."

"Yes, but at that time there were no helicopters in the Russian Air Force. But don't be so impatient. Remember, you're not dealing with that flamboyant Roman slime which masquerades under the title of carabinieri, you're dealing with the real carabinieri, those of us who, in spite of our leaders, manage to keep our reputation for thoroughness intact."

"Well?"

"Patience, patience. What are you in such a hurry about? We've already apprehended the murderer and are about to arrest his accomplice too."

"Christ—this phone call is costing me money. Spit it out." McGarr didn't know if he had enough cash to pay for as much time as they had used already, and he was anxious to call Rattei.

It seemed to McGarr that there was a flaw in the relationship Battagliatti purported to share with Rattei. The former professed only an *agon,* or competition, with Rattei, whereas McGarr believed it well might be a true hatred. Also, McGarr could well understand why Rattei would have wanted to kill Cummings and perhaps the others, but he did not understand why the killings were so clumsy. That certainly wasn't Rattei's style, unless he was being framed by somebody else. Foster too would naturally have avoided the many blunders involved in the murders. Rattei had recently completed a massive oil deal with the Soviet Union, which could explain Foster's reception at the Moscow airport, his stamped passport that provided him an alibi during the period in which Hitchcock and Browne had been murdered, and Rattei certainly had the sort of money necessary to have paid for Foster's services. McGarr well knew that in international politics a lucrative and vital business partnership, such as one based on oil, was more valuable to a state than any three men's lives or a mere ideological difference.

Battagliatti, on the other hand, had connections in Russia, access to Communist funds which were in all probability not inconsiderable, tiny feet, a hatred for Cummings perhaps no less profound than Rattei's, and a violent past in which Rattei himself figured as one of the prime antagonists. In short, McGarr just didn't believe the situation was as simple as Foster made out or that Battagliatti looked upon Rattei with as much equanimity as he professed. That was the crux of the investigation, which McGarr was anxious to explore.

"Well?"

"I got to talking to a friend of mine—he's a Communist too—about Battagliatti over skittles last night. My friend, who is originally from Colle Val D'Elsa, swears he once saw Battagliatti fly a helicopter into a rally himself when his regular pilot took sick."

"Could you corroborate that story for me, perhaps get several signed statements? Also, I'd like to see your dossiers of Battagliatti and Rattei, if I could."

"Yes, it seems I owe you several favors now. The Rattei dossier is on my desk right now. The"—Falchi cleared his throat—"rabble abandoned it when they slunk back to Rome. I can get you Battagliatti's, but that'll take several days. But, why bother? If Rattei has been framed, he's powerful enough to take care of himself. The spectacle of Rattei and Battagliatti locked in mortal combat over a beautiful, wealthy woman will divert the Italian press for whole months. The epic proportions of this struggle are really too magnificent to disturb."

"To be candid, Carlo, what bothers me most is *why* Rattei allowed himself to be framed."

"Perhaps he had no other choice."

"Nonsense. I interviewed him in Scotland about the other two murders two days before the Palio. He's a smart man. He probably knew as well as I that Cummings was going to be the next target and that he himself was a suspect in the murders. He didn't have to return to Italy to be arrested. Remember, as well, he hired Foster to begin with."

Falchi sighed, "You'll never understand the Mediterranean temperament, Pietro. Rattei is in love. He returned to see his paramour. But, if you think any other confession is imminent, make sure you contact me first." Falchi hung up.

McGarr then called Rattei's villa in Chiusdino. When Rattei got to the phone, McGarr said, "I was just talking to the carabinieri in Siena. Foster has confessed and implicated you in the Cummings murder in a way which your lawyers will find difficult to contest. You've been framed, I believe."

In a tone which seemed to McGarr strange, Rattei said, "Then you don't believe Foster."

"No. But I'm neither a jury nor a court of law." McGarr paused.

"Why would Francesco Battagliatti want to frame you?"

"Do you think *he* is the author of this thing?"

"I have no proof and Battagliatti claims you have an interesting sort of friendship, that in spite of everything you might even admire each other."

"*Il gnòmo!*" Rattei said in a hot rush.

McGarr said, "I just thought you'd like to know where things stood," and hung up. He could have told Rattei where Battagliatti would be that afternoon, but he thought it best to let Il Condottiere find out for himself. A man of his resources would quickly learn of Battagliatti's whereabouts.

Now that he had baited the bull, McGarr called the Excelsior.

"How was Florence?" he asked Noreen.

"Wonderful, as usual. Bernie and Hughie are still trying to recover from Il Latini. I had to drive home."

"Anything from Gallup?"

"Yes. They've checked the flight logs and hour meters on all the ENI helicopters in Scotland. Not one of them could have been used to fly to Ireland and back during the days in question. Tartan Limited is run on a shoestring. It doesn't own a helicopter. Otherwise, the helicopter investigation is progressing. Gallup estimates that in a day or two they'll have covered every possible landing and refueling site between Dingle and Aberdeen."

There was something wrong about the way in which they were approaching the helicopter aspect of this case, but McGarr knew not what.

"Also, British Customs reports that Battagliatti was in England two weeks before the party at the Italian embassy."

McGarr said, "I wonder if we could find out what Foster's political affiliations were. I wonder if he was a member of the Communist or Labour parties in Britain."

"I'll try to find out. Maybe Ned Gallup knows who to ask."

When he got back to the warehouse, the rally was just breaking up. The parking lot was filled with merchant mariners. McGarr leaned against the fender of his car and waited for Battagliatti. O'Shaughnessy stayed behind the wheel of the Fiat.

The little man was not glad to see McGarr. "What now?"

"Oh, just a couple details that slipped my mind yesterday, sir. It's about your friend Enrico Rattei. I know you are as anxious as I to help him. I've got a suspicion that you don't think he's guilty of killing Cummings."

"Of course not. A man like Enrico doesn't do a thing like that. It's this black, Foster, I read about in the papers. If you check into his background, Chief Inspector, you'll see why he did it. It's all there. His mentioning Rattei is just an attempt to get off with a light sentence. He's grabbing at straws. If he can say somebody powerful put him up to it, he'll look like a mere pawn in a conspiracy, the fall guy. A jury will give him a few years and that will be that."

"I never thought of it that way."

"Perhaps you should have. You're a policeman, are you not?" Battagliatti pushed by McGarr. In back of him there were twenty burly party members, the red stars obvious on their lapels. They had their hands plunged into their jacket pockets and stared at McGarr sullenly. "And, now, you'll have to excuse me, signor. I have other business to take care of." Battagliatti opened the rear door of the Lancia.

"Just one small question more, sir, if you don't mind."

"But, I do! I mind! I'm not the only source of information about Enrico Rattei, and I've got many more important things to do than talk to you." Battagliatti waved his hand to the merchant mariners.

They quickly surrounded the Fiat, in which O'Shaughnessy was still sitting, lifted and placed it several feet away from the bumper of the Lancia.

But McGarr had grabbed the back door of that car before Battagliatti could shut it. "I'm just wondering what *you* were doing in London, that's all, sir. You were there for two whole weeks, weren't you?"

"Yes—attending a party colloquium and visiting with officials of the British government. If you can remember, the Labour party is in power there at the moment."

"Two weeks?"

On a signal from Battagliatti, several of the merchant mariners began approaching McGarr.

"I thought you told me you were a busy man?"

Battagliatti tugged on the door but McGarr held it firm.

"Yes—two weeks."

"You wouldn't want to show me a copy of your itinerary or a schedule of your visits while in the British Isles, now would you, sir?"

"How right you are."

"That's because you spent most of the time meeting with Moses Foster and piloting a helicopter back and forth to Ireland twice, isn't it, Mr. Chairman?"

One man grabbed McGarr's wrist, another his other arm. Yet another shoved him with both hands.

McGarr fell against the side of the car.

The man who did the pushing then threw a flurry of punches at McGarr's head and face. The force of the blows raised McGarr up and sprawled him over the trunk of the Lancia.

Liam O'Shaughnessy bulled his way out of the Fiat, grabbed the first man he could, and placed the muzzle of his Walther against the mariner's temple. He didn't have to say a word. Nobody moved. But the driver of the Lancia drove off.

McGarr toppled off the trunk. His lip was split, one eye puffing. He wiped the blood from his mouth and felt his front teeth. One was loose. He picked himself up and, lashing out, he punched the man who had hit him square on the nose. He could feel the cartilage snap under his knuckles. The man fell back against and was held by his comrades.

McGarr walked around the car and got behind the wheel. He adjusted the seat, and then O'Shaughnessy, still holding the gun to the mariner's head, directed him into the back seat. He shut the door and slowly they drove off.

At the end of the parking lot of the warehouse, McGarr stopped the car, and O'Shaughnessy popped open the rear door and tossed the mariner out onto the tar.

Immediately, the men in the group began to shout. They hurled rocks at the Fiat.

McGarr thought he heard a couple of shots.

"Shall we give Battagliatti a scare?" McGarr asked O'Shaughnessy. His lip was swollen so that it hurt when he spoke.

"Maybe we better get you a stitch."

"Not now."

McGarr, cranking up the Fiat to its limit in all the gears, started after Battagliatti. He wanted to get on the Lancia's bumper and ride it all the way to Pisa. He had his own plan how to handle the party chairman there. The newspaper article had said that Battagliatti had been having trouble with the younger members of his party. Most of the university students believed he had sold out the ideals of communism by becoming a mere parliamentarian, somebody whom the capitalists could manipulate.

The Fiat, a 124, proved to be quick and sure-footed. Passing tank trucks and lorries, three-wheeled Lambretta farm carts and bicyclists, McGarr caught the Lancia halfway to Pisa.

Battagliatti and his associates kept looking back, worried, and twice tried to shake the Fiat, but McGarr stayed with them all the way to the center of the city.

There at the cathedral, which was near the university, McGarr and O'Shaughnessy parked and hustled to the hall in which the meeting would take place. They had just gotten inside when Battagliatti's thugs established a post at the door to check student identification cards.

In the shadows of a stairwell, which led to a circular balcony, McGarr and O'Shaughnessy sat and waited for the hall to fill. McGarr tried to smoke, but the cigarette burned the separation in his upper lip.

"Christ—you look a sight," said O'Shaughnessy.

"Consider it a dramatic mask," said McGarr. "Not one of those kids will refuse to listen to me while I'm looking like this."

"How do you mean? Surely you're not going to debate the man."

"Not actually. You just keep an eye on me to make sure I don't get mauled."

"Raped is probably a better word," said the Garda superintendent. "Will you take a gander at those painted Willies?" He was a very conservative man in every sense, and the high-heeled shoes that the hairy male students wore along with the purses they carried shocked him. Wasp-waisted jackets with padded shoulders heightened the feminine effect of their garb. Most of them wore very tight pants.

The women, as in all past generations of smart city women in Italy, had adopted the present mode of dress in a manner that was hyperbolically feminine. Somehow they wore just slightly too much makeup and their hair, worn shoulder length or longer, seemed too pampered, too perfect in shape, too—soft. They had tiny waists that emphasized hips, navels, buttocks, to which bright, chemical-weave slacks clung. Tight sweaters to match revealed the aureoles of young breasts, punctuated by the short stubs of their nipples. They chatted nervously before Battagliatti's entrance.

Here there was no drum beating, no preceding speakers. The students, McGarr imagined, wouldn't have tolerated such obvious showmanship.

Through the narrow latticed windows of the hall, which was clouded with cigarette smoke, the dim light made Battagliatti seem older and smaller. Had McGarr succeeded in frightening him, or did he simply lack confidence here before this group? McGarr couldn't credit the latter thought, and wanted to believe the former.

Battagliatti began with a noncontroversial topic: the growing strength of the party. He talked about the reasons for this—burgeoning discontent with the inaction of the regnant parties when faced with the twin devils of recession and inflation, and the fact that no other political party in Italy seemed to offer real alternatives to the many bourgeois approaches the Christian Democrats had taken over the years.

Reverting to rhetoric, Battagliatti tried to reinforce this theme. "Not the Fascists, not the Socialists, not the Conservatives, not the Liberals, but, as we always have told the Italian voter, only we, only the Communists, are the real force for change in this society!"

Nobody clapped. Stone-faced, the students stared at him. Their mood was sour.

In the moment that Battagliatti paused to compose himself, somebody yelled, "Change? Battagliatti changed his approach to the Chamber of Deputies, but the Chamber of Deputies didn't change! It's still the chamber of corrupt old horrors that it always was!"

Another student chimed in. "Battagliatti promised to change conditions in the universities, but the only thing he changed was his attitude to the barons of the lecture hall when he found he could use them!" He was referring to the outmoded system of university professorship, which made students and teachers in any one department subservient to the full professors. The students had to buy the books that the professors published themselves. The prices were scandalous. Stand-ins for the professors gave lectures, while the latter were in Rome acting as parliamentarians who had but one interest: that of increasing their own power and profits from this system.

"Battagliatti changed, Battagliatti changes, Battagliatti will change some more!"

All the students were shouting and jeering.

One of his aides now handed Battagliatti a microphone, "You ask what I am?" he roared into the mike. *"You* ask *me?* Most of your parents were *bambini* when I took this party from a group of resistance fighters and built us into a national organization. Sure—I've changed. I've had to. Otherwise, we wouldn't be here today. Remember when you read your books—this is not Russia or China. As yet, we haven't had any revolution here. Maybe we won't *need* one."

"And you don't want one!" a student shouted.

"That's right. At this rate in five years we'll have the first clear majority—sixty-five to seventy percent perhaps—of the electorate of any party in the postwar era. Why ignore the facts? We're gaining new members every day. I call that a revolution in the political thinking of the average Italian voter. White-collar workers, small shopkeepers, the borghese themselves are voting for us nowadays. They all realize we're in the same boat."

Nobody shouted again. Battagliatti had succeeded in quieting them.

It was time for McGarr to act. He got up and O'Shaughnessy followed him down the stairway, his hand placed under the lapel of his sport jacket.

As soon as Battagliatti saw McGarr, he stammered. He had to restate a sentence.

McGarr walked to the first student he had seen question Battagliatti. Bending, he said to him, "You want to see Battagliatti jump, ask him if he knows how to fly a helicopter."

"Is this a joke?"

"Sort of—but wait 'til you see what'll happen. Pass it on."

And McGarr then went to the other students, boy and girl, who had spoken out.

Battagliatti followed McGarr with his eyes. His thugs wanted to step into the audience, but they had seen O'Shaughnessy at the back of the hall.

Now all the students were watching McGarr. His puffy eye and split lip gathered their attention. He kept bending over students and talking to them in low tones.

Again Battagliatti lost his place.

When he tried to speak, a student yelled, "Question! Question! I've got a question! Signor Battagliatti, I've got a question!"

Sensing some ploy of McGarr, Battagliatti said, "Save your questions for later, I'll answer all questions at the end of the hour."

But, as in a chorus, the students began chanting, "Question, question, question, question!" until Battagliatti could no longer speak over them.

"Well," he finally demanded, "who's got the question? On your feet!"

And when a young man stood, Battagliatti shouted, "Get his name and address. What's your question? I hope for your sake it's important."

The student, somewhat intimidated now, turned to McGarr, who nodded.

"Do you——"

"Louder, speak up. We can't hear you," Battagliatti said.

The thugs had started down off the stage. McGarr, clenching his fists, made for the first one.

Suddenly, the student plucked up his courage, cupped his hands around his mouth, and shouted, "Do you know how to fly a helicopter?"

The disjunction of thought and the seeming absurdity of the question struck the students as comical. They began laughing.

Battagliatti's head snapped in McGarr's direction. "Get him! Get him!" he screamed, stamping his foot, pointing his finger.

"Do you know how to fly a helicopter?" all the students began shouting.

McGarr ducked the first punch and, kicking out with his foot, caught his assailant on the side of the knee. The man howled in pain and slumped to the floor. McGarr had broken the cartilage in the thug's knee. The leg would require surgery before he would walk again.

Another thug, however, had hopped on McGarr's back, and they both fell into the audience of students, who started drubbing Battagliatti's man.

McGarr could hear Battagliatti screaming.

Suddenly, Liam O'Shaughnessy had McGarr by the collar. He pulled him out of the melee, set him on his feet, and gave him a shove toward the back of the hall. The tall Garda superintendent then punched another of Battagliatti's bodyguards. Without once turning his back to Battagliatti, O'Shaughnessy walked to the rear of the auditorium.

The students and Battagliatti's aides were fighting in five separate places at the front of the hall.

"We'd better get the hell out of here before the police arrive," said McGarr.

As they turned to leave, they heard Battagliatti scream, "Get him! The little one! There he——" But suddenly his voice died, for standing in front of the door was Enrico Rattei.

Suddenly, a shot rang out and a slug bucked through the door a few inches above Rattei's head, yet the man stood there without moving as if nothing had happened.

Tackling Rattei around the waist, O'Shaughnessy dived through the doors, McGarr right after him.

The fighting in the hall had stopped.

Everybody was looking up at the stage where Battagliatti stood with a small automatic pistol in his hand.

McGarr said, "Jesus—I'd give anything to know what sort of gun that is."

The three of them were sprawled face down on the sidewalk. Cars were slowing to look at them. A housewife leading a small child by the hand stepped around them.

Rattei sat up. "It's a Baretta, twenty-two caliber, special issue." He picked himself up. He straightened his tan suit coat, which was ripped and smoked with street dust.

"How do you know that?" O'Shaughnessy asked. "I thought you two weren't that friendly."

They could hear the klaxons of police cars in the distance.

"Just take my word for it. I know."

A Bugatti limousine, the body cream yellow, the fenders jet black, had pulled up alongside them.

Rattei stepped in.

"Where are you going?" asked McGarr.

"Certainly *not* to jail." Rattei slammed the door and the powerful car moved off in a hush.

"Let's get out of here." McGarr's small body was a universe of pain. He had been kicked, punched, kneed, and gouged. His knees and elbows were scraped raw where he had fallen onto the street. Of course, his lip was split, a front tooth loose, and he could not open his left eye.

And McGarr needed a drink, Irish-style, very badly.

At the first roadside café they passed on the way to Siena, they ordered several rounds of whiskey and ice-cold Peroni beer. Several times McGarr asked O'Shaughnessy, "But how *could* Rattei know what sort of gun Battagliatti had in his hand?"

Finally, the Garda superintendent said, "Maybe it's common knowledge."

McGarr phoned Falchi. It was *not* common knowledge.

# 8

A day later, McGarr was sitting in Ned Gallup's office, Scotland Yard. He had a bandage on his upper lip. His left eye was still swollen and the lid had begun to turn from blue to dark green. He was dressed in a tan windbreaker and dark slacks. A soft cap rested on a folder in his lap. O'Shaughnessy was sitting beside him.

Before a large map of Great Britain and Ireland, Gallup paced. Red pins had been stuck into the map at each airport or filling station where a helicopter might have landed to refuel on a trip from the Scottish oil fields to Slea Head in Ireland. Police of both countries had been thorough—the map was shot with red marks—but still they had not found anybody who could remember pumping high-octane petrol into a helicopter in which Browne or Hitchcock and a small man had been riding.

"So there you have it," said Gallup. His moustache, wrapping about the corners of his mouth, made him seem dour. "We covered every possibility, but nothing. The chopper could have had jerry cans of fuel strapped to its underbelly or landing skids just to prevent our checking in this manner."

"That's not likely," said O'Shaughnessy. He was wearing a heavy Aran sweater, tan slacks, and ankle-cut riding boots, a brilliant mahogany in color. "They probably guessed we'd have exactly this much trouble, *if* they thought about the need to refuel at all."

"Even if they did, they had a great deal of trouble getting off the ground in an ordinary two- or four-passenger helicopter," said a young man on the other side of McGarr. He was wearing an RAF lieutenant's uniform. "That sort of machine just doesn't have the lift for, say, a sufficient amount of fuel to permit a helicopter to fly from any place in Great Britain to the southeast of Ireland. By Great Britain I don't mean Ulster." He glanced at McGarr.

"The weight of a gallon of high-octane petrol is nine pounds. Say they burned fifteen gallons an hour because they ran at top cruising speed. That's two hundred gallons, about eighteen hundred pounds. They'd never get off the ground, especially with the second chap you mentioned."

"Sixteen stone," said McGarr.

"Never," said Lieutenant Simpson.

"So, they had to stop some place." Ned Gallup dropped his hands so they smacked on his thighs. "But *where?* We've covered absolutely everywhere. We had bobbies stop at petrol stations to see if a helicopter might just have plopped down out of the sky for a quick fill-up. That's done before in a pinch, you know. We offered the representatives of all the petrol companies a hundred pounds' reward if they could come up with the copter, small pilot, and either Hitchcock or Browne aboard on the days of their deaths. We made up batches of their pictures." He pointed to his desk where two stacks of their portraits lay. "Passed those out around the country. Must have a couple thousand of them out there now. Lots of phonies, of course, but no real score."

McGarr stood and approached the map.

A drizzle had blurred the window in back of Gallup's desk.

"Maybe we've gone about it all wrong. Maybe our assumption that Hitchcock and Browne were ferried from Scotland to Dingle is wrong."

"But Mrs. Hitchcock claims to have talked to her husband on the day of his death. He had said he was in Scotland. Browne's butler had gotten a telephone call from him the night before. We've checked that. It had been placed from a Scottish exchange."

"All right, even so, suppose each of them was lured to London by an offer of some sort. The caller said a meeting was urgent and perhaps met him at Heathrow. There, on some other pretext—the need for privacy in Hitchcock's case, or the need to talk things over with Hitchcock in Browne's—they boarded a helicopter and then set off for Slea Head. Hitchcock, of course, might have chosen the

Dingle house for a meeting himself. After all, he did have a return stub in his pocket for a flight to Heathrow. Have you checked that out, Ned?"

"Yes—the Aer Lingus personnel process so many tickets every day, it's impossible for them to remember faces.

"And, I must say, all of this sounds rather farfetched. Why, if what you say is correct, did the old woman see the copter come in off the ocean? Why did she think it came from the north?"

"If I had been the murderer," said McGarr, "I would have flown out over the ocean in order to keep from being spotted by persons on land. A helicopter is a rarity in certain sections of Ireland, and the country is a small, familiar, gabby place. The assumption I would have made is that the police could place an advertisement in the newspapers and on the telly asking for information about helicopters on the stated dates."

"What about her idea that the helicopter came from the north?" Gallup again asked.

McGarr hunched his shoulders. "Don't know. Could be she made a mistake. Could be he made a mistake and flew too far up the coast. I'm not really too concerned about that since we've already checked the northeastern route to Scotland. I'd like to give this theory a go, however."

It was now up to Gallup. The RAF officer and a helicopter had been detailed to him.

Gallup looked out the window.

On the Thames, a tugboat was ferrying a Liberian tanker. A deluge of rust had spilled from its scuppers as though some ferrous atrocity had been committed on deck. Its cargo was badly out of trim, and it listed portside. In all, it seemed like a wounded hulk.

"We've tried everything else, why not this? Gad, when I think of what this case is costing us—the man-hours, the special materials."

"Now you're beginning to talk like an administrator and not a detective, Ned," McGarr remarked.

Lieutenant Simpson stepped to the chart. "Let's assume the helicopter had full tanks of petrol departing from Heathrow. We have roughly four hundred forty miles between here and Dingle, that's as the crow flies. Add another hundred or so to get around Ireland without flying over land. Then the ship would have to refuel here on the flight home." He pointed to Waterford, in southeastern Ireland. "That is, if he flew over land on the return trip."

"No reason why not," said O'Shaughnessy. "Browne and Hitchcock were no longer with him, it was night on both occasions, only his lights could have been seen from the ground."

"My guess," said McGarr, "is that the murderer would not chance refueling in Ireland. There a helicopter is too extraordinary. He probably gassed up in the south of England before making the hop over the water to Hitchcock's place. And then he would have had to stop again on the way back, right, Lieutenant?"

Simpson nodded.

McGarr opened the folder. It contained at least a dozen different facial shots of Rattei and Battagliatti, and dossiers of the men in Italian. Carlo Falchi had rushed these to McGarr before he returned to England. Below this folder was another which contained Scotland Yard reports on the two men. And below that was yet another folder from Dublin Castle. Somehow, he believed, something was escaping him and it had to do with his approach. Could it be that he hadn't gotten to know the victims well enough? "Do you suppose you could get your hands on the Cummings, Browne, and Hitchcock dossiers from SIS?"

"No!" said Gallup without thinking. Then he turned his face to the window again. "I mean, yes, I suppose I could try to get you dossiers from which certain security information has been expurgated. But what in hell are you, McGarr—a research student or a policeman?"

"Just another humble toiler in this vale of tears." McGarr smiled at Gallup, but the comment was not appreciated. Actually, McGarr wished he had a couple of days to pore over the mass of information.

"You better get going," said Gallup. "You've only got Lieutenant Simpson for the day. After that, somebody's got to start paying the RAF for his time and the use of his aircraft, and that somebody is not going to be Scotland Yard.

"And remember this, McGarr." Gallup spun around. He was nettled. "If the world contained only irresponsible administrators with the yen to play sleuth and let the paperwork, the budgets, the recruiting, and the procedures go to hell, then we wouldn't have any decent police protection."

Sheepishly, McGarr opened one of the folders, only to have something to do with his hands. He said, "My contention is that one must learn to delegate authority. If you thoroughly understood this position, Ned, you'd realize you don't really have a job at all. That, then, would free you to do only those things which please you. That's the secret to all innovative and imaginative administration. They put you in this job not because they thought you were a gifted administrator alone, but because, first and foremost, you are a gifted policeman. Why not be that?"

"Delegate authority, he says! Delegate *authority!*" Gallup began roaring at the map of pins. "He has the brass to say that when he delegated all the boring work to me and toured Italy in doubtless high style!"

McGarr quietly shut the door. He didn't think it politic to point out the high style of his upper lip and black eye.

Gallup's secretary was staring at him.

"Pressure, pressure," McGarr whispered to her.

"I don't know what you're talking about," said the secretary. "This place runs itself."

McGarr made a mental note to try and convince Gallup to let his secretary take over the s.o.p. aspects of his job.

McGarr rather enjoyed riding a helicopter across the rolling fields of southern England. What with the steady beat of the rotor blades, the sensation was like that of being mounted on a winged horse, as opposed to being in an airplane that moved like a bird.

Thus, they charged toward Bath and Bristol, the area in which Lieutenant Simpson supposed any helicopter pilot not wanting to refuel in Ireland would have stopped, going and coming.

The sun kept trying to break through the cloud cover, so that below them the green fields and bordering oaks occasionally appeared through the mist, wet and sparkling, as though elements in an aquarium of fog.

They tried the airports in Bath and Bristol, a heliport in Bristol, and an emergency runway that also had a fuel pump in Weston-super-Mare. Then airports in Cardiff, and, pushing down the Welsh Peninsula, Barry, Neath, Swansea, Llanelli, and Pembroke.

Technological architecture, McGarr speculated—like airports or petrol stations or cities that had been redesigned to accommodate the automobile—had no human history. All the airports, of need, were the same. The only changes the physical plant could tolerate were those of an advancing technology, whence the older elements would be chucked out or the entire airport abandoned.

One such place was the airport in Fishguard. Built as a Spitfire base to attack German bombers on their way to destroy the shipyards in Belfast, the concrete runways had been reclaimed by the pasture from which they had originally been carved. At several points, as the helicopter clipped in low over windbreaks, they saw cows grazing on the grass that burgeoned between the separations of the concrete slabs. A wind direction finder, once an orange-and-white-striped sock, was a tattered brown rag, blown out. Rusting Quonset-type hangars lined the unused sections of the runway. They touched down near the office of the present airport. It too was a corrugated metal structure.

It was five-thirty in the afternoon now, and McGarr had to zip his jacket when he stepped outside the toasty bubble of the helicopter.

The office door opened and a man hopped down the steps. One leg was stiff. "What'll it be, mates—fuel, directions, or the time of day?" He spoke with a thick Welsh brogue. He was wearing gray coveralls, which were spotted, and he smoked a pipe.

McGarr, as he had done at all the other airports that day, explained that he was interested in learning if a helicopter, piloted by a small man—he showed him Rattei's and Battagliatti's pictures—had stopped there on the nineteenth and twenty-sixth of June.

"If they did, I can tell you certain. I keep a record of such things. You'll have to step into the office, however. Can I get you anything first?" His face was smudged with grease, and he had needed a shave yesterday.

In one of the old hangars they had passed on landing, McGarr had seen a gleaming Spitfire. He imagined the man had restored the airship. Here, he probably had a great deal of time on his hands.

Lieutenant Simpson said their helicopter needed nothing.

A tea kettle was beginning to whistle on top of a cylindrical coal stove. The man placed it on a trivet. "Tea?"

"No, thanks," McGarr said. "We've got to push on."

"A little snort then?" The man opened a file cabinet, pulled out a bottle of twelve-year-old Ballantine Scotch, and handed it to McGarr. Rummaging around a bit more, he picked out four short glasses. Many greasy fingerprints were impressed upon the exterior surfaces of the glasses.

"That's an interesting filing system you have there," O'Shaughnessy said, helping him set the glasses on top of another dusty sheet-metal cabinet.

"The best. The very best," said the man, winking. "Never misplace a thing. If I think for a moment I have, I consult my 'inspiration.' "

The rest of the office was similarly dusty, but neat and warm. There was a mark on the top of an old wooden desk where the man placed his feet. From that seat the traffic control radio was a reach away. McGarr sat.

"Here it is." The man pulled a folder from another drawer of the cabinet.

O'Shaughnessy poured liberal drinks of the Scotch and handed the glasses around. When Lieutenant Simpson began examining the glass, the Garda superintendent said, "Sure and there's enough antiseptic in the glass to cure a thousand evils."

The man placed the folder in front of McGarr and opened it. "Seems that the only helicopter I had in during that week stopped twice. Let me check the dates." He ran the black nail of a finger across his list on the dates McGarr had mentioned. "Yup—same ship. But this one is piloted by a woman, not a man, and not the men you showed me in your pictures. Them I've never laid eyes on before.

"I remember her because she stops in here often. Horse-racing woman, she told me she was. Does a lot of training and racing in Ireland, where you're from, no?"

McGarr bent his head to acknowledge the question.

"Often she's accompanied by a black man. Big as a house, he is."

O'Shaughnessy glanced at McGarr, who asked, "Balding, close-set eyes, Jamaican accent?"

"Aye—and he's got a taste for good whiskey. Once drank a whole bottle while I greased the main bearing on the rotor of their ship. And generous, he was. He paid me handsomely for the pleasure." The man was eyeing O'Shaughnessy, who, having drunk off the first glass, was pouring himself another.

McGarr followed the entry across the page of the airport log. "What sort of registration is that?"

Lieutenant Simpson, looking over his shoulders, said, "That's a rental helicopter."

"Avis. Heathrow," said the man. "Rumor has it they'd rent you a dive bomber if you could get up the cash. Americans, you know."

"What's her name?" McGarr asked.

"Don't know."

"Do you have her check stubs? Did she ever charge?"

"Can't allow that. I'd never get my money."

O'Shaughnessy asked, helping himself to yet another drink, "What does she look like?"

"She looks good," said the man, "you know, for an older girl, that is. I got the impression the man with her was her last 'fling.' Can you understand me?" He winked. "She had this way of doting over him, waiting on him and such, although it was clear to me she hadn't waited on many other people in her life."

"How are her legs?"

"Fragile, you know. Birdlike and—nice."

"Blondish hair, bent nose, high cheekbones?"

"Yes, I'd say so."

"Hitchcock's wife," said McGarr. He stood, took five pounds out of his wallet, and placed it on the folder. He paused for a moment and put five more on top of that and asked, "May we take the bottle with us?"

"Indeed, indeed. And thank you. I buy the stuff from a fellow who comes through the international section of Heathrow. Doesn't cost me half what you put on the desk. And since you're not local police and Irishmen to boot—except for the lad, of course"— he meant Simpson —"let me do something else for you." From under the desk he pulled a case of Beamish half-pint bottles. He put six of them in a paper sack for them.

"That's some plane in the hangar over there," said O'Shaughnessy, when they had gotten outside.

"Is it fit to fly?" Simpson asked.

"Fitter than the day she rolled from the factory. And that's more than a plane, that's my retirement. I figure by the time I'm ready to pack it in, that'll be an antique some eccentric will squander half his fortune on. Are you checked out in airplanes too, Lieutenant?"

"Yes. Prop jobs and jets. Fighters, too."

"Then stop back when you have more time and I'll let you give her a run. Nothing made on the other side of the swamp could ever touch that craft."

"I'll take you up on that offer sometime soon." Simpson was delighted.

McGarr could see him reassess what they could see of the Spitfire in the now deeply shadowed hangar, looking at it this time with the eyes of a pilot who would someday fly one of the most important historical items of Britain's recent past. There was no question of his not returning and soon.

At the Heathrow Avis office, the manager confirmed the Fish-guard airport attendant's information. "Graham Hitchcock, Mrs. E. L. J. Hitchcock, Sixty Avenue Road, St. John's Wood."

"Strange name for a woman," said O'Shaughnessy.

"Strange woman," said the manager.

"How so?" asked McGarr.

"Ah—I suppose I shouldn't say. She's a good customer of mine. No—I won't say. I spoke out of turn."

"How good a customer?"

"She rents a ship a couple of dozen times in a year, which makes her a very good customer."

"Who cleans the helicopter?"

"Bobby Greene."

"May we speak to him?"

"If he's on." The manager took them out to the time clock and checked Greene's card. "You're in luck. He's got fifteen minutes. He's down in the shop."

There Greene said he couldn't remember from one day to the next what the helicopters contained, if there was mud or grease or trash on the floor of each airship. "Once I switches on the vacuum" —he pointed to the large industrial vacuum cleaner—"me mind slips into suspended animation." Earlier, McGarr had noticed the science fiction paperback in his overall pocket. "I become an automaton. You're welcome to peek into the lost and found, though. Anything I find I put in there. Come twelve month, we sell the lot for a bonus. You won't believe what people will leave in airships. I think it's because they're so glad to be down safely, they just rush away."

He unlocked a door and McGarr and O'Shaughnessy stepped into a closet so vast it shocked them. Clothes on hangers lined both walls; baggage, umbrellas, and cartons were stacked under them. McGarr didn't know what he hoped to find. "You didn't happen to come across any shell casings or shell boxes, or, say, anything like a hypodermic needle, did you?"

"Anything I found I put in here. The small stuff is in that bin. But the sort of space a dope addict is looking for can't be found in a helicopter."

There McGarr found ballpoint and fountain pens, ladies' hats, gloves, pairs of shoes, sunglasses—one pair was a wraparound type, the heavy chrome of which made McGarr's face look like the windscreen of a sleek automobile when he tried them on; O'Shaughnessy laughed and said, "Flash Gordon. I wonder why the old boy"—he motioned to the door—"hasn't taken them home with him"—rubber boots, wallets complete with money and identification, keys and rings, pocket secretaries, cassette tape recorders, cameras, even two portable typewriters.

After fifteen minutes of pawing around, McGarr and O'Shaughnessy left.

Before taking rooms at the Carlton for the night, McGarr phoned Gallup and told him what he had discovered. Gallup agreed to make an appointment to interview Mrs. Hitchcock early in the morning. McGarr would have preferred to do this at Scotland Yard, but Gallup objected. "We just can't go hauling in the widows of once powerful men for a criminal-type interrogation until we've got facts. All you know is that she and Foster might have had a 'relationship,' that she flew a helicopter and was in Ireland on the dates of the murders."

"Shoe size."

"Shoe size be damned. Another unavailing item of quite circumstantial evidence. We must see her at her house in Avenue Road."

"In state, you mean."

"Absolutely. And I hope she's regal and guiltless. I detest scandal. Everybody, even the police, loses. And, incidentally, your request to inspect the Service dossiers of the murdered men has been denied."

"What? But why? I don't understand."

"I was told simply that nobody can see them. They've been declared 'Most Secret.'"

"Is it because I'm not English?"

"No. I asked to see them myself and that request was denied too."

"But why is that? Don't they trust *you?*"

"I wouldn't know."

McGarr thanked Gallup for trying anyhow, and then hung up.

Next he phoned Noreen at the Excelsior in Siena. While McKeon and Ward were keeping tabs on Battagliatti, she was reacquainting herself with Tuscany. He told her the events of his day.

"You sound hoarse," she said. "Are you catching a cold?"

"Don't think so. Probably too many cigarettes. This case is beginning to bother me. See if you can impose upon Falchi to get me a meeting with Foster. Everywhere I turn, he's been there."

"But he'll never change his story."

"I'm not so much interested in his story."

"Well, what then? He won't permit you to learn anything about him personally. He's been around too long for that."

"I don't know what I mean. I just feel like there's something missing, my never having talked to him at length."

"You had better get some rest."

After sandwiches and further drinks in the bar, McGarr and O'Shaughnessy went upstairs to their rooms. There, McGarr got a phone call. It was Gallup again to say all was arranged for 8:45 A.M. at Hitchcock's widow's house in St. John's Wood.

McGarr undressed, climbed into bed, and began leafing through all the dossiers he had collected.

And Graham Hitchcock was indeed icily imperious at first. What was more, her barrister was present. He was a bald old man whose nose seemed to rest on his coppery moustache. After having adjusted his hearing aid and inquired McGarr's name and credentials, he insisted upon Gallup's asking all questions of his client. "A matter of jurisdiction, you see." He was wearing tails and, upon sinking into a wing-back armchair, appeared to doze off. His eyes closed, but McGarr could tell he was listening to and probably would remember every word of the interview. McGarr had run up against old foxes like him before.

Mrs. Hitchcock wore a gray pantsuit with a white silk blouse that had ruffles on the bodice and cuffs. Her shoes were black patent leather, stockings a silvery nylon. She was somewhat nervous, but confidently so. She sat very straight without allowing her back to touch the chair. McGarr imagined that even at this age—fifty-five—she was still actively athletic. Her small body seemed strong and even fetching. McGarr could imagine himself taking her down for a tumble. The way her hair was sleeked back along her narrow temples interested him most. And she was aware of his eyes on her. She smiled to him slightly before Gallup asked, "On the nineteenth and twenty-sixth of June you fueled helicopters at Fishguard airport prior to flying to Ireland. Where did you go in Ireland and what did you do there?" He was reading from his small black notebook.

"On the nineteenth I flew to Baldoyle race course. That's about fifteen miles north of Dublin. On the twenty-sixth I flew to Leopardstown race course. That's ten miles or so south of Dublin. I own, breed, and race horses. That's my profession. I'm certain the officials of both courses will vouch for my presence there and, incidentally, for at least two days after the last date you have mentioned."

"I must warn you we plan to check everything you say."

"Please do." She turned to McGarr and smiled again.

Gallup looked down at his book. McGarr had written the questions in case Gallup had to do the asking. "Let's see. Did you use the helicopter otherwise?"

"No. My barrister"—she indicated the old man—"has a signed receipt. The total mileage was seven hundred seventy-two miles, certainly not enough to fly to Slea Head and back."

McGarr had already checked that; it was true.

"Did you fly any other helicopter while you were in Ireland on the stated dates?"

"No."

"Did you leave the Dublin area on the stated dates?"

"No."

"Where did you stay on the stated dates?"

"Both times at the Intercontinental Hotel in Ballsbridge."

"Were you alone?"

She flushed a bit, but she turned to McGarr and said, boldly, "No."

"Who were you with?"

"On the first stated date, June nineteenth, I was with Sean O'Ryan. He's one of my jocks."

"What's his address?"

"How should I know? Wait a moment." She placed a finger on her temple. "Swords. I seem to remember he lived someplace in Swords. A big, gloomy room with the bathroom down the hall. That's all I can tell you."

"And on June twenty-sixth?"

"With a man named Persson. His first name is Henry, I believe."

"Address?"

"I wouldn't have the slightest idea. I met him in the bar. He went back to his room long before I was awake. Wife and all that, you know." She turned to McGarr. She was smiling. "Does this shock your Hibernian sensibilities, Chief Inspector?"

"Not at all, ma'am. I'm only bothered by the misfortune of having met you under such constraining circumstances." McGarr then directed his eyes to her barrister.

The old man seemed to revive and he glanced at McGarr. There was a twinkle in his eye.

Gallup continued. "Our records show that you own a twenty-two-caliber Baretta automatic. Where is it?"

"I don't know, haven't seen it for years. My husband gave it to me for protection while he was on assignment in Finland."

"Why did you feel you needed protection?"

"Who knows? Intruders, I suppose. He was worried about me."

McGarr broke in. "Did he know of your predilection for different men?"

The barrister cleared his throat.

McGarr glanced at Gallup, who, blushing, restated the question.

"I think so," she said. "At least, I knew of several of his affairs with my friends. I caught him *in flagrante*——"

"Ahem!" the old man snorted, and she stopped talking.

"Were you having an affair with Moses Foster?"

"Yes—if you could dignify our relationship with that word."

"Did your husband know about it?"

"Yes. I even think he encouraged it. In any case, it was he who first brought Moses around. You see, he believed that just because he was no longer interested in sex, no other of his near contemporaries could be either. Thus, he reasoned that I needed a playmate, I suppose. Somebody—how shall I put it?—somebody lesser than he, somebody . . . black, somebody who would defile me was his choice. I believe it's a common male attitude at his stage in life." This last remark was said to McGarr.

"What was Foster's attitude to your husband?"

"He hated him and everything he stood for. That's why he—I don't want to say 'raped,' exactly—that's why he 'forced' me the first time. It was at a party right here in this house. He took me into the laundry room and didn't even bother to close the door completely."

Again the lawyer cleared his throat.

"All the other men were afraid of him," she added. "And, of course, nobody had thought of carrying a gun to the party."

"How long have you been seeing Foster?"

"Years now—two, three."

"How often?"

"These questions are entirely too personal," the old man objected without opening his eyes.

"This is a murder investigation," said Gallup.

"Whenever and as much as I can. I used to fly up to Scotland at least once a fortnight. When he was in London I saw him nearly every day."

"What was the appeal?" McGarr asked.

"I don't know. Maybe my husband was right."

"You needed somebody to defile you?"

"Yes, I suppose."

McGarr kept himself from asking how Foster accomplished that, although he sorely wanted to know. Instead, he asked, "What is he like as a human being?"

"Solid," she blurted out. "When he's not trying to be cruel, that is. I mean very masculine. On rare occasions he can be extremely jolly, too, but most of the time he's just, you know, *there.*"

"Why do you think he would have wanted to kill your husband?"

"Moses?" She shook her head. "He might have killed Cummings, although I don't really believe that."

"I saw him pull the trigger," said McGarr. "He's since confessed. And twenty years of police work tells me he killed your husband and Browne too. Here is the transcript of that confession. If you don't read Italian, I can read it for you."

"Mr. McGarr, Mr. McGarr." The old man wagged his head. "If you please, remain silent."

Her mood had changed. "No—not Edward. He wouldn't have killed Edward. Edward was too—inconsiderable. Edward had always treated Moses fairly. On the other hand, Browne and Cummings——"

"Had treated him badly?" Gallup completed.

"Yes."

"But you aren't the beneficiary of a hundred-twenty-five-thousand-pound life insurance policy on either of their lives, are you, Mrs. Hitchcock?" said McGarr. "How would Moses Foster have benefited from their deaths?"

"That's enough! Interview's over." The old man began to stand.

But Mrs. Hitchcock was indignant. "If you mean to imply that Moses Foster will benefit through me from Edward's death, you are wrong, Mr. McGarr." She was on her feet now, fists clinched at her side. Her face was flushed.

"He was your lover, wasn't he? You said you want to see him whenever you can. You even went to Siena three days after your husband was killed to be with Foster. Did you even have time to attend your own husband's funeral, or was your lust so great you couldn't find the time?" McGarr asked her. "I mean—what are your *plans?*"

The old man had his hands on his client's shoulders. "Now, now, now—don't let him badger you. It's all a performance. He's trying to get you angry. Gallup will hear from his superiors about this."

But she wasn't listening to him. "Do you mean now? After what you just said—if it's true——"

"It's true, all right," said Gallup. "Here's my report, in English."

"——then, I have no plans. I wouldn't, I *won't* have anything to do with a murderer. I never want to see him again." She took the report from Gallup's hand. "Edward—he said he murdered Edward?"

"Not in so many words," said Gallup.

She had begun to cry, not as most women do with sobs, but only with her eyes. They gushed tears, although her voice remained steady. "*Not* Edward. Oh, no—not Edward." She tried to look at the page. She then tried to wipe the tears from her eyes with the back of her hand.

The barrister eased them from the room, saying under his breath, "That was a fairly masterful performance from youngsters like you two fellows, but, as gifted students of the human condition, you undoubtedly realize that my client is blameless. She's as innocent in this matter as the driven snow. A little indiscreet from time to time, beset with a touch of Indian-summer fever perhaps, but guilty of these ugly murders—never. Are we agreed?"

Gallup seemed to want to nod, but McGarr said, "I'm not agreed on anything in this case. As far as I'm concerned your client is still a murder suspect in the Irish Republic. Also, if we choose to lay charges against her, it'll be helpful to her for me to know your name. You seemed very anxious for me to identify myself; now it's your turn."

"Oh, tut-tut, young man. No need to get nasty. We're all professionals here."

That statement only made McGarr bridle more. Professing one's professionalism, no matter the area of involvement, had always seemed to him the refuge of charlatans. He had always tried to be a professional human being, although he'd never think of telling even his wife that.

"The name is——" The old man seemed to cough. "Ned knows me well. Why, I remember when he started at the Yard."

Gallup nodded and smiled.

"It's what?" McGarr asked again.

The old man's smile crumbled a bit. "Croft," he said very low.

McGarr didn't even blink. "Sir Sellwyn Gerrard Montague Croft, no doubt. The very same lawyer who represented Colin Cummings, who recommended he invest in Tartan Limited."

Croft merely blinked.

"I suppose you also advised Hitchcock and Browne to do the same?"

He said nothing.

"I don't suppose you'd like to tell me whose conception Tartan was?"

Croft flushed. "Well—it was mine. I saw a chance for my clients and me to make a handy profit, and so I established the financial basis of the concern and then hired several managers and they in turn hired the technical personnel to build the platform and sink the well."

"And you knew all along your information was privileged?"

Croft said nothing.

McGarr looked at Gallup. It was plain what Gallup had to do—initiate an investigtion of Croft's activities. And Gallup obviously didn't relish the prospect. He said, "I'm afraid I'm going to have to report this, Sir Sellwyn."

The old man was standing on the top step of the house, looking over McGarr's head into the bleary street. His eyes had glassed. His lower lip quivered. "Of course."

McGarr turned to leave. O'Shaughnessy was waiting for him in a car at the curb.

"McGarr," said Croft.

McGarr stopped and turned to him.

"I don't hold it against you. I admire your abilities. You are only doing your job. I guess I must be getting old." He turned and walked into the house.

Gallup said, "You've kicked over a hornet's nest this time, Peter. That old man represents so many powerful people it rather frightens me how this news will be received."

"Think of it as a feather in your cap, Ned."

"Nothing of the kind. You put it together. I wouldn't think——"

"Don't think. Do it. It's my way of paying you back for not telling you I knew who Hitchcock was."

"What?"

McGarr stepped into the car.

"You knew?"

"Of course. You don't think everybody from Dublin's a gobshite, do you?" He motioned to O'Shaughnessy, who drove away.

# 9

It was the middle of a torrid afternoon by the time McGarr got back to Siena. He had rented an air-conditioned Alfa Romeo at the Florence airport and didn't notice the heat until he parked in the Duomo tourists' lot and stepped out onto the hot paving stones of the piazza. The heat seemed to rise straight through the soles of his shoes. In his rush to return, McGarr had forgotten to change into light clothes. Among the shadows which the *Prefettúra* made, he undid the button beneath his tie, doffed his bowler and suit coat. Across the piazza, all the small shops had lowered their heavy blinds. Not one window in the *Ospedàle* was showing. During the middle of the day like this, the Italians tried to wall out the heat with shutters, blinds, and heavy curtains.

Not so in the office of Carlo Falchi, however. There it was dark, all right, but the coolness resulted from an old air conditioner that groaned and pinged in the aperture of one window. As McGarr opened the door from the outer office, the thermostat kicked on the cooling unit, and the lights flickered warningly. Behind McGarr, a little man with wine-stained teeth rushed into Falchi's office. He had a mop in his hands and swabbed the area in front of the straining machine. Out of the corner of his eyes, he kept glancing at Foster, who sat on a straight-back chair in the middle of the room. Perhaps on the theory that light and heat are related, Falchi had hung only a fifty-watt bulb from the ceiling and far over Foster's head. This was the room's only light. It made Foster's face all shadow, except for his single gold tooth, which shone, as now, when he smiled.

The man with the mop rushed out of the room.

Falchi directed a jet of the air conditioner toward a dark corner of the room and sat on a chair in its path.

Near the large black man, McGarr turned a chair around and sat on it backwards. "I've been back in London for a few days, putting this case in order," he said. "Do you mind if I speak English?

*"Pourquoi non? Vous me tenez à votre merci dans le procès. Les dés sont pipés contre moi,"* Foster said.

McGarr replied, *"Allez! Cessez cette comédie et soyez sérieux. C'est moi qui commande ici. Vous pigez?"*

Foster nodded, but the conversation proceeded in French, much to Falchi's chagrin.

McGarr allowed the interview to continue in that language on the off chance that Foster might want to make some admission to McGarr that he didn't want the carabinieri commandant, whose knowledge of French was slight, to understand.

"Among other things, I talked to Graham Hitchcock."

Foster's eyes flashed at McGarr. He smiled a little.

"She gives you high marks as a stud, says you serviced her quite well whenever she was in need.

"That's all you were to her, you know, especially now that she's got that hundred twenty-five thousand pounds' insurance payment. By the time you get out of prison here, she'll be—let's see—in her seventies and, I should imagine, she'll have the money all spent. Of course, you'll have the chunk of change that she put in the bank to make it seem as though Rattei was behind the whole thing, but that's less than half of her take. And then, it's you who'll have to do the time in prisons that are somewhat less than disagreeable."

Falchi looked down at the Tuscan cigar he was puffing. It looked like a piece of black twisted rope and gave off the smell of salt and pepper heated in an iron pan. The smoke was pale blue.

Foster's smile was somewhat fuller now.

"Don't believe me? Well, listen to this." McGarr reached over and removed a cassette tape recorder from his jacket pocket. He pushed a button and it played Graham Hitchcock's voice, saying in English, "I have no plans. I wouldn't, I *won't* have anything to do with a murderer. I never want to see him again." McGarr switched off the recorder. He had worn it strapped to his back throughout the entire interview with Hitchcock's widow.

Foster had begun a low chuckle that rose slowly into a stunning laugh. The chair creaked as he shook. His gold tooth flashed whenever he craned back his head.

The office door opened and the little man rushed in to mop the puddle in front of the air conditioner.

Carabinieri strained to look in at the roaring black man.

The little janitor rushed out and shut the door.

Foster composed himself, saying, *"C'est bon, c'est bon."*

Falchi glanced at McGarr, who slipped the recorder back into his suit coat, stood, and walked to the air conditioner, a jet of which played cold air onto his face. It stank of dust and refrigerators and old city smells—diesel fumes, cooking odors, fresh wax, wash hanging on lines to dry.

McGarr straightened up. "Well, I guess you've got your retirement all secured. You've earned it, if you can call killing three harmless old men work."

"Harmless?" he asked, still chuckling.

"Then you admit to killing them? Strictly off the record, of course."

Foster shook his large black head. "I question only your use of the word harmless."

"What was that?" Falchi asked.

McGarr shook his head to mean it was nothing.

Foster added, "Whoever killed Hitchcock and Browne did the world a favor."

"How so?" McGarr asked.

"Like Cummings, they were scum."

"You mean, they were disdainful of you. After all, you were worlds apart—you, a common nigger killer-for-pay and they, titled, wealthy, the very best of a very cultivated society."

Foster laughed again. "You don't believe that either, little mon. You're nothing but riffraff in their eyes too. And you know that as well as I. We're both fairly similar, you and I. We work with them because we have no other choice and we don't have to like either them or the work we do for them."

McGarr shook his head. "We're in different boats entirely. I don't murder."

"Nor I, little mon. Nor I. Have you ever killed?"

McGarr nodded.

"As have I. My killings have had the sanction of the democrati-
cally elected representatives of large bodies of people. Your executions—both the ones you did with a gun and the others you put
before juries to complete—are little different."

"Not so," said McGarr. He didn't care for the direction of the
interview, but at least he had Foster talking. "The persons I have
killed or apprehended and who then were killed after a due legal
process had violated moral strictures which have evolved among
men of goodwill since humankind was sentient, and *not* because
some self-righteous politician or bureaucrat ordered me to murder
and paid me a large sum of money to perform a deed that is so
distasteful he couldn't do it himself. And these last three murders
of yours didn't even have that pseudo-sanction."

"Morals?" Foster laughed. "Don't talk morals to me. You go and
do your homework, and then come back and we'll discuss morals.
And if you're not being paid large sums of money you're even more
of a fool than I think you are."

McGarr waited until Foster quieted some, then asked, "Why did
you feel you had to rape Graham Hitchcock? Was that just a con-
certed effort to get back at the Hitchcocks in your life?"

But that question just made him laugh some more. "Did she tell
you that?"

McGarr nodded.

"Oh—that's rich! Rich!" He kept chuckling. Finally, he said, "She
might have thought it a rape because there's such a noticeable
difference in our sizes, understand? Otherwise, it was her idea from
the beginning."

"Even the open door in the laundry room?"

"Especially the open door. She wanted her husband or, for that
matter——" He stopped speaking, then smiled at McGarr. "You're
good, do you know that? Not like some of these other——" He
looked at Falchi.

McGarr said, "When I first saw you at the inn near Foynes on the
Shannon with Rattei, had you planned to have me see you?"

He said nothing, only smiled.

"I know you were speaking Spanish. I heard you." McGarr turned
to Falchi. "Does Rattei speak Spanish?"

Falchi picked up a phone that was sitting on the window ledge near the air conditioner. He spoke into it. A few moments later, he said, "Not as far as anybody knows. Why? How important is it?"

"Extremely so."

Falchi jiggled the cutoff bar in the yoke of the old black phone. Foster cocked his head. "You're very good. I could have killed you up on that roof. I thought about it, too, you know."

"Fleetingly, I'm sure. You would then have been fired at yourself. They wouldn't have missed."

Falchi said, "The last time Rattei went to Spain on business he had to take along a translator."

"So the man you were talking to wasn't Rattei, nor was the man at Shannon, nor the man who deposited the money in the Monte dei Paschi.

"Carlo, what's the name of the bank teller who set up the account for Signor Foster in the Monte dei Paschi?"

"Vincenzo Sclavi."

"Could you get hold of him?"

While Falchi placed the call, Foster said, "This doesn't prove anything, now does it?"

"Insofar as I've confirmed a suspicion in my own mind that Enrico Rattei was one of your ancillary targets, it matters a great deal."

Foster said, "Rattei has already been indicted."

"Falsely, so it seems. *There's* the difference between you and me, Foster, the one I tried to tell you about earlier."

Falchi had Sclavi on the line. McGarr introduced himself. Sclavi said he could remember seeing McGarr's picture in the Italian newspapers years back when McGarr worked for Interpol out of Naples. McGarr asked, "Did the man whom you identified as Rattei have a Spanish accent?"

"How do you mean? In the manner that you have a slight English accent yourself?"

"Yes."

"Well—now that you mention it—before he told me his name I thought he was Sardinian, you know, some wealthy mobster."

McGarr knew nearly all Sardinians spoke Italian with a slight Spanish accent because Spain had held that island for centuries in the past. "You'd swear to that?"

"Surely."

"Would you be willing to listen to Enrico Rattei speak?"

"Of course—I'll do anything I can to help you and Commandant Falchi."

Falchi looked glum. "I know I shouldn't have let you speak to him."

"It was part of your agreement."

"At the time I didn't know you were Mephistopheles."

McGarr turned back to Foster. "After you were put on that desk job, you started to make preliminary contacts with the official, London-based Communist party. That's where you met Battagliatti, wasn't it? When he came through on his speaking tour as one of the West's leading Communists?"

Foster started laughing now. "No more, little mon. I think I've already said too much. And he"—he indicated Falchi—"surely doesn't want you to say any more either. So, you're outvoted."

McGarr wasn't put off so easily, however, and continued to question Foster for another half-hour, during which the huge black man said nothing.

It was then that McGarr's attitude toward having cracked Foster's story about Rattei changed from elation to gloom. Foster was too veteran at the business of question and answer to be caught so easily, and, what was more, to virtually admit to having been caught.

"And it wasn't an ideological change that made you seek out the Communists, was it? No. It was because you had information and techniques to sell that might be injurious to the government that had treated you so badly. Also, when Browne, feeling sorry for you, offered you a job with ENI, you took it, if only to be close to him. You knew you could find some way to exact a little vengeance, if you were watchful.

"The Tartan information gave you what you wanted. But you didn't quite know how to use it, other than getting Browne and Hitchcock sacked and maybe tried for the theft of corporate secrets —until you met Battagliatti. He said he'd pay you that lump sum— fifty thousand pounds, was it?—if you helped him pin Cummings's murder on Rattei. The situation was ready-made, wasn't it? But you weren't interested in Cummings; he had never done anything to you. You wanted Browne and Hitchcock.

"So, the plan was hatched. On some pretext, Battagliatti arranged to get himself invited to Hitchcock's vacation home in Dingle. That's who Hitchcock had been cooking for, wasn't it? He wouldn't cook for you, would he? He probably thought you only ate pig's innards and carp."

McGarr still couldn't get a rise out of Foster, who kept laughing.

"Using your old supplies of ketobemidone, you prepared a bottle of wine which Battagliatti brought when he flew the helicopter over from London. You and whoever you hired to play Rattei were in the black Morris Marina rent-a-car down the road. After Hitchcock passed out, Battagliatti waved to you. You probably made the other fellow wait in the car while you bound Hitchcock, carried him to the shed, and dumped him in. You waited until the ketobemidone wore off, searching the house for the cork. Finally, you couldn't wait any longer and one of you—Battagliatti, I'll bet; one shot in the back of the head looks like something he probably learned in the Comintern —dispatched the poor bugger.

"Browne was easier. You probably told him Hitchcock wanted a meeting at Dingle. He went along willingly enough until he saw the dark house. You clubbed him, tied his hands, and then put him out of his misery. You then drove back to Shannon and stole aboard the American jet to Russia. That way Ignacio Garcia got out of Ireland without appearing on our computer, that way Moses Foster could return to London with the alibi he'd been in Russia all the time. Even the Russian authorities—against whom he had spied for nine years—would vouch for him.

"Here in Italy, Battagliatti had arranged all the incriminating evidence against Rattei. The idea was for you to give yourself up here where Battagliatti could help you enormously. The Irish authorities would be unlikely to win an extradition with Battagliatti and the Communist party against it. And in eight or ten years you'd be out again, and this time *with* a sizable pension. It was all very neat."

Foster was still laughing. "Was?" he asked, and laughed even louder. He was holding his sides now. A tear had appeared in the corner of his right eye.

"It's only a matter of time," said McGarr.

Foster howled.

The little man opened the door as if he would rush in to mop the floor, but Falchi stayed him, then asked, "Aren't you going to say anything?"

"No," said Foster and waited until he could breathe more easily. "I don't see why I should. But, if it makes you happy, I'll say it's been delightful hearing your friend grasp at straws in French. It's a pleasant change from Italian."

"I need a drink," said McGarr. He felt foolish, having hypothesized the collusion of Foster and Battagliatti here where Falchi had heard him. And it seemed as if Foster hadn't laughed so much at what he was saying but rather at the foolish spectacle McGarr had made of himself.

And Foster laughed him right out of the office.

McGarr, Noreen, O'Shaughnessy, McKeon, and Ward dined at the Excelsior that night. Although they ordered *cacciúcco,* a rich fish stew like bouillabaisse, and drank Moscadello, a soft, sweet, golden sparkling wine that McGarr enjoyed, he was preoccupied throughout the meal and hardly ate. Twice the maître d' asked him if he found the dish satisfactory.

And later that night, he couldn't sleep. True, it was hot, but really no hotter than the other nights they had spent in Siena. He got out of bed and padded into the sitting room of the suite. There he switched on a table lamp and raised the blind of the balcony to a height at which he could duck under it.

On the balcony, he looked out over Siena. The festive atmosphere of the Palio was still present, and even though it was 2:30 many tourists still strolled along the piazza and past the air-conditioned café on the corner. He could see people standing at the marble bar drinking tall glasses of yellow or green iced concoctions. That made McGarr himself want one very much indeed, but he was at once too lazy to put on his clothes and too involved in thinking about this case to want to talk, and had a long-standing rule that he would not take a drink in order to make himself fall asleep. That smacked too much of alcoholism to him, and, whenever he had tried it, the results next day had been disastrous.

A cool breeze smelling of the country was blowing off the hills now.

McGarr eased himself against the iron railing of the balcony and folded his arms. He was wearing only pajamas, and his feet were bare.

McGarr thought about Battagliatti. What did McGarr know about him?

First, Battagliatti had appeared much too gay at the party in London. What was it he had said about the victim? McGarr searched his memory. Ah, yes—"Some would say the victim invited the crime, that some imbalance obtained in his personality that begged for an untoward act to be done to him." By that standard McGarr supposed Cummings *had* begged for his murder. He had stepped into a tight circle of friends, all of whom had loved Enna Ricasoli in some way, and had stolen her from them. Then, not walling her away, he had teased at least Battagliatti and Rattei over a nearly thirty-year period, letting them take his wife to dinner, allowing Rattei to make love to her, making no secret of his own bisexuality, perhaps even inviting Battagliatti and Pavoni and Zingiale to his home to witness all of that.

And Battagliatti was growing older now. It looked as if he was losing his grip on the younger members of his party, that he would never get the chance to rule all of Italy. Never one whom his party members loved for himself, Battagliatti would probably have to pass the rest of his life alone, with some money (that much was certain), but most probably friendless. Was that the reason he had panicked and shot at Rattei—that his soul's companion was at last free and seemed to prefer his own company to that of the handsome rival and he wouldn't tolerate any change in the situation?

McGarr then wondered if Battagliatti had any family, any brothers or sisters, nieces or nephews, who might take care of one of the grand old men of Italian politics, a national hero.

Ducking under the blind, McGarr walked to the coffee table where he pulled Battagliatti's dossier out of his briefcase. There, among the photos and news clippings that Falchi had hurriedly assembled, was his family history.

Battagliatti's father had been a *contadíno* with a small farm near Montalcino that was taken by the government after World War I as a storage area for old tanks and armored personnel carriers. Whereas the settlement seemed generous, the old man felt cheated, and indeed he was, since the land was never used for the stated purpose, and a year later was sold at private auction to the director of mines, Mussolini's brother-in-law's uncle, who promptly established a highly profitable zinc mine there. Battagliatti himself, a university student at the time, was outraged. He was arrested and spent eight months in jail for assaulting the director.

He had two brothers who had fought and died alongside him during the Second World War, and a sister who lived on the site of his father's former farm. A modest house had been built in the cavity of the excavation site and given to Battagliatti by his Communist supporters as a symbol of government collusion in schemes of capitalist exploitation. His sister was older than he and a spinster.

McGarr glanced through the balcony and down into the streets where the cafés were. Again he quelled the urge to get himself a drink.

Instead, he kept pawing through the mass of documents Falchi had supplied. Everything had been arranged chronologically, starting with Battagliatti's birth certificate and baptismal picture and running through early school diplomas, pictures of his first communion, confirmation, graduation from secondary school, and his first university picture. Then there was all the information concerning his assault on the director of mines, his prison term, his statement upon getting out that he would work for the establishment of social justice in Italy. The Fascist press interpreted that as meaning he had learned the true purpose of the present government and been converted to their cause. In that picture he looked drawn, more like a confused child than the future leader of the Italian Communist party.

McGarr turned the page and looked down at Enna Ricasoli sitting next to Battagliatti on the steps of the university mensa on Via Giovanni Dupre. Her beauty was startling. After a while, McGarr realized that the man sitting directly in back of her was Enrico Rattei. He was looking down into her hair. Was she leaning against his leg? McGarr wondered.

Then McGarr read of Battagliatti's exile from Italy, his role in the Russian Comintern—most of it speculation by the Fascist police and press and therefore not very flattering—his return as a freedom fighter, and after the war his early work building the Communist party in Tuscany, later in Umbria, and finally in Emilia-Romagna.

The succeeding pictures were all of a type. They showed him at different stages in his life, dressed in the same double-breasted gray suit, the style of which changed only slightly in accordance with popular tastes. He was either shaking hands with well-wishers and officials or on a platform or in a radio or televison studio speaking to his electorate.

Quickly, McGarr began flipping through these. But first one, then another, then a third recent picture stopped McGarr. He even stood and lifted the dossier to place it directly under the table lamp. In each of those pictures Battagliatti was wearing a pair of wraparound sunglasses, the like of which McGarr had tried on in the lost-and-found closet of the Avis operation at the Heathrow Airport in London. This was only the second time in his life McGarr had ever seen glasses like these. They had thick chrome-steel frames that ran, high and low, around the lenses, more like goggles—aviator's goggles! —than glasses. The lenses were rounded like head lamps to deflect the glare. In all, the effect was frightening. In each, Battagliatti looked more like a bug-eyed monster, some creature from another planet, than a small man. McGarr speculated that the glasses had been made especially for him, and the glasses in the lost-and-found carton had been equipped with prescription lenses which were traceable.

McGarr folded the three pictures and placed them in his pocket secretary. He then dressed quickly and went down to the café for several drinks.

There he met Liam O'Shaughnessy, who said, "Couldn't sleep. I've got that little tyke on my mind."

"Battagliatti?"

O'Shaughnessy nodded.

"Then take a look at these." McGarr handed him the pictures.

O'Shaughnessy smiled. "I'll fly back to London tomorrow. Too bad so many of us touched them." He then glanced at McGarr, who nodded. The Galwayman, elated now, kept speaking. "They've got to be prescription. Otherwise, I suspect he's blind as a bat. Well, this time make sure you're carrying a shooter, and make sure Falchi or somebody official is present. He may be small, but he's dangerous, he is."

But several things were still bothering McGarr and he remained silent. First, he felt the same deflation he had experienced when he had cracked Foster's story. Something was amiss here. If Battagliatti had dropped those glasses he would either have gone back himself or sent somebody else for them. Doubtless prescription lenses, they were far too readily traceable to him.

Next, Rattei's knowing the make and caliber of Battagliatti's weapon still bothered him. Through Falchi, McGarr had learned that was not public information. In fact, that Battagliatti saw fit even to carry a gun came as a shock to his close associates. That simply wasn't like him. The automatic itself was an unusual weapon. In the past McGarr had noted how small men were wont to carry large-caliber weapons, the diameter of the barrel seeming to vary inversely with the stature of the man. That gun was more like one a woman would use. How did Rattei come by the information and what did it mean?

The last thing that bothered McGarr was the man who was reading a *Sera* in the shadows near the corner of the tall bar. McGarr could remember seeing him not just in Siena but in Livorno, too, and—he racked his memory—*yes*, in London just today, or— McGarr checked his watch—yesterday. It was now 3:14 A.M.

McGarr ordered another round of Chartreuse drinks and asked the barman for a telephone token. He called Falchi's house and was surprised that the number answered immediately. It was Falchi himself, who explained, "Couldn't sleep."

"Me too," said McGarr. "I'll buy you a drink. It's just around the corner."

Twenty minutes later the carabinieri commandant arrived dressed in his street clothes.

During that time McGarr and O'Shaughnessy kept talking while McGarr noted every aspect of the man's appearance, which had been so devised as to fit in most anywhere. For instance, the suit was some dark gray material with a darker pattern running through it that looked almost Parisian, but it could also have been something an old, middle-class Sienese would wear, or, say, a white-collar

Englishman who had met with moderate success. The black bluchers were trim and well made, but the heels were just slightly too large. This could be vanity, but it was also an Italian preference. But Italian-style shoes were sold in Paris and London too. Likewise, the man's face was regular and clean shaven. He had slicked his hair back as older men in most European countries did when beginning to bald. McGarr himself had worn his hair like that. A gray summer fedora was on the table in front of him. He was drinking coffee, and *that* was a mistake. He was the only person in the crowded café who had ordered a stimulant. Obviously, he was still at work.

"Who's that?" McGarr asked Falchi after he had joined them for a time.

"Don't know."

"Can you find out?"

"Certainly."

The man didn't move, and a few minutes later Falchi made a call.

# 10

Nearly twelve hours later, McGarr was sitting in the Palazzo Ricasoli. The back of the tall chair concealed him from anybody who might suddenly enter the room from the hallway.

Enna Ricasoli had thrown open the windows of the room. She was standing in front of him, hands on the sills, looking out onto the Piazza del Campo. McGarr himself could see the Mangia bell tower. The clock read 2:45. Francesco Battagliatti was due to arrive at the palazzo for lunch. The day was cool and dry, a relief welcomed by all.

"What are your plans?" he asked her.

"I don't know. Everything has made me so confused. First, Edward's death, then Enrico's involvement in it, then Francesco's strange behavior. Do you know he wants to marry me?"

"No."

"He insists on it. Now, right away, so soon after Edward's death. It's unthinkable, unseemly, but he's like a crazed person. One can't talk to him any longer. I wish—— I wish that business with the police and Enrico would clear up. It's made him so strange."

"It will," said McGarr. He could hear loud talking in the hall, orders being given. He imagined Battagliatti had arrived. "You just stand right where you are, ma'am, and don't move when your friend enters the room," he advised.

"Why so?" The sun had caught in her hair, as it had during the Palio when her husband had been killed. She was dressed in black, and the plain suit became her tall and trim figure. One earring, just a gold band, glinted where her hair had been drawn into a bun at the back of her neck.

"You'll see." McGarr reached into his suit coat pocket and pulled out a pair of glasses no different from those Francesco Battagliatti had left aboard the rented helicopter in London. It had taken the Florentine police and Falchi, who was in the next room monitoring the conversation by means of a microphone that McGarr wore under his coat, all morning to find Battagliatti's optician. The prescriptions of the lenses matched those of the glasses O'Shaughnessy had picked up at Heathrow and returned with only an hour before. McGarr then removed his Walther from its shoulder holster and placed it in his lap. He covered it and his right hand with a newspaper.

Enna Cummings's eyes were wide now. "Please, no violence. No violence again. Not to Francesco, too. I don't think I can stand any more violence."

"Don't worry. There isn't going to be any if I can help it. Just act as if I'm not here."

But she couldn't. When Battagliatti opened the door and stepped into the room, saying, "Enna, my darling—how are you today?" her eyes were still wide with fright. "What's wrong, what's the matter?" Battagliatti looked around.

There in back of him in the chair and smiling was McGarr with the bizarre flight glasses wrapping his face.

Battagliatti's hand jumped for his lapel and he pulled out his small pistol.

Not before Enna Cummings had grabbed for the gun, which fired into the ceiling. "Don't!" she screamed.

"Where'd he get those? I'll kill him, the meddler!"

"Just like you killed Hitchcock and Browne, like you had Colin Cummings killed?"

Battagliatti fought with her to lower the gun.

McGarr could hear Falchi and his carabinieri in the next room scrambling to get out the door of that room and into the hallway.

That was when the door leading to the hall burst open and Enrico Rattei appeared in it. He too had a gun in his hand.

Before McGarr had time either to call out or to turn his own automatic on Rattei, Il Condottiere squeezed off a shot that struck Battagliatti right in the throat. The force of the slug lifted the little man right off his feet and dropped him on his back.

O'Shaughnessy appeared behind Rattei and promptly relieved him of his weapon.

Hands to his throat, Battagliatti lay on his back on the floor blinking up at Enna Ricasoli and McGarr. In spite of the helpless and pitiable look on his face as he tried to gasp for breath through the blood, McGarr saw that his eyes seemed calm. He was a man who had seen much and had doubtless experienced the deaths of many others.

The air stank of gunpowder and scorched blood.

McGarr then wondered if Rattei's hitting him there in the voice box was just a wild or lucky shot. Rattei's dossier mentioned that he was a championship quality marksman with most weapons. Carlo Falchi had told McGarr only a few minutes before that the man who had been following McGarr worked for Rattei.

"Francesco, Francesco," Enna Ricasoli Cummings was saying. "Why did it have to be like this?" Like McGarr, she was kneeling by his side.

"That's enough, Enna," Rattei said. All his features were animated, but most especially his eyes. They were coal black and fierce. "Get away from him."

McGarr turned to Battagliatti. "You can still blink. Help is coming, but I don't think you're going to make it." In a similar situation, McGarr wouldn't want anybody lying to him. "Did you have Cummings killed?"

Battagliatti just looked at him.

"How about the others?"

Again the little man stared straight into his eyes.

"Did you think Rattei was behind Cummings's murder? Is that why you began carrying this gun? Is that why you shot at him in Pisa? Did you think he was trying to get rid of all rivals?"

Battagliatti blinked once.

McGarr picked up the gold-plated .22-caliber automatic. It looked like an expensive child's toy or a cigarette lighter.

"Do you know how these glasses got to Heathrow?"

Battagliatti blinked.

"Were they planted there?" But Battagliatti didn't blink again. His eyes had glassed. McGarr felt for his pulse. He was dead.

McGarr turned and looked at Rattei, who, although still being held by O'Shaughnessy, looked proud and self-satisfied. The corners of his mouth just below his moustache had creased in a cruel, superior smile.

Enna Ricasoli Cummings was sobbing now, rocking on her knees, her head in her lap. Suddenly she raised her body and turned to Rattei. Her face was streaming with tears. "You're really a dreadful person, Enrico. Bloodthirsty and cruel."

"Well, if I am, you had a part in making me that way, Enna."

"This is so awful, so horrible. I never want to see you again. Never."

"Why? Because after all these years I've finally triumphed? Remember that he had shot at me before and had a gun in his hand too. And not just any ordinary gun either. Take note of the gun, Mr. McGarr. You'll find it very interesting."

McGarr looked down at the automatic and wondered yet again how Rattei could possibly know so much about it.

But Enna Ricasoli Cummings was on her feet now. "Do you call *this* a triumph? You must be ill, depraved." She had to grasp the mantel to keep from falling. "I'm tired of killing and *men*. Colin was so gentle, so trusting, so——" She began sobbing again. Her servants had pushed into the room and now surrounded her, helping her into a chair.

McGarr slid the little automatic into his pocket and started toward the door. O'Shaughnessy and Falchi had Rattei in the hall now. McGarr shut the door behind him.

Rattei was saying, "It was self-defense. You saw so yourself. I've got a license to carry the gun which is signed by a cabinet minister himself. He would have shot me, had he been quicker."

Falchi replied, "But you must come to my office to fill out a report and make a statement. It's a matter of form, signor."

McGarr gestured to O'Shaughnessy and the two of them walked down the hall toward the stairs.

"But why did Rattei go to the trouble of framing himself?" O'Shaughnessy asked him as they started across the sunny piazza toward carabinieri headquarters.

McGarr hunched his shoulders. "So the world would know that

Enrico Rattei's vow was binding, perhaps. And maybe to put Batta-gliatti—that nothing of a little man—in his place, to show him that he had neither the cunning nor the strength of will to dare to compete with"—McGarr waved his hand and trilled—"Il Condot-tiere Rattei."

"Sounds like some explanation a little boy would give for beating up the kid next door."

McGarr was then reminded of what Rattei had said at his villa—that a person is happiest who fulfills his boyhood ambitions. Surely to a northern European the swagger and bluster of Latin males always seemed childish and absurd. It had nothing to do with real worth. "I'm sure we'll never really know. He's a smart one and daring. He's given us only the implication that he engineered the whole dirty business. Unless——"

"The gun?" O'Shaughnessy asked.

"If it is the Slea Head murder weapon, then he must have had it pinched from Battagliatti at some point or other. Maybe we can get a line on it."

Less than twenty minutes later, McGarr and O'Shaughnessy were deep in the basement archives of carabinieri headquarters. Falchi had placed his entire clerical staff at McGarr's disposal, and the chief inspector had six men sifting through theft reports beginning a day before the Hitchcock murder, or June 18, and running back at least a year. In particular, he had them looking for the surname Batta-gliatti in the vicinity of Chiusdino and the report of a housebreak. McGarr figured that if Battagliatti's staff had been surprised when it heard the party chairman had been carrying a gun of late, then the gun could not have been stolen from his car or traveling bags. The carabinieri fired the gun twice into sand. The barrel markings on the bullets were the same as those on the bullets taken from Hitchcock's and Browne's skulls. It was the murder weapon.

But after an hour passed, McGarr grew anxious. He wanted to talk to Battagliatti's sister before the news of her brother's death reached her on the family farm, which was, coincidentally, in Chius-dino and quite close to Enrico Rattei's villa. Thus, he and O'Shaugh-nessy hopped into the Alfa rent-a-car and drove to the little town in the hills at speeds that made the Galwayman cringe.

At the Chiusdino barracks, McGarr explained what he wanted to the seniormost official present. He was an utterly bald old man near retirement. With a toothpick in his mouth, he was sitting, as though in state, at a massive oaken desk. His complexion was so golden that the shadows beneath his chin seemed green. Also, his eyebrows were auburn and a shade McGarr could not quite credit as real. O'Shaughnessy seemed unable to look at anything else. They were wide and bushy, and the commandant used them histrionically, raising one and lowering the other when McGarr made his request for directions to the Battagliatti farm, repeating the process when McGarr also asked for information concerning possible thefts there during the past year, then knitting both before saying he didn't think he could help the Irishmen, and finally stretching both very far when they agreed to share a small glass of cognac with him at the café across the street.

There, after much preliminary conversation, in which the policeman ascertained McGarr's background and at last placed him as the very same McGarr who had run the Italian Interpol operation for over five years, to whom, it turned out, he had had occasion to telephone once, and whom he admired, along with the great mass of his compatriots, for arresting the leaders of the drug rings which "had corrupted and debased the young people of Naples." He then repeated the old chestnut which alters Byron's quote to "See Naples and die." Finally, he said, "Why bother with records? I don't trifle with such things. Scribbling on paper is the pastime of schoolteachers, priests, and other idlers. I keep all of my records here." He tapped his golden cranium with a finger. "And have been for over thirty years. Chiusdino to Siena to Sovicili to Massa Maritima is my beat. Nothing escapes me."

O'Shaughnessy and McGarr looked at him hard. Their patience was wearing thin.

"For instance, on—let's see—the eleventh of December last year, Maria, who is Francesco's sister, called me to say——" He broke off and looked at their empty glasses. "Would you care for another small cognac, gentlemen?" He raised his eyebrows nearly onto his forehead.

"After," McGarr said, *"after,"* in a way that impressed upon Commandant Alfori the urgency of the request.

Alfori straightened up and glanced at McGarr as though the Irishman had offended his sensibilities. "——to say her house had been broken into while she was in Siena shopping. Of course, I went right over there. One doesn't ignore the needs of so important a personage."

"What was missing? In particular," asked O'Shaughnessy, who, having caught the barman's eye, gestured to the brandy bottle which was then placed on their table.

"A coin collection, their silver, an antique clock, some small pieces of crystal, the old bicycle that Signor Battagliatti had been wont to race with when he was much younger, some fowling pieces, a rifle, and some other small arms. Nothing much, really. Il Signor is a true Communist. He lives very simply."

"Including a gold-plated Baretta special, twenty-two caliber?" asked McGarr.

The phone in the café was ringing.

"Yes—I think so. Wait." Alfori tapped his forehead and arched his right eyebrow. "Yes, and not only was it stolen, but later, just about a week ago, it was recovered in a stolen automobile near the Communist party headquarters in Siena."

The phone call was for McGarr. Falchi's men had found a Chiusdino barracks report and a later *avviso* deleting the gun from the original bill of particulars stolen.

When McGarr returned to the table, Alfori asked, "Do you want the serial numbers of the gun?" as though he could recall them from memory.

"Don't need them now, signor"—McGarr put his hand in his sport coat pocket and pulled out Battagliatti's handgun, which he had again pinched, this time from the lab staff, and would only turn in on threat of arrest—"since I've got the gun itself. Have you ever been to Ireland?"

"Why, no." Alfori motioned toward McGarr's cognac glass with the neck of the bottle.

McGarr stayed him. "We've got to run, but perhaps you'll soon get the opportunity of visiting us in our country—all expenses paid, of course. Then we can share another drink together."

O'Shaughnessy was paying the barman.

"I didn't realize your inquiry was so important. If I had, certainly I would have expedited your request." Alfori stood. "Where are you going now?"

"To Signor Battagliatti's house. Can you point me the way?"

"Better—I can take you."

McGarr consented readily. With Alfori present, he wouldn't have to explain his own identity as a police official of a foreign country.

From the top of the hill above Francesco Battagliatti's small white house, McGarr could see Enrico Rattei's villa in the distance.

It was late afternoon and the Battagliatti house sat in the deep shadows of the former zinc excavation. The entire area surrounding the house had been sodded and Battagliatti's sister was working in a vegetable garden.

She was a frail woman in her sixties with a remarkably thin face and a long, pointed nose. She wore a bright red babushka and rubber boots that reached her knees. Her dress was plain gray, obviously a utility item. Her hands were black with dirt and seemed too large and coarse for her stature.

She sat on a tomato crate and offered others to McGarr, O'Shaughnessy, and Alfori.

"I've come about this gun." McGarr handed her the automatic.

"It's Francesco's!" She was alarmed. "What's happened to him? He's been carrying this with him since the Palio. I found it in his coat pocket several times. I knew no good would come of it." She searched McGarr's and O'Shaughnessy's faces, which were impassive, and then she looked to Alfori. "How did they get this? Where's Francesco?" She started to rise.

McGarr put his hand on her thin arm and eased her back onto the tomato crate.

Behind her McGarr could see a large hare loping slowly toward the fringe of the garden. Strange, he thought to himself, how funereal were the purple shadows the cliff cast over the house while the western slopes of the hills beyond were brilliant with the same startling ocher light of the dwindling sun that he had noticed some days before.

Alfori was saying, "To tell you the truth, Maria, I don't know how these gentlemen obtained the gun. Can you enlighten us, sirs?"

"What can you remember about the theft of the gun, ma'am?" O'Shaughnessy asked. "Thinking back on it now, is there something you can remember that you forgot to tell Signor Alfori at the time? It's important."

But she just kept staring at the two Irishmen, trying to read their faces. "I don't know. I don't like this. Who are these two men?" she asked Alfori.

"As I told you before, Maria, they're policemen from Ireland."

"Why Ireland? I've never been to Ireland. Where's Francesco? I want to talk to him first."

McGarr said, "This gun has been to Ireland. It killed two people there."

Her hand jumped to her mouth. "I don't believe it." She looked at Alfori.

He said, "It's true. These men don't lie."

"But Francesco's never been to Ireland. If he had visited that country he would have brought me something from there. That's his way whenever he goes someplace new."

"The gun killed those people while it was stolen, before it was found in the automobile again."

Her neck jerked and she glanced down into the valley and at the bright hills.

Alfori said, "We're too well acquainted, Maria, for me not to know that you've got something to tell us."

"I can't," she said. "It's not right. I'm not really sure. That's why I never said anything before, not even to Francesco. And he's a poor man anyhow, a mere servant."

"Who?" asked Alfori.

"I must talk to Francesco first."

McGarr picked up a stone and tossed it at the hare so it scampered out of the garden. "You can't talk to Francesco anymore."

She lowered her head. "I thought that's what you'd say."

"It's why we've come," McGarr explained. "We need to know about that gun. If we act fast——"

"His name is Cervi." She looked up at McGarr. She was not crying. Her voice was clear and strong. "He has a three-wheel van, a Lambretta, I think it is. The day we were robbed I saw him going down the hill," she pointed over her shoulder. "I was in the bus. It's high. When he passed, I looked back and I thought I saw the hilt of the sword Francesco brought back from Russia. It was one of the things stolen from the house. I couldn't be sure because of all the dirt on the windows of the wagon and the dust from the road. And then we were going fast. I only got a glimpse of it. Anyhow, it wasn't 'til much later that I remembered it, and I thought all of the things taken we could easily do without. We don't——" She paused. "——we never needed much."

"*Paolo* Cervi?" Alfori asked.

She nodded.

McGarr and O'Shaughnessy stood.

Alfori said, "Are you going to be all right, Maria?"

"Of course," she said. She was looking toward the garden.

The hare had reappeared.

McGarr could see at least two others.

"Perhaps Signor McGarr can tell you——"

"I don't want to know. They'll tell me soon enough, I'm sure."

But as McGarr turned to go, she asked, "Was there pain?"

"No," he lied.

"Do you mind if I use your phone, Maria?" Alfori asked.

She flicked her wrist toward the house.

While Alfori called his office for somebody to come out to the house and keep her company, McGarr and O'Shaughnessy watched her watch the *lepri* nibbling on the plants in the garden.

"You don't think she'll do something wild?" O'Shaughnessy asked McGarr. "She gives me that feeling."

But she was on her feet now, shooing the hares out of the garden. She then began to replace the tall chicken-wire fence that kept them out during the night.

McGarr had not correlated the name Paolo with the man's occupation, servant, and the butler from Rattei's villa until the door of the hillside *casòtto*, more a shelter than a house, opened, and he saw him standing there, for the briefest moment that it took Cervi to react.

He slammed the door in McGarr's face and threw the bolt. The chief inspector could then hear him rushing through the house.

One thing about McGarr, he could always run with the best of them. As a lad on Moore Street, he had not once been caught by the Garda after nicking fruit from vendors' wagons, and as a wing on any football team he couldn't be stopped once he broke clear.

McGarr shoved by O'Shaughnessy and Alfori and sprinted around the house, out of which Cervi had long since debouched. McGarr could see him up on the hillside, running through a herd of goats which were scattering, their bells clanking and ringing. A caged guard dog lunged at McGarr and then coursed from side to side barking savagely.

The air was cool in the shadows on the hillside, yet McGarr's lungs burned. He smoked too much. He promised himself he'd quit as soon as he got back to Ireland, and he knew he was lying to himself. Anyhow, he wished he could quit.

The diminutive butler kept looking back, as McGarr gained on him. His eyes were wide with fright. McGarr could see he wasn't carrying a weapon, since he wore only a light cotton shirt, which flapped as he ran, and tight black pants, no doubt his work garb, that would have shown the bulge of a gun had he been carrying one.

Just at the line where the setting sun peeked over the neighboring hill and struck Cervi, McGarr clapped his hand on the man's neck and forced his face into the hillside. He pulled handcuffs from the small holster on his belt and jerked Cervi's wrists into them. Then he pulled out Battagliatti's Baretta Special. He held it so the sunlight glinted off the gold plating, so Cervi would see. McGarr figured that as long as Alfori and other witnesses were beyond earshot he'd try to frighten the little man. McGarr was sure Rattei would supply Paolo Cervi with his best lawyers the moment he was booked.

"See this, you little bastard?" he whispered in the man's ear while leaning all his weight into the handcuffed arms. "You know what it is, don't you? Twice you pulled this trigger and dispatched the old men. Did you know who they were? Did Rattei tell you? Or did you read about it later in the papers? They were big men, important men, and you're in trouble now.

"Rattei told you they'd never extradite you, right?" McGarr jerked up on the handcuffs.

The man winced with the pain.

McGarr glanced behind him and could see O'Shaughnessy and Alfori weaving through the bushes and goat droppings as they started to climb the hill toward him.

"Well, he was right, like always. Your boss is always the man with the proper information. But this time he didn't tell you one thing —the British don't do things regular when it's a case like this. No. The British are ruthless themselves, you know that. When I went to London they offered me a lot of money, whole piles of it, not—mind you—*not* to bring anybody back for a court trial—that's too long, too messy—but to 'solve' the problem, get me? And that's what I'm going to do. I'm going to 'solve' you. Down there in that chicken shack. It's not a standard Irish chicken shack, but we'll see how much you can course around after I put a bullet in your brain."

McGarr flashed the gun in Cervi's face, then, stepping off him and using the handcuffs, pulled the small man to his feet. McGarr started down the hill with him, rushing him toward O'Shaughnessy and Alfori so that Cervi stumbled and tripped and fell. McGarr just kept on tugging at the handcuffs, so that the little man seemed more to sledge down the hill on his chest than to use his feet. The front of his shirt and pants was smeared with animal slurry.

"He resisted arrest," said Alfori, when McGarr passed the two policemen. He began tsk-ing. "More people seem to make that tragic mistake daily. Ah, well—it'll save the Italian people the expense of a trial."

McGarr twisted the wooden latch of the shed and tossed Cervi into the shadows without caring that the hutch was filled with chickens which burst out of the confinement with a flurry of wings and feathers and dust and squawking. It all added to the show, McGarr believed.

He shouted, "Son of a bitch—stand away from the building, Liam. I don't want to hurt any witnesses to his resisting arrest. He's got a gun, you know. The very same one he used to kill Hitchcock and Browne." McGarr dropped the gun so that it lay close to Cervi's nose. He then pulled out his own Walther, slowly checking the clip to make sure it was fully loaded. He pushed forward the safety, cocking it. Compared to the little gun in the dust of the chicken coop, the 9-mm automatic looked like a weapon of terror.

McGarr spoke all the while. "You've got the advantage over them though, my friend. I was remiss. I failed to remember to bring along any twenty-two-caliber ammunition. This gun"—he waved the Walther—"will blow the front of your head right off. Sorry about that. Nobody's perfect. You'll just have to be satisfied with a closed casket. *Buona notte!*" McGarr had only to place the metal barrel of his fountain pen on the back of the man's neck and Cervi began to speak in a rush.

"He made me do it, signor. I had no option. I'm just a poor man. We don't have complete control over our destinies. Sometimes we have to do what other men—bigger, richer men—desire. That's the only way we can survive."

"Why tell me?" asked McGarr. "After I kill you I'll be a bigger, richer man."

"Don't!" he howled pitiably.

McGarr slipped the Walther into its holster and kicked open the chicken coop door. He waved O'Shaughnessy in.

The tall Garda superintendent already had his notebook out. Alfori had one too.

"Rattei's responsible for the murders, then?"

"Yes. He hired the Negro, he asked me to accompany him."

"And you did."

"I had no choice. I know Rattei. It was not really a request. If I had said no, he wouldn't have trusted me any longer. Then, because of other things I know, it would have been only a matter of time before——" his voice trailed off.

"How did you get to Ireland?"

"ENI company jet to London. I took the train from there. I stayed in a bed-sitter in Limerick for a week and a half. I met the helicopter outside the city in a field near the river."

"Why you and not some bigger man?"

"I didn't know at the time, but later I put it together. It was because Francesco Battagliatti and I were the same size." Cervi broke down and sobbed. "And the Battagliattis have been so good to me. His sister used to send his old clothes and shoes—and not even when they were old or used either—over here to me."

"And still you burglarized their home?" McGarr asked. He had lit up a Woodbine now, which burned his throat. He tossed it into the dust.

"I had to, I had no choice."

"Did you pull the trigger of this gun twice in Ireland?"

"I had to. Yes."

"Did you murder Hitchcock and Browne, then?" O'Shaughnessy asked to get Cervi on record twice admitting to the crimes.

"I had no choice. I didn't know who they were. They were just two old Englishmen. It was them or me, really, signor. The way Rattei asked me, I saw how it was."

"What did Rattei give you to kill Hitchcock and Browne?"

"Some of his private shares in ENI. Believe it or not, he has little else. He's gambled everything on the new drilling."

"And you were willing to go along with him?"

"Don't you see I had to? And in a few years the shares would be worth millions. Signor Rattei is never wrong."

O'Shaughnessy said, "He certainly was when he asked you to kill two men."

"I mean, in business."

"Who was the man who 'played' Rattei in Ireland?"

"I don't know. I never saw him before, I never saw him again. He let it slip that he worked for ENI in Spain, though."

"Shouldn't be hard to find," O'Shaughnessy said to McGarr.

"Where was he when you pulled the trigger?" McGarr asked.

"Right outside the building."

"And Foster?"

"Standing alongside me."

Alfori, who had gathered enough information to conclude that this was no ordinary burglary arrest, asked, "Where did Rattei make this request, here in Chiusdino?"

"Yes. Can I sit up now?" Cervi's face was still in the dust of the chicken shack.

McGarr undid the handcuffs and pulled him to his feet.

McGarr had often noted in the past that people who didn't really like the taste of whiskey could in no way appreciate the flavor of Irish whiskey. He was sitting in the breeze of Falchi's air conditioner. On the window ledge were also a telephone, a bucket of cracked ice, some tumblers, and a bottle of fourteen-year-old Jameson whiskey that McGarr guessed was at least twice that age. The café owner across the street had found it down in the farthest recess of his wine cellar, or so he told McGarr's runner when mentioning the premium price; and now McGarr and O'Shaughnessy sipped tall cool glasses of the peat-smokey liquor. Even over ice, the crisp whiskey flavor and musky aroma were unmistakable. Alfori, who entered the room now, had had to cut his whiskey with water. But McGarr figured the Chiusdino barracks commandant would have drunk the mixture if it had been laced with hemlock, for the glass itself gave him high status here in Siena headquarters. Only Falchi, who was standing on the other side of the door, had been offered a drink and had refused.

In the middle of the room sat Paolo Cervi and some ten feet away from him Moses Foster, who was reading the statement Cervi had given McGarr, O'Shaughnessy, and Alfori.

After a while, Foster folded the statement and motioned it to Falchi, who took it from him. Foster then turned to Cervi. "That's your signature at the bottom of the pages?"

Cervi nodded. He did not once look at Foster.

"And you gave that statement freely, not under duress?"

Cervi glanced at McGarr. He was still somewhat frightened. "What's the difference? It's the truth."

Foster too glanced over at McGarr, but he smiled. He shook his head. "Do I get a touch of that thing?" He meant the bottle of Irish whiskey.

"After," said McGarr.

"O.K.—but *I* did not pull the trigger on those guys in Ireland, get that? Even he"—Foster indicated Cervi—"swears to that. I just went along for the ride.

"Now, don't put any water in that glass, just booze and right to the top." He added, "Please," and smiled broadly.

While Foster drank, he recounted the details of the assassinations of Hitchcock and Browne. Everything matched Cervi's story perfectly. Foster signed the statement. McGarr gave him another drink. Foster said, "You little runt—I don't know why I should like you, but I do."

McGarr said, "Sure, you'd say that to any old leper brandishing a whiskey bottle."

That was when Rattei was brought into the room. For a moment the sight of Cervi and Foster together seemed to disconcert him, but he quickly regained his aplomb. Two lawyers carrying briefcases flanked him.

Falchi handed him Cervi's statement.

From the outer office McGarr could hear a typewriter clacking. When Foster's statement was ready, a copy of that was handed Rattei. He and his lawyers never took seats but just stood like a triptych under the bare and dim light bulb reading the statements.

All the while Foster kept sipping from the glass, keeping his eyes on Rattei. One thing that Foster had never mentioned was how much Rattei had paid him or where the money was. McGarr knew that Foster, unlike Cervi, would never have accepted any payment but cash.

When, at length, Rattei looked up from the second document, he looked right into Foster's eyes, which were shining now. Foster was smiling the same smile McGarr had seen in the Siena train station before the Palio—that of a large black house cat smiling down into a saucer of milk.

Rattei said, "This means nothing." With a flick of the wrist he tossed the copies at Falchi. They fell on the floor by the carabinieri commandant's foot. "The testimony of two *scarafaggie*—one a killer, the other a common thief. I denounce these statements as nothing but inept attempts at character assassination. Some one of my enemies has put them up to this."

Rattei's lawyers were watching him, admiring him. One began smiling.

As did Foster, but more fully. "A *what* assassination?"

Rattei turned to him sharply. "A *character* assassination—that of me, Il Condottiere Rattei, the founder of ENI, chairman of AGIP, . . ." he began to enumerate his titles and accomplishments.

But Foster's laugh drowned him out. It was stunning and contagious. Even Rattei's other lawyer managed a thin smile by the time Foster had exhausted himself.

McGarr poured him yet another drink. He had earned it.

Rattei's face was flushed. He tried to leave in a huff, but Falchi stopped him in the outer office. For the third time in a week, new charges had been lodged against him. This time it was conspiracy to commit the murders of Hitchcock and Browne. Rattei had hatched those plans in Chiusdino.

McGarr imagined it would be many months before the Irish Republic brought the four men to justice.